DEN OF THIEVES

KATHARINE STALL

A FIRESIDE BOOK
PUBLISHED BY SIMON & SCHUSTER, INC.
NEW YORK

COPYRIGHT © 1987 BY KATHARINE STALL
ALL RIGHTS RESERVED
INCLUDING THE RIGHT OF REPRODUCTION
IN WHOLE OR IN PART IN ANY FORM.
SIMON AND SCHUSTER/FIRESIDE BOOKS
PUBLISHED BY SIMON & SCHUSTER, INC.
SIMON & SCHUSTER BUILDING
ROCKEFELLER CENTER
1230 AVENUE OF THE AMERICAS
NEW YORK, NY 10020

SIMON AND SCHUSTER, FIRESIDE AND COLOPHONS ARE REGISTERED
TRADEMARKS OF SIMON & SCHUSTER, INC.

DESIGNED BY BARBARA MARKS
MANUFACTURED IN THE UNITED STATES OF AMERICA
10 9 8 7 6 5 4 3 2 1
10 9 8 7 6 5 4 3 2 1 PBK.

LIBRARY OF CONGRESS CATALOGING IN PUBLICATION DATA
STALL, KATHARINE.
  DEN OF THIEVES.

  "A FIRESIDE BOOK."
  I. TITLE.
PS3569.T317D4 1987   813'.54   87–12893
ISBN 0–671–64588–9
    0–671–64055–0 PBK.

FOR ALL MY FRIENDS,
ESPECIALLY
LUCIA, FRANK, AND GAYLE

CONTENTS

WILL YE STEAL, MURDER, AND COMMIT
ADULTERY, AND SWEAR FALSELY, AND OF-
FER UNTO BAAL, AND WALK AFTER OTHER
GODS WHOM YE HAVE NOT KNOWN, AND
COME AND STAND BEFORE ME IN THIS
HOUSE WHEREUPON MY NAME IS CALLED,
AND SAY "WE ARE DELIVERED," THAT YE
MAY DO ALL THESE ABOMINATIONS? IS THIS
HOUSE WHEREUPON MY NAME IS CALLED
BECOME A DEN OF THIEVES IN YOUR EYES?

—JEREMIAH 7:9–11

PART
I

I cherish the greatest
respect toward every-
one's religious obliga-
tions, no matter how
comical.

—MELVILLE

CHAPTER 1

ROSIE HAD BEEN BUGGING ME ALL WINTER TO join the break-in team. I wouldn't do it. I had a thesis to finish, and ordination exams to try to get through after that; those weren't my only reasons, but they were the ones I gave her.

"But who else can we trust?" she said.

"I don't know; hell, get anybody. We're all good Christian folks around here," I said. "Besides, I've already got one jailbird in the family."

Rosie scowled. "Come on, P.K., nothing's going to happen. We've got it all worked out. It's foolproof!"

"No, it isn't, either," I said. It couldn't be. Nothing could be foolproof when you were up against professionals. "Desperate people," I told her. "You're amateurs; what do you know about burglary, anyway? You'll get creamed."

"Oh, P.K.," she sighed. "You're such an asshole. Honest to God."

Yeah, well.

I was right, though. They did get creamed.

The professionals in question were two burly men in raincoats, driving a late-model blue Buick, who had pulled up to the curb in front of the Second Presbyterian Church of Shaker Heights, Ohio, on the Sunday morning before Christmas, while worship services were in progress. They'd waited there until the last burst of organ music—something from one of Handel's oratorios, with all the stops out—when the minister, Rev. Norman Wanley, appeared in the doorway with a smile on his face, waiting to have his hand shaken by his parishioners on their way out; and then, in a blur of motion, the two burly men emerged from their car, grabbed Rev. Wanley by the collar and the seat of the pants, tossed him into the back seat, and took off. They were so quick about it, they were out of sight before any of the worshipers even realized what was happening.

Rev. Wanley hadn't been heard from since. The two men in the Buick had, though. The following Sunday they'd shown up at a Lutheran church in Bloomington, Minnesota—or perhaps it was two other men in another Buick; the Lutherans didn't get any better a look at them than the Presbyterians had. Some of them said the men looked like Hispanics or Indians; others said they were blond. One woman thought they'd been carrying pistols; others thought not. All they could agree on was that there had been two of them, and that they'd had Rev. Lutz in the back seat when they'd left.

A week later it was an Episcopal church in New Canaan, Connecticut. The next week it was Nashville; the next, Tucson—and it went on like that, Sunday after Sunday, from December to March. Thirteen preachers so far, in thirteen towns scattered all over the map. Every one of them yanked right out of his church door in broad daylight.

All the victims were white, male, fortyish, middle-class, Protestant. They were nice-looking and well liked—so said all the neighbors and wives and deacons interviewed on television. Former Boy Scouts, most of them. Former class presidents. Former football players. Nice guys; got along with everybody; wouldn't hurt a fly.

Ludicrous, of course, the idea of anybody's wanting to kidnap a lot of preachers. Especially these particular preachers, none of whom, as far as anybody could tell, had an enemy in the world. Absurd; bizarre; even insane; but there it was. Somebody obviously wanted to do it, and was doing it very well indeed.

The FBI was "following up every lead," as the TV repeated week after week, and there was a toll-free number you could call if you had any information, but it looked bad. They couldn't very well stake out every middle-class white Protestant church in the country, nor check up on every late-model blue Buick. Worse, there were none of the usual ransom notes for them to trace. No tape recordings delivered to radio stations in the dead of night. No revolutionary messages slipped under doors. No phone calls. No corpses. Nothing.

Just another nice guy disappearing every Sunday morning, with no end in sight.

Rosie and I were in the middle of our senior year at Union Theological Seminary that winter. Union is on upper Broadway in New York City, just above Barnard and Columbia: a little Gothic fortress, all stone and bell towers, sitting in the shadow of Mr. Rockefeller's Riverside Church like Jonah under the gourd. There were several hundred of us there, behind the leaded windows, all busily studying exegesis and systematic theology and ethics and hermeneutics and whatnot, by way of preparation for the Protestant ministry to which we hoped, or suspected, or feared, we'd been called; but on Sunday nights we put away the books long enough to gather around every available TV set to catch the latest kidnapping on the evening news.

We wouldn't have missed it for the world. It wasn't every day you got to see a cosmic joke being enacted right before your eyes.

"And so the question remains," the reporters intoned, standing lugubriously on sidewalks in front of empty churches. "Who can be doing this terrible thing? And where will they strike next?"

"And why do they bother?" we hooted in reply.

"Who'd want 'em?"

We tried—gleefully—to guess who the burly men could be. Who *would* they be? Moonies? The JDL? The Islamic Jihad?

Nah. The Baader-Meinhofs, the Invisible Empire? Scientologists, maybe? Secular humanists? Crazed veterans of the Bay of Pigs? We went through every group of lunatics we could think of, all the unfunny gangs with the funny names—but none of them would do. None of them would be crazy enough to go to the trouble. Or dumb enough, either.

Not for the likes of Wanley and Lutz.

Because, at Union, we knew just what kind of preachers the poor victims were. We read between the lines; we knew they were duds. Drones. Zeroes. They'd been the butt of jokes, richly deserved, for centuries on end. Nice guys; wouldn't hurt a fly; they were the ones whose sermons sounded like the *Times*'s editorials on spring. They were so pleasant, so mild, so inoffensive, that you would leave their churches of a Sunday with, at best, a vague feeling of optimism—a feeling strong enough, maybe, to last you until you got home, but nowhere near strong enough to get you through the newspapers.

That is, if you'd managed to stay awake through the sermon in the first place. Which you probably hadn't. That was why the kidnappers were having such an easy time of it, we told each other: all the witnesses were snoring in the pews. "What! Another one gone?" we cried every Sunday. "How can they tell?"

The trouble was, we were too accustomed to the ludicrous at Union. We were jaded. The clergy we were about to graduate into was filled to overflowing with implausible characters and bad writing. Soap opera. On the one hand we had the old, tired mainline church, led by the Lutzes and Wanleys of the world, earnest and plodding and innocuous—the Opiate of the Masses, whose sweet old-fashioned comforts just wouldn't cut it in a world filled with neutron bombs and suchlike. As the pain got worse, it kept requiring a bigger and bigger fix, and so, for years, the old church had been losing members by the truckload. They'd gone over to the New Church—bouncing, vibrant, belligerently Spirit-filled, frothing at the mouth with love and praise and happiness, offering the world (gladly

and at top volume) the idiotic cure-all of being Born Again.
Soap opera was what it was.

"Sickening, is what it is," Rosie used to say.

Rosie was my roommate at Union; we'd roomed together
ever since we'd first gotten there three years ago. That had
caused some confusion in the dorm for a week or two, back
in the beginning, since the two of us looked enough alike—
same height, same skinny excuse for a figure, same dark hair
and eyes—to be mistaken for each other, at least by strangers.
But as soon as Rosie opened her mouth, all that was cleared
up. She was about the angriest woman in New York; she
cursed like a mule-driver, and her warmest curses were reserved for Christians, whom she hated as passionately as she
loved the Bible.

"I swear I don't know how you can study with all that crap
going on out there," Rosie would tell me. "It's madness. Everywhere you look, there's another of their goddamned prayer
breakfasts, or another 'Buy Christian' campaign, or another
school where you can't get 'Little Red Riding Hood' out
of the library. They're everywhere! They're like the Body
Snatchers," she'd say. "They're turning the whole world into
a bumper sticker!"

"Aw, Rosie, don't be so apocalyptic," I'd tell her. "The
world needs a little comic relief."

"Hah! They laughed at Joe McCarthy. They laughed at
Nixon."

"Oh, swell."

"Well, they did, didn't they?"

Actually, it's not fair to say she hated *all* Christians. She
hated Fundamentalists, Crusaders, Inquisitors, Catholics, Protestants, and Orthodox as a general rule; but there were a few
individuals, through the centuries, who she would admit—if
pressed—might have been worthy of the name. She hadn't any
use for the Church Fathers, except Augustine, who wasn't too

bad. And the Apostle Peter, if only because he was such a buffoon. Dietrich Bonhoeffer, perhaps, for his attempt to assassinate Hitler; but not for his books, which she considered pious, narrow-minded bullshit. Martin Luther King was all right, but she had her doubts about Martin Luther. She liked Zwingli, though, because he was supposed to have said, "For God's sake, do something brave."

On a less exalted plane, she approved of Dorothy Day, the Berrigans, and my father.

Rosie had grown up on Long Island in a little white house with green shutters, and a patio and a barbecue grill, and a little patch of lawn with a chain-link fence all around it to keep the neighbors' crabgrass from coming over and eating the dandelions, and her parents had never let her go into Manhattan by herself for fear she'd be mugged. Trying to shelter her, like the Buddha's daddy, they'd sent her to a Methodist girls' college in Virginia. To their surprise, she had majored in religion; to their shock and dismay, she'd gone from there to Union, which they thought of as being "practically in Harlem."

In fact, it *is* practically in Harlem, and if you take the subway up from midtown and forget to change for the local at 96th Street (because nobody told you to, since you didn't know anybody who had ever ridden the subway that far north), then when you get off you'll be in Harlem not practically but completely.

That was what Rosie did on opening day, her first year at Union. She got off the Long Island train at Penn Station and got on the uptown IRT, in her Pappagallos and her London Fog and carrying her two matching pink Samsonite suitcases, and she came up out of the ground not at 116th and Broadway, by the Columbia gates, but at 116th and Lenox—only a few blocks away, but, as the theologians say, a different Sitz-im-leben.

She thought she must be on Mars.

There were people selling watermelons out of the backs of

trucks, for God's sake, and kids playing in the flood of water from open fire hydrants. There were old men, sick men, dead men, and beggars. Junkies nodded in doorways. Music blasted out of the few stores that were open; the rest of the stores were closed and barred and locked and boarded up. People had written their names on the boards.

The language was English, and Rosie realized she wasn't on Mars. She was *from* Mars.

Then this must be Earth.

"Pardon me . . ."

"Where? The Union Theological Seminary?"

"Cemetery?"

"Don't believe I ever heard of that. . . ."

"Which one?"

The sidewalks were broken. The trees were stunted. The streets were paved with garbage.

"What's that, a school?"

"She wants the theological—"

"Oh, the theo*log*ical cemetery."

"Gonna be a preacher, huh?"

"That right?"

"Hey, the Reverend's lost."

Curtains stirred behind dirty windows. Plants died on fire escapes.

"Near what? Columbia?"

"Where?"

"*Broad*way! Honey, you a long way from Broadway."

A finger pointed toward the western horizon, and Rosie picked up her suitcases and set off. She passed young men lounging on stoops who looked as if they ought to be in the hospital; the buildings behind them looked like Dresden. They looked like Troy, like Carthage; like Jerusalem after Nebuchadnezzar got through with it, not one stone left on a stone. There should have been hyenas and jackals picking through the rubbish.

She went on, beginning to get the picture, trying not to stare but staring anyway, as though if she could only stare hard enough she would see it all, and when the street ended at Morningside Park she stared some more. Across the park, at the immense, soot-darkened cliff rising up into the sky on the far side like the wall of a canyon, encrusted with buildings all along its rim—St. John the Divine, St. Luke's (blessed be ye poor), and the Beaux Arts apartments of the Heights—fancy, white, sunlit, looking as though they were made out of ice cream.

Rosie's face hardened into a scowl.

Head down, chin out, she marched straight across the park—never mind the muggers, big deal, she was too mad to give a shit about that—and started up the long flight of stone stairs that were built into the face of the cliff, about the steepest and most interminable stairs on earth. It was like climbing up out of Hell. She lugged those pink suitcases step by step all the way to the top, panting and wheezing and getting madder by the minute; it was a long way indeed, and by the time she got up there her head was spinning.

She paused there on the rim, gasping for breath, and looked wordlessly back down into the valley of Harlem, and up again at the wedding-cake buildings, and down again at the valley.

Then she turned on her heel and went on, and tramped right through Columbia and all the way up to Union without seeing a thing.

The suitcases went to the Salvation Army the next day. So did the shoes and the London Fog.

She never rode the subway again. She went back to Harlem, though—and East Harlem and the East Village and the South Bronx; if the ghetto of her choice was too far to walk to, she'd drive there in the little green Volkswagen she bought herself. For three years she kept this up, after classes, whenever she could spare an afternoon. She was a glutton for it; she never got used to it; she always came back to the seminary in a cosmic rage.

She would trudge into our room and flop down at her desk without bothering to take off her coat (the army surplus model which she now wore). She'd sit there for several minutes, silently radiating anger; then she'd start picking up pencil stubs or paper clips from the desk, glaring at them like a character in a Sartre novel, as though their very triviality offended her, and putting them down again.

"What a shithole," she'd say.

"Yup," I'd say, not looking up from my Hebrew.

More brooding. Several minutes later: "You know who that idiot had on his show last night?" This was a reference to Rev. Anderson, her most unfavorite TV evangelist.

"Who," I'd say, still trying to read.

"The guy that broke the land speed record in his little rocket car, that's who," she'd tell me. "What's-his-name. Six hundred and some miles an hour; ain't that terrific?" Pause. Fidget. "He's a Christian, of course."

"So?"

Whirling around to face me, Rosie would say in outraged tones: "So he broke the fucking land speed record for Jesus! Doesn't that make you *sick?*"

I would sigh wearily. "Don't tell me it surprises you."

"Yes, it does! It sure as hell does," she'd declare. "And you want to know why?" And then she'd be on her feet and stomping around the room, making a speech about unemployment, rats, arson, absentee landlords, and children starving in Harlem. "And these assholes don't know a thing about it!" she'd yell. "They don't even *want* to know about it! They're so busy breaking the speed record, they don't have time!"

Rosie's most fervent wish, I knew, was that God should smite the Christians. She pined for the old days when He indulged Himself in things like that, blowing a city off the map every once in a while, just to let people know He still cared: "Just passing through; noticed how corrupt you'd gotten to be. Regards, the King of Kings." Though she did admit that fire and brimstone were probably more than the Christians deserved. Dropping piles of shit on them, she said, would be more apt.

• • •

So when this kidnapping business started, Rosie was tickled pink. She had even less sympathy for the poor old dud preachers than the rest of us. As far as she was concerned, it was good riddance. Hadn't Ezekiel said it was all going to start at the temple? "Who knows—maybe they're angels," she said of the burly men in the raincoats. "The Lord works in mysterious ways."

Back in December, if you had suggested that Rosie would be plotting, before spring, to ruin those same angels of the Lord, you'd have been laughed out of the seminary, with Rosie laughing hardest.

It wasn't out of the goodness of her heart. She didn't suddenly turn into a saint; it wasn't that she loved the victims more, but that she loved Rev. Anderson less.

Rev. Anderson's Gospel Crusade. "Winning America to Christ," his motto. He'd materialized on TV as if from nowhere only a few years before, with his three-piece suits, his suntan, his prematurely snow-white hair, and his smooth, round, mellow baritone. Gentle yet manly; everybody loved him; Redford should look so good; and his show had gone straight to the top of whatever charts the Christians used. By our senior year in seminary, he was right up there with Falwell, Swaggart, Schuller, and Bakker, "The 700 Club." He owned a whole string of TV stations, and a great big ritzy Gospel Crusade Center just outside of Washington, and branch offices in major cities—the works. Rev. Anderson called it a miracle, of course, evidence of the wonderful power of Jesus' love. Rosie called it frightening.

She watched his show all the time; she was a glutton for that, too. She'd sit there muttering in the dorm's common room as he flickered before her on the screen, pounding his Bible, shouting and moaning, and pausing at appropriate moments to wipe his eyes. "Don't be afraid to ask Him for a miracle," he'd be saying, pleadingly, into the camera. "Come and join God's winning team."

He horrified her.

I guess she was hoping to see a pile of shit drop on the

Reverend while she was watching. No such luck, though. Instead, quite the reverse: people were coming out of the woodwork to follow the man. They packed football stadiums every time he went on tour. They bought his books and listened to his cassettes. They came in tour busses to his Crusade Center like pilgrims to Elvis's house, and went into ecstasies in the studio audience. They sent him so many requests for prayer, and so much money, that he had to have his own zip code.

"How can they *fall* for it?" Rosie would demand. "It's such a fake!"

"Oh, well, people'll buy anything they see on TV," I'd tell her. "Fast, fast, fast relief."

She'd scowl at me.

"I think it sounds kind of nice, actually, don't you?" I'd say. "I mean, don't you *want* Jesus to tell you you're okay? And don't you *want* Him to fix up the world, all by His little old self?"

She'd glower.

"It's a lot cheaper than cocaine, you've got to admit that."

"But it's *wrong!*"

"Of course it's wrong, so what else is new?" I'd say. "You're acting like everything was perfect until Anderson came along."

And Rosie would exclaim, "Oh, for Christ's sakes!" and storm out of the room, clutching her head.

Divinity schools are weird places; they attract all kinds of people—idealists, street poets, burned-out stockbrokers, jailbirds' daughters, publicans, sinners, women taken in adultery. Radicals, too; and, as you might imagine, by our senior year it was at the radicals' lunch table, off in a dark corner of the refectory, where Rosie was spending a lot of her time.

They were old-fashioned radicals at Union; they still wore beards, ate granola, and listened to Crosby, Stills and Nash. Most of them had been hanging around for years on end, writing dissertations on hopelessly ambitious topics like "Vietnam, Imperialism, and the Problem of Evil"—trying, and failing, to say it all. They sat at their corner table day after day, huddled together like conspirators, arguing endlessly about the masses and liberation and struggle and praxis—but what they were really doing, like exiles everywhere, was dreaming of home. Home: the Glorious Sixties, their brave little conquered nation, more thoroughly lost than any piece of mere real estate could be; and here they were, leftovers, sojourners in the eighties, carried away into (God help us!) the Yuppie Captivity; by the waters of Perrier we sat down and wept, when we remembered Kent State. So they sat and kept their vigil, and went through the rituals, and spoke the language of the old country (dead as Ugaritic, but it was theirs), as if they hoped to conjure up the old god of the barricades. Maybe he'd come and deliver them.

Rosie got along well enough with the radicals—though, she thought, they were a little long on the talk and short on the action. Not that they weren't interested in action. They dreamed up plots all the time, she told me; they were going to pillage Bloomingdale's, going to raid City Hall, going to abduct busloads of first-nighters from the Met and dump them in the middle of Bedford-Stuyvesant. They were always on the verge of doing something, but the trouble was, they never seemed to get around to it. Some of their plots actually made it as far as the research phase, complete with maps and floor plans—but, every time, some snag would develop at the last minute. Somebody would always find something to object to, and they'd split up into factions and start calling each other names, and finally the project would be abandoned.

"I hate it," Rosie would tell me, back at her desk, in between chapters of Hosea or Amos. "They'll take a perfectly good idea and run it straight into the ground. It's amazing. There's never anything wrong with the plan; it's always some crap about ideology."

"Uh-huh," I'd say, reading about the Israelites bickering in the wilderness.

"And, you know," she'd say, "they almost seem happy

about it, too. After they've scrapped it. It's like now they can go back to talking about the Third World."

"Uh-huh."

"Keep it theoretical, right?" she'd sniff. "Typical theologians. They just don't want to admit they don't have any nerve."

She got what she was looking for at the end of January, when the new semester started and J. Ashley Rittenhouse IV came back to school from one of his many leaves of absence. Ash was gaunt and rawboned and wild-haired, dressed in jeans and a fatigue jacket; like the other radicals, he looked pretty much as though he'd stepped through a time warp from Chicago in '68. Unlike them, he had actually been there, as president of the New Trier chapter of SDS. He had a sharp nose and a sharp chin, and a mustache that belonged on a pirate, and a pair of hard, bold, beady eyes—perfect for a revolutionary, though he also looked a lot like his father and grandfather, J. Ashley III and Jr., investment bankers, both of whom had long since disowned him.

Nerve was something Ash had plenty of—it ran in the family, I guess. Besides Chicago, he'd been in most of the antiwar riots of the late sixties, and in the thick of them, too, throwing bottles at cops and yelling through bullhorns and getting tear-gassed and all the rest of it. Some of the minor riots he had started himself, while on leaves of absence from Yale; it was a fairly easy job in those days, since merely to pronounce the name of Nixon, or Agnew, or Kissinger, was enough to make people fly into a rage, the way Georgians would when they heard the name of General Sherman.

In recent years, of course, after the Movement broke up and everybody went to business school, rioting and marching were out; Ash had been forced to change his tactics. He hadn't given up, though; he was indefatigable. He kept wandering from place to place, in between stints at Union, scouring the country for diehards from the old days and leading them into assorted raids and acts of sabotage.

Raids increasingly modest, it must be admitted, the times being what they were. Strictly on the local level. Grass roots. But raids nevertheless.

This time, Ash told the seminary radicals at their lunch table, he'd been staying with an underground group that called itself the Soldiers of Jeremiah. This news got nothing but blank stares from the radicals; they'd never heard of the Soldiers of Jeremiah—which wasn't surprising, since Ash's Movement friends all seemed, lately, to be obscure, lonesome little bands nobody had ever heard of.

Except Rosie, who turned the name over in her mind a while, and said, "That's Louise Macdonald's gang, isn't it?"

Ash looked at her with interest.

"Didn't they pull something on a bunch of Senators a while back?" she asked him. "Busted up a prayer breakfast—something like that?"

"Yeah," Ash said, impressed. "Something exactly like that."

Well, he said, he thought the radicals would want to know that the Soldiers of Jeremiah were at that moment working on the cases of these kidnapped preachers.

Rosie's eyebrows went up.

"The pigs are out looking for somebody to pin it on," Ash told them, "and they're making it pretty hot for the religious Left. So, the Soldiers figure they'd better find out who's doing it, before the pigs catch up with *them*. They're putting on a nationwide investigation," he said. "They've got people all over the place working on this thing—and so far all the evidence points in the same direction."

He paused dramatically, and murmured, "Rev. Anderson."

Rosie fell for him like a stone.

The rest of the radicals were astonished by Ash's news, and delighted by it—for a few minutes. Until he told them he had come back to the seminary not merely to report what was going on out there but to enlist their help. He had a plan. He wanted volunteers. The Soldiers had somebody working under "deep cover," he said, posing as a secretary in Rev. Anderson's fund-raising office right here in New York; this contact had passed along some information about a safe in that office. Ash's assignment was to go in and get the contents of the safe.

"This is hot stuff," he told them. "We do this right, man, it's going to turn into something really big."

"You should have seen how fast they chickened out," Rosie told me afterward.

"I did," I said.

The rest of us in the refectory hadn't been able to help but notice it. One minute the radicals were welcoming Ash back to their midst, and hugging and cheering and carrying on, and the next, they were growling at him, and at each other, like a lot of tomcats; and then, one by one, they got up and left the table, looking sullen and contemptuous, until Ash and Rosie were the only ones left.

"They didn't like his analysis," Rosie said.

"Was that it," I said.

"Yeah. They thought it was bourgeois." She made a face. "Usually it takes 'em a couple of weeks to get to that stage," she added, brightening. "If they dumped him in one day, I don't guess he can be all bad."

So the next day, and all the following days, Ash and Rosie sat at their own table, in a different corner of the refectory. They became an item; they went to classes together, went to the library together, watched Rev. Anderson's show together—looking for clues, no doubt—and drank coffee together until all hours at an all-night diner called Jake's, a few blocks down Broadway. I'd almost say they slept together, too, except I'm not sure they slept at all; they were too busy working on the break-in.

CHAPTER 2

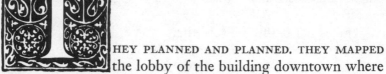

HEY PLANNED AND PLANNED. THEY MAPPED
the lobby of the building downtown where
Rev. Anderson's office was, and found out when the lobby
guards changed shifts and took coffee breaks; they rode up
and down the elevators with stopwatches. They made diagrams of the night watchmen's comings and goings. They
studied traffic patterns in the street, noted when the police
cars went by, and timed escape routes down to the second.
They had their own cars tuned up—Rosie's Volkswagen, Ash's
Porsche. They even took up jogging to get in shape.

It took them almost two months to pull it off—an awfully
long time to put together a fairly simple break-in, you'd think,
even with a full load of theology courses on the side. What
really held them up, though, was the search for a safecracker.
They couldn't do it without one. The safe in Rev. Anderson's
office was a modern one, according to Ash's contact—whose
name turned out to be Muffy. Muffy said they couldn't just
pry the hinges off this thing, or drill holes in it, or whatever.
They had to get somebody who knew what he was doing.

"I can't believe we can't find anybody," Rosie grumbled
one day. "We've been looking all over the place. Nobody
knows how. There aren't any radicals around with any skills."

True enough, I thought to myself. The radicals with the
skills were all down on Wall Street, having it all. So much
for the Counterculture. "Why don't you try the Mafia," I
said.

"They think we're Commies," she said.

"Who?" I said, startled. "The Mafia?"

"Yeah."

"You mean you *asked* them?"

"Of course," she said.

"Of course," I repeated to myself later, in the same haughty tone she'd used. "Of course"—accusingly, as if only a hopeless jerk would have asked in the first place. It was hard enough for me to keep my mind on my thesis without having to put up with conversations like that. Shreds of them kept wandering into my mind; I'd be sitting at my desk, minding my own business, plowing through the commentaries ("Moreover, the numerous behavioristic abnormalities exhibited by Ezekiel, in particular his protracted period of dumbness [3:2ff] and his symbolic lying on his side for three hundred ninety days [4:4–8], while attributed by the prophet to divine commands, have nevertheless been interpreted as symptoms of a more or less profound mental disturbance [Klostermann], with pathological features consistent with those of paranoid schizophrenia [Broome, Baentsch, Giesebrecht, et al.]"), when suddenly my eyes would glaze over and I'd hear myself murmuring, "Of course."

The trouble was, Rosie wanted me to go along, too. She would accept no substitutes. The plan called for four people in all—two upstairs, two posted in the lobby. There had to be a fourth; it had to be me; that was all there was to it.

And she dedicated herself to that task all through the winter. Heart and soul, and with all the righteous indignation, which was considerable, she could muster. Let Ash run all over New York looking for a safecracker—he had the experience for that, after all, and the right kind of acquaintances. Sooner or later, he would turn somebody up; meanwhile, she would work on me.

"Well, they got another one this week," she'd tell me, over my shoulder, while I tried to study. "A Baptist," she'd say. "From Orlando, Florida."

"I know," I'd say, not turning around.

"Home of Disney World," she'd add, bitterly. "Christ."

"I'm not going with you," I'd answer.

She'd spend the next few minutes pacing moodily up and down the room behind me. "That's number eight," she'd say, in a voice full of reproach, as though I were fiddling while Rome burned.

"Forget it," I'd say. "No."

She'd give me time to pretend to read a page or two while she stared at the back of my neck. Then she'd snap, "This ain't exactly cowboys and Indians, you know. I can't understand why you won't take it seriously."

"I do take it seriously; I just don't want to be in on it, that's all."

"Oh, excellent," she'd say. "And from the Preacher's Kid herself, yet. P.K., I have to hand it to you for taking such a principled stand. It's so very moral of you."

"Moral!" I'd say. "Oh, that's a good one. That's fine."

She'd stand there and grin at me.

"Moral," I'd say. "Shit."

I'd have to remember to ask my father, next time I went up to see him in the clink, just how good it felt to be moral.

We already had one jailbird in the family; that was my problem. Maybe you heard of him, the Rev. Sam Mather, if you were following the news back in 1972. He was in the papers, briefly, for blowing up an army train full of bombs on their way to Vietnam. It was a nice gesture, blowing up weapons to end the war, only of course the war didn't end; and now, all these years later, while the country pretended for all it was worth that there'd never been a war in the first place—or if there had been, then it had happened to someone else—or if it happened to us, then we won—my good old moral father was still in jail, going gray.

Moral indeed, I thought.

1972; imagine that. God, that was a long time ago.

It seemed much longer ago than it ought to.

Rosie knew all that stuff; I didn't have to go through it all over again for her. It wouldn't have done any good if I had, anyway; she thought it was wonderful. "Shit, he's a hero. What kind of a problem is that?" she'd say.

So all I said to her was, "Quit asking me."

Well, she didn't.

Our room at the seminary had bars on its windows. Whether they were supposed to keep burglars out or seminarians in, I never could decide. Considering the view, I imagine it was the latter; the windows looked out across a narrow alley onto the backside of the Riverside Church—cold limestone, gray and grimy—which towered so high that you had to crane your neck to see a piece of sky. Doves made mournful noises in the eaves up there. The bottom of the alley was in almost perpetual shadow, like the bottom of a well; the sunlight made its way down into it for about six minutes a day, and then it was all gloom again.

I spent a lot of time looking out there that winter. Piles of books on my desk, most of them my father's; he'd said he wouldn't be needing them but I would. His spiky, illegible handwriting all over the margins. Underlines. Exclamation points. Asterisks. "Yes!" he'd scribbled. "No!" "Bullshit!"

Piles of typing in the wastebasket, all of it mine.

Looking and smoking and looking some more. I kept hearing Rosie saying, "Very moral of you," from behind me. Trying to shame me into it.

And me saying, "Give me a break. You're talking about a felony here."

And her saying, "Of course it's a felony!" And throwing her hands in the air. "You think we haven't thought about that? Believe me, P.K., it's going to be worth it!"

Worth it, I'd be thinking. I'd have to ask him was it worth it, too.

I envied her. Things had been that simple for me, too, once; I'd spent my childhood as a junior-grade hippie, a little peace cadet, and I'd loved it. Parlous times, back then. Nobody was laid back, nobody was mellow, nobody had it all; a whole lot of people had nothing, or death. That was simple enough, right? People were killing each other; God said not to; period. A child could grasp it. A mind uncluttered by mitigating factors, pragmatism, Realpolitik. No wonder Jesus liked children.

Everybody marching and screaming and hollering and handcuffing themselves to buildings and sitting down in hallways and committing felonies. True believers. It was like being for the Red Sox in the World Series, only better, because even a kid could understand that this wasn't a game, it was life and death, it was good and evil, it was Truth.

"Worth it," I'd mutter. "Swell."

Though the Sox had their consolations; when they lost the Series, life went on.

"You're a real total-depravity freak, aren't you," Rosie would say.

"Yeah," I'd say. "Wait'll you hear me do my Kafka imitation."

"Why don't you do the one about the guy who turns into a cockroach," she'd say. "You'd be good at that."

I looked out the window some more, and thought about Wykeham, Massachusetts.

Wykeham is the kind of Boston suburb that calls itself a village. If you can forgive the paved streets and cars and electricity, it looks today very much the way it did in Colonial times; it's laid out around the original common, with the Congregational church at one end, the sides lined with little red brick shops with Old-English-lettered signs on them (even if they say "Pappagallo," they have to be Old English, by village law and ordinance), and handsome old houses with brass plaques from the Landmark Commission. The high school band is a fife-and-drum corps; they're called the Patriots, and every Memorial Day they lead the parade, in their Continental Army uniforms, from the red brick A&P into town and around the common, ending in front of the church where the speeches are made and the Brownies lay the wreath, in honor of the numberless dead, against the Revolutionary cannon which serves as a war memorial.

The church at the end of the common is the village's pride and joy; it's older than the rest of the buildings by a good seventy years. Puritans built it, the way only Puritans could, or would want to—tall and narrow and austere, with a steeple sharp as a sword, the better to poke God with. The First Congregational Preservation Society takes fanatically good care of it. They've spent hundreds of thousands on it over the years; it has new wiring, new plumbing, a new roof, and fresh paint outside and in, in historically correct colors. They've even found a craftsman up in New Hampshire who can match the original windows, if one should break.

Wykeham is where I grew up. First Congregational was my father's church from 1961, when they hired him, until 1972, when he went to jail.

I've always thought they must have hired him mainly for aesthetic reasons—because he belonged in the building. The Preservation Society and the church Session are made up of pretty much the same people, and they're all Colonial history freaks; they know, and care, more about the seventeenth century than the twentieth. Back in '61, they spent half their waking hours (and I suppose they still do) puttering around with Chippendales and Queen Annes—most of them lived in the houses with the plaques on them—and they knew an original when they saw one. They might not have set out deliberately to find a preacher the same way they'd have looked for a settee to put in the foyer, but when they saw the name Samuel Mather among the dossiers they'd gotten, they probably couldn't help themselves. "Do you think—?" they must have asked each other. "It's not *such* a common name, after all. . . ." And when he arrived for his interview, they steered the conversation around to the subject of Wykeham's Colonial heritage. One of them, who had been put up to it, came out and asked him if he mightn't by any chance be related to the Puritan Mathers, the learned Cotton, the upright Increase, the ferocious Richard. Why, yes, my father said, as a matter of

fact he was. And they all beamed at him, already imagining
the effect he would make in the pulpit of their dear old
church. Because he looked the part: tall and dark-haired and
thin—though not as thin as he got to be later—with a narrow
face and a scholar's high forehead, and bright black eyes with
plenty of fire in them.

Maybe a little too much fire, actually. Surely somebody
on the Session—or the Preservation Society—must have noticed that, even back then; somebody must have felt a twinge
of misgiving, and whispered to his neighbor, "Don't you think
he's awfully *serious?*"

But if the rest of them thought so, they discounted it. Or
they might even have chalked it up in his favor; after all,
what else could you expect of a real live Puritan descendant?

He didn't disappoint them when he showed up for his trial
sermon. Congregational ministers tend to wear suits and ties,
maybe with a choir robe thrown over, even in stuffy towns
like Wykeham, as a democratic gesture—priesthood of all believers and so forth. Not my father. He wore what my mother
liked to call full battle dress: his flowing black doctor's gown
and a clerical collar, and not your ordinary collar, either, but
the formal Calvinist collar and bands. When he got up in the
ancient pulpit, in that old, old church with its dark wainscot-
ing all around, its balconies up above, its narrow windows,
its old, cool, dusty odor—some people said it was enough to
make them wonder, for a second, what century they were in.

And what topic did my father choose to preach on, that
first day—Love? The Good Shepherd? The Efficacy of Prayer,
maybe? Nope. My father told them about Belshazzar's Feast.
Most people would have given them something sweeter at
first, and slid the bitter in afterward. But he thought it was
only fair to let them know what they were in for.

He didn't tell any football stories to warm them up, either;
he simply got on with it, straight from the prophet, no chaser,
reciting Daniel's awful warning in the same low, menacing
growl which must have scared the daylights out of poor Belshazzar to begin with. "O thou King," he said to them.

The most high God gave Nebuchadnezzar thy father a kingdom, and majesty, and glory, and honor:

And for the majesty that he gave him, all people, nations, and languages trembled and feared before him: whom he would he slew; and whom he would he kept alive. . . .

But when his heart was lifted up, and his mind hardened in pride, he was deposed from his kingly throne, and they took his glory from him:

And he was driven from the sons of men; and his heart was made like the beasts, and his dwelling was with the wild asses; they fed him with grass like oxen.

The words rolled around the church like thunder, bounced off the old polished wood, and hung in the air like bells tolling, like muffled drums.

And thou his son, O Belshazzar, hast not humbled thine heart, though thou knewest all this;

But hast lifted up thyself against the Lord of heaven; and they have brought the vessels of his house before thee, and thou, and thy lords, thy wives, and thy concubines, have drunk wine in them; and thou hast praised the gods of silver, and gold, of brass, iron, wood, and stone, which see not, nor hear, nor know: and the God in whose hand thy breath is, and whose are all thy ways, hast thou not glorified:

Then was the part of the hand sent from him; and this writing was written . . . MENE, MENE, TEKEL, UPHARSIN.

This is the interpretation of the thing: MENE; God hath numbered thy kingdom, and finished it.

TEKEL; Thou art weighed in the balances, and art found wanting.

PERES; Thy kingdom is divided, and given to
the Medes and Persians.

He went on to tell them that Belshazzar was alive and well
in Wykeham, Massachusetts, and that the handwriting was
still up there on every wall in sight, uppercase and underlined
(and not in Old English lettering, either); furthermore, that
because of stories like that one, the Bible was as dangerous
as dynamite, for it could blow their smug little world to pieces
in the twinkling of an eye; and that anyone who didn't like
that idea had no business being in church, for such a person
was not on the side of God, but of men.

After a performance like that, I wouldn't have blamed
them, or anyone, for handing the man a one-way ticket to
whatever booby hatch he'd come from. But they didn't. Far
from it; they were thrilled. "Doesn't he sound magnificent!"
they said to each other. "The acoustics . . . Marvelous. . . .
As if they'd built the place just for him!" It was a fine old-
fashioned talk, they said. Stirring. Wonderful delivery. Oh,
very thought-provoking indeed; they'd hung on every word;
hadn't heard anything like it in they didn't know how long.

"Well," my mother said, "at least they had good taste."

In retrospect it seems fitting that he should have mentioned
dynamite, since that was what he used, later on, to blow up
the train; but that wasn't until 1972. A lot later on. The Preservation Society can be forgiven for not having guessed he'd
be capable of anything like *that*. This was only 1961, after
all. They didn't know what was coming. Sure, the Freedom
Rides had begun by that time; there were sit-ins, the occa-
sional shooting—down South. We had plenty of Green Be-
rets already at war—over in Asia somewhere. Those were
causes for concern, yes, but nobody dreamed they were signs
of a future full of dynamite, one long deafening explosion
from Birmingham to Watts to Chicago to Saigon to Massachusetts and back again.

So they hired him.

· · ·

Well, he *was* a Puritan. I don't know what else to call him. Not that that's necessarily a compliment; I might as well call him an extremist or an utter misfit, or say he exhibited signs of a more or less profound mental disturbance. It's possible that the Bible had addled his brain; when he read things like "Be ye perfect as your father in heaven is perfect," he thought they were for real. He didn't believe in witches, or in government by the elect, as the Puritan Mathers had, but he did see just about everything in life as a moral matter, from foreign policy right on down to cleaning your plate at supper. And none of your modern notions about morality—no situation ethics, no relativism, no enlightened self-interest. For him it was "As ye did it unto the least of these, ye did it unto me."

You, mind: because Belshazzar was you. Everything was connected to everything else. If you had ice cream, whole nations starved; not only that, but you piled another brick on the tombs of the prophets, and handed another drink of vinegar to Christ on the cross.

Not a fashionable point of view. We don't tend to think that way in the twentieth century; if the world is killing itself all around us it's because of entropy, or Congress, or the Arabs; but for my father, it was sin and judgment. Sow the wind and reap the whirlwind—that was his idea of cause and effect. It was written out plain as day in the Bible, he said. You had to be blind to miss it. And deaf, too—thanks to TV and radio, you had the cries of your neighbors around you every minute, floating in the very air. You ignored your neighbors' cries at your peril; they would be your cries soon.

The Kingdom was real to him—as real as the Revolution is to a Communist or Justice to a judge. He went through the sixties in a slow, smoldering rage as the vision that was already in his mind took on flesh. Masses of people marching and crying out for justice, for peace, for equality—and meaning it! Naturally they touched my father's heart. They were saying what God had been saying for six thousand years.

Meanwhile, the nation went right on cranking out the napalm and bombs and Saran Wrap and electric can openers.

My father was incredulous. It just didn't fit his sense of logic. "Even Belshazzar had enough sense to be scared," he'd snap.

He took it all personally, my father. That was what his problem was. He had no sense of geography; when riots broke out in Watts or Harlem or Detroit, he had trouble distinguishing them from Sodom and Gomorrah, or from Wykeham. And when the four little girls were blown to pieces in the Birmingham church, he wept and carried on as though they'd been his own children—and the next Sunday he took it out on his congregation as though they'd planted the bomb themselves.

He thought they had.

He had the American flag taken out of the church. He quit giving the benediction on Memorial Day. He sold all the furniture in the parsonage (proceeds to the SCLC, I think it was); we sat on cushions in the empty living room, hippie-style. He gave away most of his salary, and so did my mother; we ate rice and beans, and our clothes came from the Salvation Army. The house was always full of Civil Rights people, draft dodgers, Quakers, all kinds of zealots; we could hear them downstairs, after we'd gone to bed, arguing all night long. And we went to all the marches, my father holding my hand and carrying Jonah, and later Sarah, on his shoulders. "Peace now!" we shrilled, waving our chubby little fists in the air. "The whole world is watching!" And we believed it was. History was being made; great changes were beginning, at last, at last, and our family was right in the middle of it. My father spoke at all the rallies; he was famous. People began to come from all over the Boston area to hear him preach.

He got up early on Sunday mornings, went downstairs in his grim black clothes (with us peeping at him from the landing), ate no breakfast, talked to no one, withdrew into his study and shut the door. What he thought about in there was a mystery—maybe he thought about the monks burning themselves to death on the streets of Saigon, or about the Chicago cops, or about destroying villages in order to save them—but, whatever it was, when he came out again he was madder than ever. He strode off across the lawn, head down, fists clenched, his gown streaming out behind him—the grass still dewy, the bombs going off in his head—and by the time he got to church he had the fierce, rapt look of a man about to take vengeance for a dreadful wrong. The choir began to sing; nobody paid them any attention; they watched him instead as he sat there brooding, chewing his knuckles, glaring furiously at the floor. There was a hush as he rose to speak—and he didn't speak, he roared. "The land is full of blood, and the city full of injustice." His eyes blazed; his fingers clutched the edges of the old pulpit as if he meant to break it in half.

He told them about Jeremiah. He told them about the rich man and Lazarus. He yelled at them. He browbeat them. He told them they were stupid, blind, violent, miserable wretches. He told them they had to change or die.

And it was just as well that he was attracting new people to the church, because bit by bit the Wykehamites were leaving—sneaking over to Lexington and Concord in search of more reassuring fare. Puritan or no Puritan, they thought, he'd gotten to be a little hard to take. "All that gloom and doom, every single week," I heard one of them grumble. "The man never lets up. What ever happened to the Good News?"

But the newcomers more than made up for the loss. Anti-war kids, most of them, from Harvard and Radcliffe and B.U., longhairs in army clothes. They filled the balconies to overflowing—and the collection plates, too—earning the grudging acceptance, or at least the toleration, of the Preservation Society. The college kids loved my father's tirades; he freaked them out. "Right on!" came the growls from upstairs. They thought he was subversive; a prophet; a walking symbol of a terrible time.

Time passed, though.

CHAPTER 3

IME PASSED AT THE SEMINARY, TOO. WINTER dragged itself toward spring. It was Lent; the ice began to melt off the surface of things, dull roots, spring rain, and the dogshit began to thaw, and the streets began to smell like garbage again, and the bodies came up out of the Hudson where they'd lain submerged since Thanksgiving and Christmas and New Year's Eve; the cops went out in boats and fished them out with hooks, fishers of men.

Preacher number nine disappeared without a trace, right on schedule. So did number ten. We still watched them on the news around the seminary, but our jokes were starting to wear thin. There was still no comment from the FBI.

The latest President announced the latest humanitarian aid program for the latest military dictatorship, to be financed by cutting back on food stamps. This was greeted with apathy by everyone except, presumably, the victims and God, neither of whom got any air time.

Ash was still out in the streets, wandering in search of his safecracker. I was still looking out the window. Rosie was still breathing down my neck.

"All you have to do is be a lookout in the lobby," she told me. "Come on, it'll do you good. Get your nose out of those books."

"Rosie, dear," I said.

"What?"

"You're asking me to help you commit a felony because of a rumor."

"But it's not a rumor!" she said.

"It is too! All it is is Ash says Muffy says the Soldiers say—"

"Yeah, and the Soldiers have been watching Anderson for a whole year!" she said. "They *know* he's doing it."

"Well, how come they're the only ones who do? There hasn't been a peep about it in the news; what is it, the Messianic Secret or something?"

"No, dammit!" she said. "What's wrong with you? They're the Underground. Fugitives—get it? They have to work under cover. They've got Muffy in the New York office, and this other guy, Nathan, at the headquarters down in Arlington—but they have to keep it all secret, see, until we can get some hard stuff out of that safe."

All this talk gave me a queasy feeling in the pit of my stomach. Lookouts. Lobbies. Fugitives. Networks. Why couldn't she say, "Hey, P.K., let me borrow your hair dryer, huh," like a normal person? We should have been talking about beer and boys and parties. "General Hospital." The Dead Sea Scrolls. Lots of things. Not all this cloak-and-dagger nonsense. She was supposed to be in one place, one frame of reference, and the Soldiers of Jeremiah in another. Somewhere else, with the Weathermen and the Symbionese. Elsewhere.

Worlds in collision. "Does this mean Daddy's a criminal?" my sister Sarah had asked, the first time we went to see him in the slammer. She was only nine, and scared. "Naw, you dumbbell," Jonah had told her, though he didn't sound very sure of himself. Mother said there was nothing abnormal about being in jail, and I believed her, because there was nothing much else to believe. I was sixteen, the oldest; I was cool; I could handle it.

I'd been handling it for a long time now. Worked hard at it; had it down to a science. I didn't care for that queasy feeling coming back again, after all that work. I fought it off as best I could.

But Rosie kept after me.

"You want to know where he's taking them?" she said one drizzly March afternoon, after number eleven, a Methodist from Grosse Pointe Farms, had vanished in the back of the eleventh blue Buick.

"Tell me later," I said. "Tell me at dinnertime."

"Muffy says he's taking them out West somewhere and converting them."

"Converting them?" I shook my head. That didn't make any sense at all. "He's already converting people by the thousands. Legally," I said. "What would he take a chance like that for? For a few measly preachers?" Kidnapping was hardly necessary, not in this screwed-up country; surely Rev. Anderson knew that. He had his armies of blue-eyed boys and girls on all the street corners downtown ("The 'Harvest Workers,' " Rosie had said, making a retching noise), right next to the Children of God and the Hare Krishnas and everybody else. All they had to do was stand there and reel them in. The kids out there were so estranged—hell, not only the kids, everybody—so uprooted, so mind-boggled, so weirded-out, that they joined up willingly. Gratefully. It was a gold mine out there, an endless crowd; they would swallow any kind of fairy tales, and do slave labor and shave their heads, too, they didn't care—anything, just for a chance to belong to something. Just to drown out that silence inside. And, now that Jesus was in vogue, Rev. Anderson had it easier than ever; his missionaries were all but turning them away, they were so swamped.

"Anderson's already got it made," I said. "You must have the wrong guy. Wait and see; he'll do what all the rest of 'em do. Build a university or a prayer tower or something. Start a think tank. Get a few million more people to vote Republican. Then he'll sit back and clip his coupons."

"Uh-uh. Not this guy," Rosie said. "He doesn't want a prayer tower. He wants to win America to Christ."

"Well, sure, but—"

"But he's serious, P.K.! You don't watch him like Ash and I do. The guy is absolutely stone-cold serious."

"So, fine! Let him be serious," I said. "It's a free country; if people want what he's selling, let 'em have it."

"Ah," she said, holding a finger up.

"Ah, what?"

"That's his problem," she said. "Plenty of people want it, but plenty more don't. See, they're so far gone, and full of sin and secularism and everything, they don't even know what's good for them—and, after all, it's their immortal souls at stake. So, he has to figure out a way to *make* them want it, right? He can't do that with the methods he's using—so he tries another method. A little experiment. With the preachers." She lit a cigarette and leaned back in her chair. "He tries thought reform."

"*Thought* reform?" I said. "My God. Rosie, you've lost your mind."

She blew a cloud of smoke into the air.

"Come on, now, that's really bizarre," I said. "That's too much."

" 'I will put my laws into their minds, and write them on their hearts,' " said Rosie. "It's right there in the Bible. You can't fight the word of God."

"Is that what Anderson says?"

"Every chance he gets."

I frowned. "That's ridiculous," I said. "Besides, it would never work."

"Yeah? How about the Moonies? Or the People's Temple?"

"But that's with their consent," I protested. At least, to begin with it was. I frowned again.

Rosie waved her cigarette. "What does he need consent for, when he's already got these guys shanghaied? I bet there's a lot of stuff you can talk people into once you've got 'em locked up somewhere. Especially with something as slippery as religion. Look at those poor jerks," she said. "Good old mainline Protestant mush-heads. They don't even know what they believe in when they're safe at home in Grosse Pointe. They've never had to find out. What do you think's going to happen to 'em under pressure?"

"This is insane," I said.

She said, "You bet your ass it is."

Write my laws on their hearts, I thought. Winning America
to Christ—good Lord, we were living in a nuthouse. I had
heard some crazy things in my time, but this took the—well,
no, it didn't, either. That was the whole trouble. It didn't take
the cake at all.

I tried telling myself he couldn't possibly be as crazy as she
made him out to be. Or not as malicious, at least. Put my
laws into their minds—great image, something we could all
wish for—but nobody could connect it with brainwashing,
not in a million years! Could they? All right, granted, Christians had a time-honored tradition of absurdly literal readings
of Bible passages. They got snake-handling out of the Bible
somehow, and slavery (but of course they'd seen the light on
that one, hadn't they). And no dancing and no movies. And
creationism. And heading for the hills when the numbers in
Revelation said to. Harmless little quirks for the most part.
A trifle inconsistent, perhaps—why couldn't they beat their
swords into plowshares while they were at it?—but for the
most part harmless.

Sort of.

But once you started taking the Bible for a recipe book,
where did you stop? If you really and literally believed you
had to preach the Gospel to every living creature, and so on,
otherwise they'd burn in Hell for all eternity; if you really
believed the End was near (which wasn't too difficult); if
you took to heart all the rhetoric about how urgent it was,
how crucial, to drop everything for the sake of saving those
immortal souls—if you believed all that, then you might just
get zealous enough to think brainwashing was a pretty hot
idea. For their own good. In Jesus's name.

Well, why not? you'd say. Use every possible means to
get the message across. You could use TV, couldn't you? And
advertising—billboards, bumper stickers, lapel pins, T-shirts?

And songs on the radio? And movies? All those evil marketing techniques that used to be frowned on, that used to belong to Mammon, until Christians woke up, got with it, and realized they could be used, too, to sell God? Why, even the monasteries were advertising in *Playboy!* Every possible means—so why not brainwashing? Wash the brain. Reform the thoughts. That was all it was, after all, you'd say; what was wrong with that?

You wouldn't even have to be especially crazy, I thought. Just passionate. Crazy for Jesus. Just taking certain things to their logical conclusions. Onward, Christian soldiers! Let's get out there and save that village!

Never say dictatorship. Of course you wouldn't call it that. You'd call it the Kingdom of God on earth. You'd call it peace. And that's what you'd believe it was, too, as long as you were in charge of it.

Well, I supposed the law-and-order problem would be solved, at least. Everyone would certainly be well behaved.

"I told you he was a motherfucker," Rosie had said. "And that's exactly why he's getting away with it: nobody sits down and *thinks* about what he's saying. They're so used to preachers being full of nothing but bullshit, they can't believe it when one comes along and actually means what he says. It might be a saint one time, or a creep like this another time— but, either way, nobody's going to be listening."

"And now, from the Nation's Capital . . ."

The tube in the common room showed an aerial shot, panning from the Capitol Building over across the monuments and the Potomac, and then zooming in on Rev. Anderson's Gospel Crusade Center, which they didn't bother to mention was not in the Nation's Capital but in Arlington. "Right next to the cemetery; ain't that a kick," Rosie said.

While the Gospel Crusade Choir sang "America the Beautiful," we got a postcard view of the place—acres of grass, and fountains, and flowers, and white columns and plate glass.

And flags, of course. Stars and Stripes everywhere; the place was dripping with them. It was a perfect parody of itself, and just the kind of thing that used to make us grind our teeth, way back when.

I'm not going to get mixed up in this, I'd told myself; I ought to be studying; I'm farther behind than ever—but there I was anyway, watching the show with Rosie and Ash. Rosie had told me I had to see for myself the look on Anderson's face when he quoted his proof-text. "Jesus, it'll make your skin crawl," she'd said, in such an appalled tone of voice that I thought maybe I'd better.

And there was the Reverend now, front and center, suntan and three-piece suit and all. "Ah, yes, God shed his grace on thee, praise the Lord," he said resonantly, and his delighted audience yelled, "Praise the Lord," back at him.

Most of it was the usual evangelical stuff. There were hymns by the choir, and a talk show-style interview with a young couple who said that Jesus had gotten them off welfare, and an appearance by the Harvest Workers of the Greater Cleveland Area, grim, bright-eyed youths who had been flown in to get some kind of an award.

All this was punctuated by obscenities from Rosie and Ash, as I expected. But when it came time for the sermon, they both sat up and got very serious.

"The Pilgrim Fathers came to America to found a Christian nation," the Reverend began. "I want you to think about that with me today. A Christian nation; think of it—what a marvelous thing it is! No other nation on the face of God's earth, in all the history of mankind, can make that claim!" Smiling a dazzling smile, he told how the Pilgrims trusted in God to get them across the stormy ocean and thanked Him once they got here, in that touching scene with the Indians and the turkey, and how they vowed to walk in God's ways and keep His commandments, and how they were going to build the New Jerusalem in the New World, totally rejecting the corruption of the Old, and so forth.

The audience in the Crusade Center ate it up, as the camera

showed us from time to time. And small wonder; it was a nice story and he told it very well, making those iron-hearted old Christians sound as meek and gentle as lambs. They would have loved it back in Wykeham.

"But, today, look around you," he said. "Everywhere you look, you'll see our great land groaning in travail and confusion." His voice went from sweet to sour, and so did his face, as he told us how thoroughly we had forsaken the Pilgrims' wonderful faith, so that every man did what was right in his own eyes, with the inevitable and tragic results: the breakdown of the family, abortion, the banishment of God from our schools, sex and violence on television, and of course a weak and ineffectual foreign policy and the loss of the world's respect, so that every two-bit country in the world was thumbing its nose at us.

Ash looked merely disgusted, but Rosie looked as though she could hardly restrain herself from smashing the TV set.

"But there is a way out of this, and one way alone," the Reverend said, "—to bring every soul in this great nation to the love and conviction of Jesus Christ!" Then would the confusion melt away, the doubt, the despair. "You who know the marvelous love of Jesus know what I mean," he said, his voice beginning to rise. "Picture it—I ask you—a whole nation, indivisible, under God—and if God be for us, who can be against us? Think of it—if everyone in your city, in your town, in your community, opened up his heart to the power of . . ."

Rosie dug her elbow into me. "See that? See?" She and Ash were both on the edge of their seats.

". . . we've got to *win* America back to Christ! And *win* America's hearts and souls and minds! Praise the Lord, we're going to *make* America Jesus-minded!" He was hitting his crescendo, and the crowd was in an uproar. "Yes! *Jee*-sus-minded!" he yelled. "'I will put my laws into their minds, and write them on their hearts'—and that's exactly what we're going to do!"

I'd been sitting back, up to that point, figuring it was the same old junk these guys always said; but now it was getting weird. *He* was getting weird. "We're going to wash all the sin and corruption and doubt and all the laws of the earth right out of their minds, praise the Lord, and put the love of Jesus in, right back where He belongs. . . ."

And Rosie was right. It was unbelievable. My skin did crawl—not at the words, which were creepy enough, but at the way he said them. He didn't look deranged, or possessed, or anything as picturesque as that. There wasn't any strange fire in his eyes, and his face didn't twist into an insane leer—no, it was only the barest, tiniest hint of a smile. Just a little old smile, a smug little smile that said he knew something we didn't know, and, boy, were we going to be surprised.

"There! What did I tell you!" Rosie said fiercely. She leapt to her feet as the show closed on Anderson sweeping triumphantly up and down the aisles, holding his arms high, while his audience yelled, "Praise the Lord," over and over again.

"Just like the cat that ate the canary!" she said. "Look at that! Every goddamned *time!*"

She went over and snapped the set off, and stood there for a minute, seething.

I was still feeling a little numb, wishing I hadn't seen what I'd seen, when to my surprise I heard Ash begin to giggle.

Rosie turned and said, "What are *you* laughing at?"

"Oh, I'm just thinking," Ash said merrily.

"Thinking! Oh, swell, he's thinking," Rosie said to me.

"Uh-huh," Ash said, getting up off the couch. "Just—just thinking how he's going to look next week."

"Next week, what the hell's next week?"

"Next week, shweetheart"—he did a terrible Bogart, and put his arm around her—"he's going to have a little salt on his tail."

"No!" Rosie said, breaking into a grin. "You didn't!"

He giggled at her.

"Why, you old son of a bitch, you found one!" Rosie cried. "Come on, P.K., drinks all around! Oh, I'll be damned!"

• • •

I am really not going to get mixed up in this, I told myself over my third beer. No way.

We sat around a corner table in the room over the refectory—dubbed, inevitably, the Upper Room—which the seminary had kindly allowed the young theologians to turn into a beer hall. For our stomachs' sake, of course. The room was all full of oak ceiling beams and leaded windows, and the lighting was nice and dim.

Good. Maybe nobody would see me.

". . . So this turkey goes dragging his ass around the place all day long," Rosie was saying—giving Ash a little squeeze, while he looked pleased with himself—"telling me he's used up all his leads and doesn't think he's ever going to find anybody!" She laughed and shook her head. "I'm telling you!"

She was telling it to a guy named Bill Garfield, who could hardly have looked less like a safecracker—but then Rev. Anderson didn't look much like a kidnapper, either. Garf (his Yale name; that was where Ash knew him from) looked like the perfect preppie, with a boyish face and blond hair that kept falling in his eyes. Suit, tie, and briefcase, too; he'd just come uptown from working late.

He wouldn't have looked that way back at Yale, not if he had Ash for a friend; he'd have had a ponytail and a headband, and a beard, if he could have raised one on those peach-fuzz cheeks. He'd had some interesting summer jobs as a student: he'd spent a couple of summers on a wrecking contractor's crew, demolishing buildings, which was how he'd learned about dynamite; and he'd worked for a security consulting firm, which was how he'd learned about safes. He was a banker now, which I guessed said something for the dotty old people who insist on keeping their money in their mattresses.

"Yeah, well, you can imagine how *I* felt seeing Ash walk into the Yale Club, for God's sake," Garf was saying. "All clean-for-Gene, with his hair all plastered down—what a sight! And wearing a tie! I thought I'd died and gone to Hell!"

"I thought I had, too," said Ash.

"The Old Boy Network strikes again," said Rosie.

"Gets struck again, you mean!" said Garf. And they all thought that was hilarious; they hooted and yocked and clunked their mugs together.

I smiled along with them, though, I imagine, a bit wanly. I was having a hard enough time getting used to Rev. Anderson without—now, barely an hour later—sitting next to, in the flesh, a safecracker dressed up as a businessman. Unreal, man, as we used to say back in the old days.

But it had all been real, back then, too, hadn't it. We'd had White House staffers dressed up in red fright wigs, and *agents provocateurs* dressed up as hippies, and mass murderers dressed up as army officers, and crooks dressed up as Presidents. It was ridiculous. You couldn't have made it up. A lunatic couldn't have made it up, but it was real anyway.

Rosie and Ash were giving Garf the whole story, from the kidnappings to the Reverend to the Soldiers of Jeremiah and back again. They told him all kinds of neat things about safe houses and couriers and secret telephone networks for passing messages along. Then Ash got out his maps and diagrams, and they spent a long time going over those. Garf kept rubbing his hands together and saying, "Whoa, this is going to be fun."

Yeah, lots of laughs, I thought. The room was filling up with seminarians, each new bunch pausing in the doorway to let their eyes get used to the gloom—and, it seemed to me, to cast a dubious glance at the four of us. I squirmed.

"Now, your friend Muffy's got a key to the office?" Garf was saying.

"Yeah, but we don't want to blow her cover," Ash said. "It won't take 'em long to figure it out, but we want to make sure she gets a head start before they do."

"We thought we'd just break the lock," Rosie said. "Use a hammer or something. Make it nice and messy."

"Good enough," said Garf. "So you'll take care of those

supplies for me—Tiny's a great guy, you'll love him—and I'll get the specs on the safe."

"Check," said Ash.

My stomach was going bad on me again. You're amateurs, you'll get creamed. . . . Listen to them, I thought; they sound like a lot of little kids. Make-believe. Raiding the icebox. Sneaking into the vacant house down the street, pretending it's the gangsters' hideout. Check! Whoa, this'll be fun!—But what happens if it turns out to *be* the gangsters' hideout? What do the kids do then?

Things get out of hand, I wanted to tell them. Don't you know that? Don't you remember? You were there—all those balmy afternoons at the end of spring semester that used to start out as fun little fuck-the-war rallies, until somebody decided it would be even more fun to start throwing things, and before you knew it a lot of kids had their heads bashed in? What if your Reverend turns out to be just as bad, and nasty, and dangerous, as you think he is?

—Oh, Mather, lighten up, will you, I told myself. For pity's sake. You're being paranoid. Pathological. Have another beer.

Garf got up and got me one—the perfect gentleman—and I gave him a sunny smile.

CHAPTER 4

MASSASOIT FEDERAL CORRECTIONAL FACILITY IS in southeastern Massachusetts, just off the interstate, to the east of Providence. That's where my father is doing his five-to-thirty—the five for being a minister, the thirty for blowing up the train.

Once a month I drive up from New York to see him. Third Sunday of the month is my turn; first Sundays, my mother makes the trip down from Boston, where she lives now. The scattered disciples. Somebody else lives in the parsonage in Wykeham—a younger preacher, I hear, calmer and more realistic, who has put the furniture back in the house and the flag back in the church. Sarah and Jonah have both ended up in New York, though we don't see each other very often; I usually bother to call them up, along about Thursday or Friday, to ask if they want to come with me. They never do. "Oh, hell, P.K., I've got this big exam coming up," Sarah says. Freshman economics, usually. Sarah is a realist, too; she's going to major in economics. And Jonah usually says he's pulled weekend duty again; he's a New York City cop. On the bomb squad. He calls himself Joe these days.

So on Saturday I gas up the old Plymouth—the family car, which I inherited—and on Sunday, after church of course, I go and make my visit.

It takes about three hours to get there from New York— plenty of time to think things over. This time I had more to think over than usual. It was the third Sunday in March, and the break-in was all set for Monday night. That was tomorrow; hardly any time left at all. I felt awful.

Rev. Anderson had bagged his thirteenth victim that morning. UCC, this one, from Shawnee Mission, Kansas; I heard it on the car radio on my way up. And, according to the radio, the FBI still didn't have a suspect. Still none, after all this time.

That had been the last question I'd had for Rosie. The ultimate question: Why don't you just *tell* them? I'd been proud of myself for thinking of it; I'd been sure she wouldn't have a decent answer. My ace in the hole. It had come to me the other night, over the beers in the Upper Room, while the three of them put the finishing touches on their plan, and while I sat there going through my paranoid act. I haven't *got* to go with them, I'd told myself. It doesn't have to be *me*. All they need is an extra lookout; that doesn't take any talent. Anybody could do it. Besides, I thought, I'd be too nervous, I'd probably screw it up somehow and get them all caught. . . . And then it came to me in a—yes, in a flash—Why not eliminate the break-in entirely!

There'd been no point in putting it to all three of them at once; they'd have been obliged to gang up on me, if only to save face. So I'd suppressed it until the next morning, when Rosie came by our room to pick up some books for class.

"Why can't you just let the FBI do it for you?" I asked her. Such a brilliant idea. Occam's razor. "Give them an anonymous tip," I said. "Call their toll-free number. It'd be perfect; you wouldn't have to take any chances at all."

She looked at me in mild surprise. "We can't," she said.

"Why not?"

I'd expected her to say that they'd gone too far now and couldn't turn back, or that too many people were in on it already, or—well, I don't know what I expected. But what she said was, "Because the FBI already knows about it. That's why not."

"They already—?"

"Yeah; they've been sitting on it all this time. And they're going to keep sitting on it, too. That's the whole idea."

"Sitting on it," I said dully.

"Sure. The guy's got friends. You know. In Washington?"

"Washington," I said even more dully. I sat down.

"You remember Washington. That's where they have the government."

"Uh."

"Takes a lot of money to run for re-election these days," she said. "And besides, it's not nice to cross a guy who's got a mailing list the size of Anderson's."

Slowly, gently, noiselessly, I felt the bottom dropping out. "They'd do that? For him?" I said, after a while.

Rosie rolled her eyes. "Oh, P.K., come on! Where the hell have you been?" she said. "You know how these things work! Of course they'd do it. The guy's powerful!"

"And you know this from the—"

"The Soldiers, right."

Them again. Damned Soldiers everywhere.

"You remember the prayer breakfast thing," she said.

Yes, I did. Rosie had reminded me of it several times. She even had newspaper clippings, from Ash's scrapbook. It was the Soldiers' way of celebrating the Bicentennial; they'd broken in on a Senate prayer breakfast somehow and poured blood all over everything and everybody, and turned out all the lights. "I thought they were just trying to be funny," I said.

"Oh, no. You remember who was there—Rundel, Hackett, Mumford, Quackenbush, all those guys. Well, it's interesting: you go down the list, and they're all on Appropriations, and on all the law enforcement committees. They're the big shots."

"Still?"

"Still."

"Oh, wow," I said.

• • •

Oh, wow. Very articulate. And this from a scholar, yet, soon to become (perhaps—if they—we—they—got away with it) a Master of Divinity. Hey, good work, Mather, I told myself on the interstate, on my way to the slammer. Good work; your head is chock full of great ideas, advice for the heartbroken, words to live by in a fallen world; you've got all the Law and the Prophets to pick from, and the Church Fathers, and the mystics and the rationalists and the neo-Platonists too; but when it comes to what's actually going on in front of your nose, this is all you can come up with.

Oh, wow. That had been what I'd had to say, at sixteen, when my father was arrested.

Evidently I hadn't made much progress.

It poured down rain, I remember, that night in '72 when we drove him to the airport. We took the Mass. Pike in from Wykeham, which is a holy terror in a hard rain; all the nuts in Boston seem to get a sudden inspiration to go out for a joyride, and they go careening around you, cutting from lane to lane, splashing up bucketfuls of water in your face. The defroster in our old Plymouth hadn't worked in years, so my mother had to keep swabbing the fog off the windshield while my father drove.

He drove the way he always did: fast.

I don't seem to remember much else; I didn't know it was a special occasion and that I was going to wish I did remember it.

They'd brought all three of us kids along. I ought to have taken note of that, since we seldom made such a big deal out of going to the airport. My mother's idea, as it turned out. In case anything went wrong, she didn't want us to feel bad about not having said a proper goodbye. Bringing us along blind was the best she could do, though. It was a felony, after all. She couldn't be compelled to testify against him, but possibly we could, and that was too big a burden to expect children to bear.

So we believed what she'd told us, that it was just another peace conference he was going to, and that he'd be back in a few days. Believing that, we conducted ourselves in the back seat with our usual lack of dignity; Jonah and Sarah heckled each other (under their breaths, so as not to incur our father's wrath), and I—full of sixteen-year-old moral authority—told them (under my breath too) that they were being babies and pains in the ass.

I was in a bad mood. Not that I suspected anything—I could tell you now, in retrospect, that my father had been tenser and more silent than usual that spring, that he'd spent more time than ever in his study, that all the pencils in the house seemed to have teeth-marks on them all of a sudden—somebody had been chewing on them, and it must have been him—but I didn't notice any of that at the time, or, if I did, it didn't register. No, this was just a normal sixteen-year-old's bad mood.

Well, normal for a sixteen-year-old peace freak in the spring of '72. I was having a terrible time of it that spring. I was working harder than ever, immersed in the peace movement up to my eyebrows—I had meetings and marches and rallies to go to about three days a week, and I was out there with the Vigil Committee on the village common, or the steps of the library, or at the A&P, every spare minute—but it wasn't working any more.

I was getting sick of shoving leaflets into my neighbors' hands and seeing their eyes glaze over. I'd been doing this to them for years—the preacher's kid, skinny little girl in a fatigue jacket, getting taller every year—and they were sick of me, too. Half the time they crossed the street to avoid me, whether I was handing out leaflets or not.

A lot of time had passed. Everybody was tired; everybody's nerves were shot. The Kent State Four were cold in their graves in '72, already fading from memory; so were the dead and wounded of Jackson State, Wisconsin, everywhere; the years of tear gas and sirens, napalm and body counts. It was all winding down, as they said in Washington. American boys were coming home, planeload by planeload. They came home in wheelchairs, boys hardly older than I was; weeping, they threw their medals at the White House—unnoticed by the President, who was busy watching a football game.

Meanwhile, the planes they'd come home on were going back across the Pacific full of bombs. They flew more missions that spring than they had in years, bombing schools, hospitals, whatever was handy—but bombs didn't look like war. They were technology; they could be dropped from a lordly altitude, from high up in the firmament, making for dull footage on the evening news. Didn't spoil your dinner. It was like a bad movie: no close-ups, no houses blowing up or people screaming. After a steady diet of screams, for all those years, it was suddenly hard to make the connections.

Maybe that was why the protesting that spring was only half-hearted. We cranked up the mimeograph machines and marched again, struck again, cursed Nixon again—but wearily, with an air of self-mockery. We sang the old songs again, but not very loud; and it seemed to be raining all the time.

Business as usual. Maybe I knew that already, and just didn't want to admit it: the war was ordinary by then, a part of everyday life. Nothing to shout about. The older peace freaks—the ones I'd always looked up to, who had been at Columbia or Chicago or in the balconies of my father's church—were going back to school in '72, writing their theses, getting on with their careers. And the younger ones were, already, too young to remember Kennedy or King. Already they were getting the peace symbol mixed up with the Mercedes Star.

Mercedes Stars, in spray paint, on all the walls.

Mene, mene, tekel, upharsin.

That was the season my father chose to blow up his train.

. . .

And did he give us any special goodbye at the airport? Did
he hug us all perhaps too hard, exchanging glances with our
mother? Did he tell us, perhaps too sternly, to be good? I
doubt it; he wasn't the type. I didn't notice, at any rate. After
all, it was only an old peace conference, this time in California, but otherwise no different from the rest of them.

So I didn't give it a second thought until two days afterward, when my mother was already home from work when I
got back from school.

"What's the matter, Mom, you sick?" I called on my way in.

"No, honey, I'm fine." She was standing in the middle of
the kitchen as if she'd forgotten what she'd gone in there for.
"Sam's been arrested," she said.

"Is that all!" I said. He was always getting arrested. Especially at peace conferences. People who went to those things
always seemed to find some way (last item on the agenda:
Putting Those Ideas Into Action) to get themselves thrown in
jail for the night. It seemed to make them feel better.

"Well, no," she said, "this time I expect it'll be different."
And she leaned against the refrigerator and explained to me,
very calmly, that it hadn't been a peace conference at all, but
an army train full of bombs. The train had been on a siding
in California, waiting to be routed through to whatever air
force base they flew the things out of, and, along with five
other preachers, my father had blown it up.

And I said, "Oh, wow."

We gathered on the living room floor to watch the evening
news. My mother quietly sipped a large bourbon. Jonah and
Sarah quivered with excitement. I don't know what I did. I
was so stunned, I guess I just sat. I didn't want to watch it, to
go over it all again, the whole damned thing—but there it was
anyway, no matter what I wanted: the train, or what was left
of it, burning and burning, great gouts of black smoke rising
slowly into the sky.

Jonah was sorely disappointed that we didn't get to see the explosion itself; he liked explosions.

"They couldn't get a camera crew there in time, dummy," Sarah told him.

"I bet it was *huge*, man," Jonah said, ignoring her. "Look at that smoke!"

I probably made a face.

We didn't get to see him lying on the escarpment, either, where a piece of shrapnel intended for the Enemy had hit him in the leg because he hadn't had enough sense to take cover. In spite of all his sermons about dynamite. He'd gotten the instructions out of an underground magazine, *Ramparts* or something, and it had told him where to buy his materials, how to place them to do maximum damage, and how to detonate them, but not how far and how fast to run; so he had just stood there in the open, admiring his handiwork—*fiat lux!*—and it had knocked him ass over teakettle.

And we didn't get to see his noble band of co-conspirators scrambling away up the hill to their getaway car, in spite of the vow they'd taken to stick together. Nor the MPs, who arrived soon afterward, first bandaging his leg, then passing the chain around his waist and snapping his wrists into the handcuffs attached to the chain. All we got to see was him being hustled out of a car and up the steps of the federal courthouse in Sacramento.

"There he is, Mom!" Sarah and Jonah crowed in unison. "All *right*! Right *on*!"

He was surrounded by a crowd of MPs, cops, and reporters. He was wearing his clerical collar, as always, and his pants leg was slit as though he were on his way to the Chair. They took him up the steps, with him limping; when he got to the top, he turned and smiled at the camera.

"That's for us," Mother said quietly. "To let us know he's okay."

Oh, perfect, I thought.

But Jonah and Sarah were beside themselves with joy. Our

very own father on Walter Cronkite—think of it! They wondered if the war would end. They wondered if the FBI would come to the house and interrogate us. And if he'd have a big trial the way the Berrigans always did. "Maybe we can get Kunstler, Mom, what do you think?"

Well, no. I'd figured that out by then. It all slid into place, lined up in neat straight rows, like tumblers in a lock. Ding. Click. The answer was No.

No, he wouldn't be needing Kunstler; he wouldn't have a trial at all. Not because of the expense, or because the war had been put on trial before, and acquitted, or because blowing up trains was passé by then, but simply because our father—being our father—would plead guilty. The reporters in the courtroom would sigh and toss their pencils down, done out of a story. "Well, I *am* guilty," he'd say. Back home in Wykeham, Jonah would break a boy's nose at school for calling our father a Commie faggot, and I would go bail him out of the principal's office and take him home, both of us marching angry and dry-eyed across the common like a couple of Hester Prynnes—while, back in Sacramento, at about the same hour, our father, not content to stop with the guilty plea, would be preaching a sermon at the judge and getting the book thrown at him.

I understood that it would go like that, and it did. I wasn't clairvoyant; it just figured, that's all. Local Minister Turns to Violence. "Can't Believe It"—Neighbors. I could have written the stories blindfolded. Mather Goes to Jail; Doesn't Pass Go. War Continues.

"How do you feel about all this, Sarah?" The Boston *Globe*, looking solemn and sympathetic, on my way to school.

"I'm not Sarah," I snarled.

"Oh, sorry; then you must be Olivia."

"Nobody calls me Olivia."

"Well, uh, how do you feel about it?"

"Swell. I feel swell about it."

I wished I did.

• • •

Oh, I wished I did. I wished I could force myself to be as proud of him as Jonah and Sarah were—at least, as they were at first—or as quiet and contained as Mother. Something dignified, at least. No such luck. I couldn't even come close, because the one thing I couldn't understand, that didn't figure, was—for what?

For what, Dad! I wanted to yell at him. Five-to-thirty—and for what? To blow one train off one siding? Hey, swell, that ought to hold them up for about five minutes. Face it, Dad, we're already beaten. They're painting Mercedes Stars on the walls; soon they'll be voting for Presidents; McGovern will get creamed, and we'll get Watergate after that. Give it time, and we'll get Love Canal, and Three Mile Island, and the Moral Majority, and an actor from Hollywood who likes to play with guns. It's a whole new ball game, Dad; get used to it. It'll be as if we never existed; all we'll have to show for it will be designer jeans and white wine. Out with the sixties, in with the eighties; nothing changes, you can't beat war, the whole world is made of it. It makes the world go 'round.

Peace, man. Keep the faith. Childish things, put away. Blown away.

Face it, Dad. We were dreaming. It's over.

They finished Massasoit just in time for him; they were just seeding the lawn and planting the petunias around the parking lot when we got him transferred there from California.

It's a nice place, Massasoit. It doesn't look like a prison at all; it looks more like an electronics factory. They've concealed the guard towers, and hidden the razor wire, behind a plain blank wall wrapped all around the building. From the highway, all that's visible is the shell, with a long driveway and a water tower.

They did their best, considering the needs of maximum security. There are two sets of motorized barred doors at the entrance—they had to have those—but, inside, the visitors' waiting room is reasonably cheery. They've hung calico curtains around the bulletproof windows; there are Colonial settees to sit on, and a rag rug on the floor. There's Muzak.

I hated it from the moment I saw it. There ought to have been turrets and battlements and portcullises. There ought to have been a sign over the door: "Abandon All Hope, Ye Who Enter Here." Did they think we wouldn't realize where we were? Where he was? I hated everything about it. But I went in, with Jonah and Sarah and my mother, and I tried to act like an adult. It's not so bad, I told myself. Nothing abnormal about being in jail.

It *was* bad, the first few times. We had to hand in our coats and pocketbooks to the guard at the door, who wore a gun. They made us sit there a while, and then they called some names—Jenkins, Lopez, Martinez, Mather—and we went still further inside, down corridors not so nicely decorated. Mothers and children, herded along in a huddled little group, through more sets of doors shutting forever behind us. We knew damn well where we were by then; this was the Jug, the Slammer, the End of the Road. And then at last we came to the Visitation Room, so-called, and we sat down at the counter where they told us to. It was a semi-partitioned booth, soundproofed, eerily resembling the language lab at school—and there was our father, across the counter from us, behind a pane of blue glass.

No wonder Jonah and Sarah won't go back any more. They were too young, I guess; didn't handle it too well. It was bad at first, it's true. But I got used to it.

Blue glass with chicken wire in it, to separate the crooks from the innocents, the just from the unjust, the ghosts from the living, so we couldn't pass any weapons back and forth, no talismans, nothing of any use. Couldn't touch the museum piece, the relic from the past. Divide and conquer. They had an armor-plated telephone in there; that was how we talked to him. They were taping the conversation, so we'd heard, somewhere in the building. From our mouths to the warden's ear.

Bearing that in mind, we could say anything we wanted.

The only trouble was, he didn't talk back. That was the real trouble; forget the settees and the curtains and the rest of the scenery. It was his silence that got me. Some people go on hunger strikes in jail; my father went on a talk strike from the moment he got there. A real basket case, this one. Like old Ezekiel in the Bible—ask him a question and get back an oracle. After all those years preaching, he wouldn't shut up, he was too furious; he slaved away over those sermons, hammer and tongs, endlessly rewriting so the point would be perfectly plain, so any dummy could understand it—and now all I got was Doctor Zen.

"For what, Dad?"

"God is not mocked," he said through the phone.

Sitting there behind the glass, looking neither happy nor unhappy, the anger all gone out of him.

"But a bomb, Dad?" Rotten little kid. "Dynamite? After everything you said?"

"Not peace but a sword," he said.

"A sword?" I said. "Come on, Dad, this isn't fair. What the hell do you mean?"

And he said, "They have Moses and the prophets; let them hear them."

After a while I got used to that, too.

Going up to Massasoit, once every month, seedtime and harvest, year in and year out.

My mother calls the whole thing "Father's Little Adventure." A tough lady, that one; she's a shrink, has been a shrink all along, in a mental hospital in Boston. The state hospital, where, as she puts it, the real nuts are. None of your neurotic housewives, no anorexic little girls from Wellesley. That's the way she talks. They get that way in those places, living and working amid the peeling paint, brown linoleum, and old dead furniture, where everybody knows where they are, where there's no hope at all; they get tough. Nothing surprises them or drives them to tears. At least, not in public. Maybe they tell Jesus, when no one is listening; but otherwise, they speak of the bitterest, most painful things wryly, almost casually, the way cops do, or ghetto dwellers—as though they happened every day. Which of course they do.

Father's Little Adventure. Well, I suppose she's seen worse.

I admired the way she handled it. God, was she cool. What endurance, what fortitude. What a role model. She never complained or flung a tantrum; just went right on with it. I decided I would do as she did. Not a conscious decision; I sort of fell into it over the years. It seemed the easiest way.

Done properly, of course, it's the hardest; done close to the bull, as Hemingway put it. But if you're going to do it properly, you have to remember everything. It's a lot easier to forget everything, and you get about the same result.

Same outward and visible sign.

So the doors rolled open, that Sunday afternoon in March, and rolled shut again behind me, and I handed over my belongings and took a seat on one of the settees, and waited, miserably, for my name to be called.

Back at dear old Massasoit. Same guard on duty after all these years; same sour face; he hadn't changed a bit. Neither had I, evidently. All grown up now, but having made no progress at all.

As Rosie put it.

Let the dead bury their dead. And was he living? No, he wasn't living any more, as far as I could see. It was hard to tell, what with all the barriers they had erected between me and him, but as far as I could see, he was just sitting there. Well behaved, going gray. He looked as if he was on Thorazine—as if they had body-snatched him, taken him away somewhere, and substituted a look-alike zombie.

• • •

And what had they substituted for me?

There's Rosemary, that's for remembrance. It's curious, really, how suddenly these things can happen. After all the time you've put in. You've gone along, you've gotten used to things; the seasons pass, you get hardened, you adapt. Welcome to the real world. Well, you say to yourself, so what if this Rev. Anderson has bought himself a bunch of Senators? So what if he's going to brainwash everybody? That figures, too, doesn't it. You know how these things work. Probably won't make much difference anyway. You've learned to think, not exactly that it's normal, but that it's just the way things are, that's all. Can't beat City Hall. The System. Everything. Principalities and powers. The military-industrial complex. The Man. This mortal coil. It's all rigged, it's all a fake; the truth (supposing it exists) is so completely overpowered, the good guys (ditto) so hopelessly outnumbered—why should I spend my life beating my head against a wall, you think. People get the leaders, gods, et cetera, they deserve. So let 'em have 'em.

The hell with 'em.

And then, just when you think you have it under control, when you've gotten to a point where you can just about stand it, Rosie comes along and drops a pile of shit on you.

"But if he's as powerful as all that, you haven't got a prayer," I'd told her. "No matter what you get on him, he'll weasel out of it with a fifty-dollar fine and come back and flatten you guys."

"You know," she'd told me, "sometimes I think you really missed it."

"All right, look. Suppose everything goes off absolutely perfectly, and you get away with it. Put him out of business," I said. "Great; good for you; but what happens after that? Somebody even worse comes to take his place. There's plenty of them out there, and they're getting stronger all the time. People want it, Rosie! It's what they want! Knock him off and what do you accomplish? You're right back where you started. You can't change anything on this freakin' planet. It reverts. They just change the names once in a while, that's all, to keep it interesting."

She looked at me for a long time, letting me listen to myself. "It's important to do it," she said at last.

"Oh, Rosie, don't give me that! That's so dumb!" I was all heated up by then, mad at her and everybody and everything.

"Of course it's dumb! It's an act of faith, asshole!" she yelled. "My God, I'd have thought even *you* could have figured that out!"

"Jenkins, Kaplan, LaRussa, Mather . . . Mather? You coming or what?"

"Oh. Yeah."

When I got up and followed the group down the corridor, I realized my hands were sweating. I couldn't believe it. Ridiculous, I told myself; come on, Mather, be cool, can't you?

I was going to have to ask him about it. I only had until tomorrow night. Rosie had said they were going to go without me if I didn't hurry up and decide, and if that happened they'd probably get caught, and it would be my fault, and I'd be an asshole for the rest of my life. Or words to that effect.

Act of faith indeed. How ironic: ask the jailbird. Was it worth it after all, Dad? Was it fun? Would you recommend it to a friend?

Even though it's over?

The end of the corridor. The guards herded us into the Visitation Room and took up their positions by the door, and there I was again, fidgeting on the edge of a plastic chair, facing him through the glass.

"How you doing, Dad?"

God, he looked so gray. I'd forgotten.

"Treating you all right?"

Shrug.

"What's new?"

No new thing under the sun, dummy.

What's the meaning of Zen, Dad? Does a dog have Buddha-nature?

What did you come out to see? A reed shaken by the wind?

"Listen, Dad, tell me something."

Please.

"You, uh, read the papers in here; you know about these kidnappings, don't you?"

He nodded, slowly. A cautious nod? Don't blow it, idiot, I told myself. Don't say anything to alarm the boys with the tape recorders.

"Well, um . . . What if I . . . what if you knew something about—something like them. That nobody else knew. I mean, very few people."

Did his eyes narrow ever so slightly? Brows move? A flicker of the old stern expression?

"Well, would you—would you do something about it?" I said helplessly. Couldn't say more. It was a conspiracy, after all, and this, I supposed, was an Overt Act.

He looked out at me from behind the glass for what seemed like twenty minutes or so; and then he said, in a low voice, "An evil generation seeks a sign; but no sign shall be given it except the sign of Jonah."

Well, I'd asked for it. And I'd gotten it, and now I was stuck with it. He sure had my number. How many times had he preached about Jonah, back home? How many times had he dinned it into us? He didn't mean the sign of the fish, God rescuing His prophet from the belly of the whale. That was a nice ending, but it wasn't the part of the story he liked. He liked the beginning better: how Jonah got swallowed by the whale in the first place, because God had told him to cry against Nineveh, that great city, and he wouldn't do it.

Click. Ding.

And then my father did a very peculiar thing.
He winked at me.

I don't know how I got back to New York. I have a vague
memory of nearly rear-ending somebody at a tollbooth around
New Haven. If that was you, by any chance, I apologize.
Dark-haired woman, in an old white Plymouth with Massachusetts plates, who stared at you as if she hadn't the faintest
idea where she was? Yup. Me. Sorry.

Back in my room at the seminary, I poured myself a good
stiff one and sat down and put my feet up on my desk, where
my thesis lay in a heap, unfinished. I sat there for several
hours, smoking, drinking, drifting. Staring out the window,
across the dark alley, at the colossal backside of the Riverside
Church. Thou shalt see my hinder parts, but my face shall not
be seen. Ho ho. Somebody ought to paint that on the wall out
there, I thought. A message to the seminarians.

"Oh, God," I sighed.

All you need is love. All you get is the sign of Jonah.

And a wink. Through the glass.

Damn it all, I thought, why did everything have to be so
fucked up? Act of faith indeed. Sign of Jonah indeed. Fine
way to talk. Fine old ancient wisdom, and meanwhile, every
few minutes—in between acts of faith—another siren would go
by in the street outside, beyond the backside of the church,
announcing somebody else done for, another ten-year-old
murdered by a twelve-year-old, another Viet Vet Slays Wife,
Kids, Then Self, another Grandmother Freezes to Death in
Unheated Tenement, which would come out in the papers
tomorrow opposite an artificially emaciated Bloomie's model
in three-hundred-dollar cowboy boots.

God! What a shithole!

Happens every day.

But it's important to do it.

Damn him, I thought; it's all his fault. Damn Rosie, too.
Damn them both to hell.

• • •

I was still sitting there around one o'clock in the morning, with my mind going around in circles, when the phone rang. I nearly fell out of my chair.

"P.K. It's Rosie. You better be awake."

"What? What are you—"

"Can't talk now," she said. "Let me buy you a cup of coffee at Jake's."

I looked at my watch. "Right now?"

"Yeah, right now."

"Is something wrong, or what?"

"No, but—well, yeah, something's wrong. Just get your butt down here."

"Gimme time to put on some shoes," I said, but she'd already hung up.

Oh, Lord, I thought, putting my shoes on. Oh, help. What now. I wasn't ready for it, whatever it was.

The Jake of Jake's Diner had left for New Jersey years ago. The place was now run by a man named Angel, but the decor was just the same as always—lunch counter up one side, shabby red leatherette booths up the other, patched and re-patched with cloth tape where they'd been worn out by generations of Columbia students' bottoms. Angel's coffee was, if anything, even worse than Jake's was said to have been, though he scrubbed out his coffee urns day and night. "What can I do," he'd tell you wearily. "They poison the water. Stupid city."

I could see him in there now, scouring away and shaking his head, as I pulled up to the curb behind Rosie's old green Volkswagen.

Six or eight other people were inside, talking and studying. Rosie was in the last booth in the back, near the pay phone, nervously watching the door, and looking angry and scared. The fluorescent lights put dark smudges under her eyes.

She'd ordered two cups of Angel's dreadful coffee, and she shoved one of them across to me as I slid into the booth.

"What's wrong?" I said.

"What do you think's wrong, dammit? We blew it, that's what."

"But you—!" I was stunned. "But it was supposed to be tomorrow night!"

"Keep it down, will you?" she whispered, glancing past me toward the other booths. "Garf has to fly out to L.A. tomorrow night for his crummy bank. He just found out about it this afternoon."

"Oh, man." I wasn't ready. You're supposed to get a nice long dark night of the soul, in which you struggle and suffer and finally make your peace with yourself; then you can rise up calmly in the morning, and set your jaw, and go do what a woman's gotta do. That was what I'd been counting on. You're not supposed to get a full-blown disaster dumped on you before the night's half over with.

"So here's the deal," Rosie was saying. "We got in, got the stuff, got out, just fine—just like I told you; nobody got hurt or anything—but then somehow the getaway got screwed up, and I lost 'em. I don't know where the hell they are!" She lit a cigarette and shook the match dead. "We were supposed to rendezvous down on 72nd Street. We took different routes over there—you know, that's so they don't catch all of you at once—so, all right, I go on over there, no problem, and I'm waiting and waiting and waiting—and they never showed up! I waited an hour and a half for the fuckers. Nothing. Not nobody."

"Ow," I said.

"You're damn right, ow," she fumed. "Old Genius Rittenhouse was going to give us the address of a safe house someplace in Pennsylvania. I should have been halfway there by now; instead, here I am with my ass hanging out."

A safe house, I thought. It gave me a chill.

"I mean, how much trouble can you get into in thirty blocks?" she said in disgust. "Christ, that was supposed to be the easy part!"

"Maybe they didn't get caught," I said helpfully. "Maybe they had a flat tire or something."

"There's a subway, ain't there?" she snapped.

I guessed there was.

"So help me out, P.K.," she said. "I can't go back to Union. The cops'll be all over it in the morning—maybe before morning. And don't tell me to hide under the bed, either. Then we'd both be up the creek."

Both! But of course; I was her roommate; I knew all about it, didn't I? Or so the cops would think. And everybody had seen us together in the Upper Room the other night. Was that an overt act, too? Or would it be misprision? Aiding and abetting? Jonah would know, I guessed. Though he was hardly the man to ask.

And hadn't I just come back from seeing my father, the crook?

I suppressed that train of thought. No time for it. Think, woman! I told myself.

"I guess your family's out," I said.

"Huh!" she snorted.

"Preacher, maybe?"

She looked pained.

"Well, how about this Muffy? Or did she leave town already?"

"Left on Friday. Right after work."

Damn. "You must know somebody else in the Soldiers."

"Yeah, swell," she said. "I'll tell you everything I know. Won't take a minute. I know 'George and Ellen in Pennsylvania'—they're the ones with the safe house. And 'Beth in D.C.,' and 'Zeke in Colorado.' No last names, no addresses. For their protection. You only get the details when you're actually on your way there. It's the 'cell system.' Great, huh?" She cursed and drank her coffee, which made her wince. "All very devious," she added. "Meaning stupid."

"And that's all he told you?"

She nodded wearily.

"Jeez! Rosie!"

"Don't get me started," she said.

We brooded for a while.

"That shithead," she muttered. "You should have seen me sitting there, trying to be cool, with all these freaks walking around. . . . Christ, I'm going to kill that guy." She sighed and poked at the ashes in the ashtray. "I don't know, P.K.," she said. "I just don't know. I've racked my brains tonight. The only people I can think of are the ones the cops would think of, too."

As if on cue, a police car at that moment went screaming up the street outside. We both flinched, and Rosie turned paler than she was already. "Shit!" she said. "I can't deal with this."

"Just hold on. Hold on. Lemme think." I didn't care for the way my heart was jumping up and down.

"Fine. So think. Watch my purse, will you; I'm going to the john."

So I sat and watched her purse and tried to think what in the world I'd do if I were in her shoes. Hotels were out, I figured; too expensive, not to mention the high visibility of checking in at this hour. Even in New York, that would be remembered. Where else, then? Runaway shelters? The Salvation Army? No; they worked too closely with the cops. What did that leave? The subways? The steam tunnels under Grand Central? Not exactly your viable alternatives. But for the life of me I couldn't come up with anything better. What did I know about cops and robbers? Jail I knew about. Staying out of jail I didn't. Rosie was supposed to know about that stuff; if she and Ash were such hot-shot radicals, why hadn't they thought of this before? The whole thing gave me the creeps.

Some people can pray at a time like this. The Born Again folks have that luxury; they just get on their knees a while, and let the old Bible fall open, and close their eyes and put their finger down, and they get the answer. Sell the house. Buy the dress. Not the red one, the blue one. Very simple; it must be nice.

But meanwhile the cops were careening around the streets,

probably looking for her already. Think, dammit! I told myself. Think clearly! This is an emergency!

I'd never heard Rosie say there was anything she couldn't deal with.

. . . Well, it was irrational. A sorry way to operate, but there wasn't any rational thing to do. Fallen world, and all that.

I'd been fishing in my pocketbook all the while, and then in my coat pockets, for my cigarettes. I sure wanted one. But evidently I'd left them home, or out in the car; so I reached over and lit one of Rosie's, and smoked it while my mind went barreling up and down its blind alleys. Under duress, of course, the mind turns to irrelevancies—mine does, anyhow—and I found myself thinking how foul Rosie's cigarettes tasted. Nothing like menthol when you're not used to it. She smokes Kools, you see, and I smoke True Blues; that used to be our joke, way back freshman year, when people couldn't tell which one of us was which. "She's Kool; I'm True Blue." (No, no, I told myself. It would never work.) We thought it was a riot. People kept sneaking looks at our cigarette packs. We thought they were crazy—*we* didn't think there was any resemblance at all—but it took them weeks.

To tell us apart.

I stared at her pocketbook on the table, her Kools, her car keys. I don't believe this, I thought. And furthermore, I don't believe I'm even thinking this. But, sure, it would work; it had to work. Hell, it was too ridiculous *not* to work!

I put some change on the table for the coffee. Quickly, before I could think better of it, I took my car keys from my coat pocket, and put them in my pocketbook, and put my pocketbook on the table. Then I picked up Rosie's pocketbook, and Rosie's car keys and Rosie's Kools, and walked out of the diner.

PART

II

Men never do evil so completely and cheerfully as when they do it from religious conviction.

—PASCAL

CHAPTER 5

BY THE TIME ROSIE CAME OUT OF THE BATH-
room, I was half a mile away, at the wheel
of her Volkswagen, driving north on Broadway with a silly
grin on my face.

"You turkey!" I yelled happily, scooting past the Columbia gates. "You freak, you must be out of your mind!"

All the lights were green. I coasted down the hill toward
125th Street, waving at Union Seminary as I went by, and
hung a left under the subway tracks. Heading for the George
Washington Bridge—in Rosie's car, for God's sake. Impersonating a felon; what a joke; it was ridiculous! Idiotic! Much
too crazy not to work! I pictured the look on Rosie's face
back at Jake's Diner and giggled to think how mad she'd be.

"Whoo-hoo!" I said.

I went banging and bumping over the ruined pavement,
letting out another whoop with every pitch of the car. I
passed the drug clinic and the meat-packing houses and got
up onto the West Side Highway, and a couple of minutes
later I was circling up the ramp to the bridge.

And over it I went, over the dark Hudson, my first state
line—(interstate flight while impersonating a felon)—driving
very conservatively past the tollbooths on the Jersey side, so
as not to exceed the speed limit, and resisting the temptation
to honk the horn. I wanted to, though.

There was of course no reason for this inordinate giddiness.
No reason on earth why I should feel so swell just at this
moment. I knew that. I was being stupid, rash, reckless, fool-

hardy; there was no end to the things I'd failed to take into account. I knew it perfectly well, but I didn't care.

Something had been let loose in me. I didn't know what it was, or what I was going to do with it, but it was loose.

I shifted up into fourth and headed west.

Back at the diner, Rosie was at least twice as mad as I'd imagined.

"What the hell is *this?*" she cried, staring at the empty booth where I'd been sitting. "Angel! Did you see her go out?"

Angel, who made it his business to stay out of other people's business, turned around from his coffee machine. "Something the matter?" he said mildly.

"She took my purse," Rosie said, holding up my pocketbook.

Angel looked blank for a moment, and then he shrugged. "Call a cop if you wanna," he said, waving his dishrag at the pay phone. "I didn't see nothing."

The other people in the diner were turning around to look at her, too. "Probably just a joke or something," she said, trying to smile.

She rushed out the door.

And she stopped short on the sidewalk, as she saw my old Plymouth waiting for her at the curb, just behind the empty space where her Volkswagen had been. "Oh, my God," she said. She looked wildly up and down Broadway. The traffic lights had changed to red, but there weren't any Volkswagens under any of them. She couldn't have spent that long in the john, could she? Two minutes? Three?

She ran to the end of the block and looked down the side street. No sign of me there, either.

"Bitch!" she said.

She couldn't believe it. Of all the goddamned stupid boneheaded things to have done. And with the documents, and the cash, carefully tucked behind the seat. . . . "Shit," she said.

The very notion of *me* running around loose with that stuff made her head hurt.

"You freak!" she yelled at the empty street. "You must be out of your mind!"

All right, she told herself. Just don't panic. Panic was what killed you, as Ash, the genius, was fond of saying. There must be something she could do. Try to catch up with me? No— with all the routes I might have taken out of Manhattan, she wouldn't have a chance in hell of picking the right one.

Well, then, she thought, she'd have to get in touch with the Soldiers. There must be some way to do it that she hadn't thought of. She could warn them, if nothing else, that the job had gone all to shit. Get onto their phone network. Ash had told her there was a code you had to use, though naturally he hadn't given her a phone number. Him and his goddamned secrets. She could go back up to Union, quick, before the cops got there, and search Ash's room—maybe he'd been careless and left something lying around, or . . .

"Christ almighty," she wailed. "My *keys!*"

She stared down at her hand, in which she held *my* keys. They'd get her into our room all right, but not into his.

Another police car, somewhere to the south, began its unearthly bleeping noise. Rosie jumped.

Blithering idiot, she told herself. Acting like a perfect asshole. The lobby guard had probably untied himself long since; before long there would be cops everywhere. If there weren't already. Nothing to do but get into the damned Plymouth and beat it; she'd have to worry about what to do later, later. Just act like you know what you're doing; Ash had said that, too, blast his hide. At least he'd gotten that right. Just act like you do, even if you don't.

As she started my car, she noted with disgust that I hadn't even left her a full tank of gas. But she found my cigarettes. They were right on the dashboard, where I'd left them.

Meanwhile, Ash and Garf were sitting, in handcuffs, in the

back of a police car on 98th Street between Broadway and West End Avenue.

"A fucking red light," Garf muttered. "I can't believe you ran a fucking red light."

Ash closed his eyes.

"Mister Big Shot," Garf said. "Mister El Bandido."

The car's radio squawked.

The street was blocked off in both directions by several more police cars with their lights flashing. Just beyond them, in both directions, knots of people were gathering to get a look at Ash's Porsche, which, a little while ago, had come whipping up West End Avenue with three squad cars right behind it, turned the corner of 98th Street at about forty, swerved to avoid a double-parked van, and hit a large pothole. After a short trip through the air, the Porsche had come to rest in, and around, and under, an extensive collection of garbage cans, all of which had been full at the moment of impact.

"And you couldn't just pull over and let them give you a ticket," Garf went on. "Oh, no. Not you. You had to do the chase scene from *The French Connection.*"

"Just shut up," Ash said through gritted teeth.

"What a man," Garf said bitterly. "Great getaway car. Look how well she corners."

A cop was climbing out of the Porsche with their share of the documents and several fat bundles of bills.

"There it goes," Garf said.

Ash took a look, and groaned, and shut his eyes again.

"Simple little job," Garf said. "Easy as pie."

"Well you could have thrown it out the fucking window like I told you."

"Well, you're stuck with it now, aren't you?" said Garf.

"Me?" Ash gaped at him.

Another cop came over and got into the front seat of the squad car, and said something incomprehensible into the radio. Then he made himself comfortable and began writing it all down on a clipboard.

CHAPTER 6

A TALL BLONDE, MADE EVEN TALLER BY THREE-
inch spike heels, strode briskly into the lobby
of an office building on North Michigan Avenue in Chicago
on Monday morning at seven o'clock sharp. She wore a stunning suede coat, pearl gray, over an equally stunning blue silk
dress, set off by gold earrings and a little gold cross around
her neck. Under one arm she carried the *Sun-Times* and the
Trib. Her nails, long and beautifully manicured, were lac-
quered a dark crimson.

Seven o'clock was the time she always arrived at work. The
lobby was empty at that hour except for the lone security
guard, who was lounging against a pillar. He looked up at the
sound of her heels clacking smartly on the marble floor.

"Morning, Kelly," she said, passing him without breaking
stride, and noting, with her usual satisfaction, that he invol-
untarily stood up straighter as she went by. "Beautiful day,
isn't it?"

"It sure is, Miss Masters," the guard said, with feeling. He
gazed appreciatively after her—wishing, as he always did, that
he were twenty years younger and five inches taller—as she
swept through the lobby, past the building directory, on
which her name was not listed, and disappeared into an express elevator.

She emerged again on the twenty-third floor.

Suite 2308 had a blue door, and on the door was lettered, in
gold, "Bliss Publications. National Sales Coordination." That
name wasn't on the building directory either; nor was it in
the Chicago phone book. The main office of Bliss Publica-

tions, purveyors of devotional books and magazines, religious tracts, liturgical aids, Sunday school teaching materials, calendars, posters, and greeting cards, was not in Suite 2308, but in an industrial park in Schaumburg, Illinois, some thirty miles away.

Harriet Masters took a set of keys from her pocketbook and unlocked the door.

Her assistant, Ralph Simpkins, was already in the office. A clean-cut lad, handsome and dimpled; a recent graduate, in speech and communications, from a good conservative Baptist college in Indiana. Ralph had come to her after a year's seasoning in Senator Quackenbush's press relations office, and the Senator's staff had trained him well; he worked almost as hard as Harriet did herself.

At the moment he was kneeling on the floor in front of the Associated Press teletype machine, gathering up the waves of yellow paper that had spilled out of it during the weekend. He looked up at Harriet and beamed. "*Good* morning!" he said heartily.

"Morning," Harriet said, smiling down at him. "How are things going? Heard from Mike and Bruno yet?"

"Uh-huh; just a few minutes ago."

"They made it to Salina, I trust?"

"Yup. Right on schedule. They'd made the drop-off; they were just about to start back."

"Excellent." Stepping around the cascade of paper, Harriet moved from Ralph's anteroom into her own office, where she shucked off her coat and tossed it into a chair.

"They said the Reverend had a little reaction to the tranquilizer," Ralph called after her. "Nothing serious, though. Just a little nausea."

"Mmmm," Harriet said, fluffing out her hair in a mirror behind the office door.

"And they said to give you their love."

She smiled at herself in the mirror. "Well, wasn't that nice of them."

Her office was done in shades of cream and beige, with two

sleek chairs and a coffee table facing her large, sleek desk. The chairs were seldom used for anything but Harriet's coat; visitors were few and far between.

It was a large, sunny room. The wall behind the desk was all glass, with a fine view of Lake Michigan. One side wall was filled with bookshelves, from floor to ceiling, holding a huge collection of reference works—directories, atlases, phone books, and college yearbooks by the dozen; legal manuals; psychology texts, with a heavy emphasis on the behavior modification school; and binders full of back issues of *Security & Surveillance Magazine*. On the other side wall, next to the door, was a giant highway map of the United States, divided into thirty territories and studded with colored pins.

As for the back wall, it contained two Bliss posters, one of an ocean beach at sunrise (or perhaps sunset) and the other of a meadow full of wildflowers, both with inspirational messages in script across the bottom. Between these two posters was a photograph, taken through a long lens, of President Kennedy, Jackie, and the Connollys riding in an open limousine. Jackie's suit and pillbox hat stood out bright pink.

Pink indeed! thought Harriet, going over to the picture and standing contemplatively before it, as she did every morning. She was no admirer of the Kennedys; far from it. She had not been fooled. She had felt while Kennedy was President, and still felt, that he was part of an extremely sophisticated, high-level, international conspiracy to deliver America into the hands of the Roman Catholic Church and, through it, to the Communists. His presidency marked the beginning of permissiveness in American culture, from the Warren Court to the welfare state, from whose poisonous effects the country was still reeling. Had he lived, there was no telling how much worse things might have been. Harriet had prayed every day for Kennedy's death—so had her whole family—and as far as she was concerned, it was the mighty hand of God. He had gotten exactly what he deserved. Harriet's mother had even written to Jackie to tell her so.

Harriet's own political career had already begun by that

time. She was secretary of her high school student council; the following year she worked for Goldwater while also running for president herself (he lost; she won). In college she rose to the state chairmanship of Young Americans for Freedom, and when she graduated, with her B.A. in psychology, she joined Senator Quackenbush's campaign staff.

It had been the best training experience anyone could wish for. It was 1970, and the Senator was in the middle of the toughest reelection battle of his life, against an up-and-coming young liberal by the name of Sidney Goetz. Goetz was dynamic, ambitious, and smart, with a strong civil rights record (and, it went without saying, he favored total retreat from Vietnam), and he was killing Quackenbush in the early polls by portraying him as an old fogy with antiquated ideas.

"Old fogy, my ass," said Quackenbush one day. "I'll tell you where he got *his* ideas—got 'em from Karl Marx, that's who." Which gave Harriet an idea of her own. She sat down and wrote the campaign letter that turned the tide, the one that ended, "Rise up! Join with me in smashing the warmongering lackeys of capitalist-imperialist oppression!" They sent it out over Goetz's name, on Goetz's letterhead; and for good measure she had the envelope stuffers spray each letter with perfume as it went into the mail.

It did the trick; Quackenbush won easily. It also made Harriet's reputation. She got job offers from campaign committees and public relations firms from coast to coast—even Chuck Colson paid her a visit—but she turned them all down. She had other things in mind.

Winning elections was not enough for Harriet; how could it be, for a Christian? She knew that the only campaign worth winning was the Lord's. That didn't depend on electing a few Christians to a few seats in Congress. Compromises and committees, a bill here and a bill there—there was no time for that. The Lord didn't tolerate compromise. He didn't tolerate majority rule, either, when the majority was in the grip of godlessness and subversion. No. He demanded a radical change—not on Capitol Hill, but in the hearts and minds of the electorate.

That was where the real battle had to be won. It was total war, and it called for total victory.

And Harriet intended to bring it about. As soon as the 1970 election was over she had set to work, rereading everything from her psychology courses and more besides; and within a year, she had worked out a plan. Senator Quackenbush had backed her all the way—he was never one to shy away from bold measures, and of course it was not lost on him that a Christian nation would be in need of a Christian President.

All that remained was to find the right religious figure to spearhead the movement. They wanted a sincere Christian and a real American, with just the right image—gentle, yet manly—to prepare the way and make straight the path. It was a tall order, and the search took Harriet all over the country, but it was time well spent, because of course the man she found was Rev. Anderson.

Proof, if any were needed, of God's mighty hand.

Harriet turned from the Kennedy photograph with a little sigh of humble gratitude and went over to the highway map of the United States. She was pleased that things were on schedule this morning. She took a blue pin out of Shawnee Mission, Kansas—the one that represented Mike and Bruno's progress—and stuck it in at Salina.

"Coffee ready yet, Ralph?" she called.

Ralph rustled his AP wires. "Not quite. Half a sec."

"That's fine. Take your time."

She settled into the leather chair behind her desk, took a slim gold cigarette from her bag, lit a slim cigarette, and opened the *Sun-Times*. The kidnapping story was back on page six this time, under a larger story about an unemployed steelworker who had shot several people in a supermarket. Splendid, she thought. They were getting tired of running the same old thing every week, with no new developments.

Humming absently to herself, she leafed through the rest of the paper.

After a while Ralph came in with her coffee, but he had a

worried look on his face. He handed her an AP wire and said, "I think you'd better see this."

The wire went as follows:

> NEW YORK, NY—After a high-speed chase through Manhattan's West Side late Sunday night, two men were arrested for reckless driving and a variety of related charges.
>
> But documents in the suspects' car led police to the scene of a burglary in the New York regional office of Rev. Anderson's Gospel Crusade, Inc.
>
> Burglars had entered the building on Madison Avenue, according to police, around 11 P.M. Sunday. They allegedly bound and gagged a security guard, went upstairs by elevator, and broke into a safe in the evangelist's office.
>
> Apparently the office had no alarm system.
>
> The suspects were being held for questioning. They were identified as J. Ashley Rittenhouse IV and William F. Garfield, both of Manhattan.

Harriet spread the wire out in the middle of her desk and pondered it. Then she leaned back in her chair and slowly blew smoke at the ceiling.

"Well," she said. "Maybe they're not as incompetent as I thought."

"Who?" Ralph said.

"The opposition," she said gently. "Subversive elements. The underground."

"Oh." Ralph looked uncertain.

"Rittenhouse," she said. "You don't recognize a name like that? For shame, dear. Look here." In one of her desk drawers she kept a series of black looseleaf notebooks; she pulled out the one marked "P-Q-R," flipped through it, and turned it around for Ralph to see.

Ash's face glowered up at him, once from a photo clipped from an old Yale yearbook, and again, in the midst of a crowd, from a newspaper shot taken at a demonstration against American policy in El Salvador. Under the photos were six or seven lines of notes in Harriet's handwriting: school career, activities, and known links with radical groups.

Ralph peered at the pictures. "He looks like bad news."

"That he does," said Harriet. "But not as bad as he thinks, if he managed to get caught. Now, you'd better get back to that machine. If anything else comes in on this, I want to know, and quick. You think Wilson knows about it yet?"

"I doubt it," said Ralph. "That one just came in; it's probably not even on the radio yet."

As he left the room, Harriet swiveled around in her chair and slid open the doors of a low cabinet that sat beside her desk. Inside the cabinet was a Megatronic 8500, the state of the art in scrambler/debugger equipment. There was one like it connected to every telephone in the organization, including the mobile units. Expensive, but worth every penny. Anderson and Quackenbush had squawked when she'd told them what the system cost, but she'd won them over in the end. Penny wise, pound foolish, she'd told them. Secure communications were absolutely vital to their success, after all—and it wasn't their own success she was speaking of, but the Lord's. It simply didn't do to get stingy with the Lord.

She flicked a few switches inside the cabinet. Then she picked up the phone and called Wilson, the head of the New York office. She called him at his home; it was only a little after eight in New York, and, knowing Wilson, she figured he would still be dawdling over his breakfast.

She nodded at the green light that glowed in the cabinet. "Good morning, Fred," she purred. "This is Harriet."

"Why, hello, Harriet. What a surprise."

"I'm just calling," she said sweetly, "to ask what you're doing about the break-in."

"The what?"

"The break-in, dear. Or haven't you heard? The underground broke into the safe in your office last night. I assume they took everything, unless I hear otherwise."

There was a pause, and then Wilson said, "Oh, Jesus."

"Yes," Harriet said even more sweetly. "Now, Fred, we did discuss this, didn't we? And you did tell me you were going to get rid of those papers, didn't you?"

"Oh, gosh, Harriet, I was going to, I—"

"Well, now, let's just pretend you did, shall we? When you talk to the police—I'm sure they'll be around to see you—suppose you just tell them about the cash. Tell them you don't know about any papers. Now how does that sound?"

"Well, I—"

"Good, good." She smiled. "And of course you won't want to say the cash was payroll; what will you say it was?"

"Donations," said Wilson.

"Donations, that's right," Harriet said. "Oh, and one other thing you ought to know: one of the burglars is a neighbor of yours, from Union Seminary. His name is Ashley Rittenhouse. Ring a bell?"

"Uhh—"

"Or maybe you might have hired someone lately who'd know him."

"I'll have to check, Harriet."

"Do that for me, won't you? But carefully."

"Okay," Wilson sighed.

"Very good, dear. I'll be in touch."

Harriet sighed, too. The weakest link in the chain, she thought. Everything had been going so smoothly up until now. Hardly a soft spot anywhere along the line—hardly. It was a good organization. A fine organization. She'd put it together carefully, patiently. Everyone on the staff, coast to coast, completely dedicated to the cause. Not the kind of thing to simply write off for the sake of a few lousy pieces of paper.

She wouldn't permit herself to be angry with Wilson; that would be un-Christian. Worse, counterproductive.

She lit another cigarette and smoked it thoughtfully. Third-rate burglaries had a way of getting blown out of proportion if the press weren't handled properly from the beginning. She was going to need to take evasive action on this one. Probably, she thought, she should throw it back onto the underground itself—whichever faction Rittenhouse was representing this time. She could make it look as though they had fabricated the papers themselves—all they'd have needed was a typewriter and a rubber stamp—and planted them in an effort to frame Rev. Anderson. She could leak a few clues through the usual channels; it would be quite plausible, and pleasantly confusing. . . . No—much as she liked it, it would be too messy in this case. Too time-consuming, too. She wasn't going to feel safe with the papers floating around loose.

Ah. Yes, she thought. Jensen. Much simpler.

She picked up the phone again and called him. Her best agent in New York; ex-Agency man; very sharp.

He was in. Again the green light glowed in Harriet's cabinet. She told him the news.

"And we're in a bit of a bind," she said. "The safe held the month's payroll—which is all right; we can replace that—but also the records on our operation."

Jensen whistled. "All of them?"

"Just about. Anyway, enough to cause an awful lot of trouble."

"Well, then," Jensen said. "I guess I ought to pay a little visit downtown."

"Oh, would you? That would be awfully sweet."

"Sure. Nothing to it, the way they run things down there. You just leave it to me."

"Of course," she said, "I'm authorizing you to use any means you deem appropriate."

"Sure thing."

Harriet hung up the phone, patted it, smiled, and sipped her coffee.

CONFIDENTIAL. EYES ONLY. DO NOT FILE. Stamped in red

across the top of every sheet. I'd found them by that time, of course. First time I stopped for gas, at an E-Z Off-On place in Stroudsburg, Pennsylvania. It was about four in the morning, still dark outside.

I'd gone into the ladies' room, first thing, to find out what was in Rosie's pocketbook. It contained the usual handful of ballpoint pens, and matchbooks, crumpled cigarette packs, and other debris. A checkbook. A hairbrush. A Mace Purse-Pak, a jackknife, a wallet. No gun, I was relieved to see. I'd been beginning to wonder if she carried one.

The wallet was leather, with a change purse in it, and bound around the edges with a spiral of white plastic cording. On the front, stamped on the leather, was, "Niagara Falls, New York."

My word, I thought. I missed her already.

The wallet had forty-two dollars in it—more than I'd left her with, I realized. But, then, she had my MasterCard, which she could use all she wanted. I now had hers. "Rosemary D. Flood," it said. Same on her driver's license, and on her Union Seminary I.D. card.

I didn't know what the D was for. I trusted nobody would have occasion to ask me.

The Union I.D. was the only one with a picture. And what a picture; a nastier-looking scowl I'd never seen. She looked like a terrorist. But aside from that, there was a reasonable resemblance. It would do.

I tried scowling into the mirror, but the image was so ridiculous that I laughed. "Forget it!" I said, and went out the door.

The kid pumping the gas had found them before I did. He was peering into the back of the Volkswagen while he waited for me to come over and pay him.

He looked at me strangely and said, "You with the CIA or something?"

I looked in the window and saw what he'd been peering at, and tried to keep my eyes from popping. They must have vibrated themselves loose on the way; there they lay on the floor, behind the driver's seat, in plain sight, stamped very legibly in red. With a whole lot of money on top of them.

I turned back to the kid, who looked about eighteen. "Nah," I heard myself saying. "State Department. CIA's full of nuts. Going up to Binghamton," I added confidentially. "Got a visiting Russian professor up there who wants to defect."

He liked that a lot. He didn't smile, but his eyes lit up.

I handed him Rosie's MasterCard. "Got a coffee machine around?"

"Sure do," he said warmly.

"Good. I could use some."

"My God, Mather," I said to myself, driving out of there as fast as practicable. "*You* said *that?*"

CHAPTER 7

IGHTEEN NORTH," SAID A SIGN. "SHARON. Greenville. Exit ½ Mi."

"Sharon," Rosie said to herself.

Eleven-fifteen Monday morning, western Pennsylvania, Interstate 80. A bright morning; snowy hills, bare trees, mill towns. It was cold. Rosie was glad, at least, that she had a hat and gloves, since she'd had to drive the whole freaking way with the window open, since my old Plymouth's defroster didn't work.

Crappy car, she thought. Everything falling apart. What a country, to have started out with the Bill of Rights and ended up with this.

She supposed she ought to thank me, but she didn't feel like it.

I was twenty miles or so behind her just then, as it happened, just passing the cutoff to Pittsburgh. She had no idea, and neither did I, that she had driven past Stroudsburg while I'd been goggling at her papers in the gas station. Just one of those things.

But Sharon—she wondered why that rang a bell.

She was boiling mad, of course. She'd been mad ever since Ash and Garf had stood her up last night, but that was nothing compared to how she felt now that she knew why. A red light, she thought. Good God. It was more than she could stand.

"According to a spokesman for Rev. Anderson," the eleven o'clock news had said, "several thousand dollars in donations were stolen."

Donations, Rosie thought. Hah. But the radio hadn't said a word about the papers. That was peculiar—and probably very bad. It had to mean those papers were as important as Muffy had said they were. Which had to mean Anderson would not want the cops to have them. Which meant he would find a way to get them back. Using his pals at the FBI, no doubt. They'd probably tell the cops it was a matter of national security.

And when some other cops, somewhere along the line, caught up with me in Rosie's Volkswagen (as they surely would, she thought, considering what a dope I was) then he'd find a way to get the rest of them back, too.

And then the whole thing would be down the tubes.

All that sweat, and all that planning, for nothing.

Boiling mad, she decided, wasn't the word at all. Something stronger was necessary, to account for what she wanted to do to Ash.

"Down the fucking *tubes!*" she said aloud, pounding her fist on the steering wheel.

It had all looked so beautiful, lying there, when Garf popped the safe open. The money, all in small bills, all in bundles, just like in the movies, and then those gorgeous red-stamped papers. Do NOT FILE—how poetic. She'd wished she'd gotten a chance to read the damned things. They would have finished Anderson; she was sure of it. If only. If only.

But not now. Anderson would tighten up his security and make sure that nothing like that ever happened again; probably manage to find Muffy and Nathan, too, and get rid of them. Ship them out to Colorado, no doubt, with the preachers, and then go merrily along with his plans. Stronger than ever. And pretty soon the whole country would be on his side, yelling and screaming for Jesus to drop-kick them through the goalposts of life.

And also screaming for the blood of anybody who might not be worthy to be on Jesus's team.

She wondered how long it would take.

And all for a red light, she thought. So the radio said. Absolutely unbelievable.

Damn his ass. Look at him, she thought. God's gift to the Revolution, right? What a guy. All those daring exploits in the Movement, leaping around from one riot to the next. And she'd bought it, hadn't she, the jerk. Jogging, stopwatches, diagrams, the whole bit. Bob Dylan on the stereo, Che Guevara on the wall.

For all she knew, he'd never given a shit about Anderson to begin with. He'd been having too much fun playing Errol Flynn.

Well, but *she* gave a shit.

Then she had to find the Soldiers, dammit. She must. They had to be out there somewhere.

Sharon, she thought. Sharon?

She went over it for the thousandth time. The phone network. Something really simpleminded: you rang once, hung up, waited a certain interval, and rang again. That much she knew; but who were the people, what were their phone numbers, where did they live?

All he'd have had to do was to have told her one lousy crummy Christalmighty phone number.

But there was something he had told her—damn his ass. She could swear he had. What was it? Weeks ago—something about the guy called Zeke, in Colorado.

Something about the towns they picked to settle in. There was method in it. A kind of private joke, he said.

And what was it that Zeke did? Ran an ashram or something. A retreat center, or a farming commune, or something like that? Home for wayward souls, up in the Rockies. Blending in with the Young Lifes, the Vacation Bible Schools; protective coloration. Nobody would notice if he had people going in and out all the time. They were all up there together, getting holy in the mountains—where, of course, it was easy to get holy, there being no distractions, no people to spoil the pretty view by trampling on the needy and grinding the faces of, of, of—

For God's sake, yes, she thought: Sharon was a Biblical name. Of course! All the towns they lived in had Biblical names!

She swerved the car over onto the shoulder and grabbed the road atlas from under the seat, where I kept it, and consulted the index.

"Beth in D.C." would probably mean Bethesda. Or Alexandria. Too big. Never find her. She could look up Beth's name in a newspaper file; but she wouldn't be using her real name, would she.

"George and Ellen in Pennsylvania"—well, there must be 37,000 Pennsylvania towns with Biblical names.

But in Colorado there were only three. Corinth, B-6. Manassa, G-6. Timnath, B-8.

She looked them up.

Manassa and Timnath were in the flat part of the state.

Corinth was in the mountains.

She smiled. It couldn't be too hard to find somebody called Zeke, running a retreat center, in Corinth, Colorado.

She did a zero-to-sixty as fast as the poor old Plymouth would go.

CHAPTER 8

JENSEN CALLED BACK IN THE MIDDLE OF THE afternoon. By then the blue pin on Harriet's highway map had moved from Salina to Limon, Colorado. Everything was going smoothly; the Reverend would be at home base by nightfall, ready to begin his education. The first day of the rest of his life, Harriet liked to call it. Number thirteen—Phase I was almost done now. Three more weeks and everybody could relax. Phase II would be the easy part.

"Got 'em," Jensen said.

"Wonderful," Harriet said. "You *are* a dear. Have any trouble?"

"Nah. Piece of cake."

"Lovely. May I see them?"

"Oh, sure. Just let me get the machine turned on here."

"Ralph?" Harriet called, putting her hand over the phone. "Pick up on five, will you? We've got a fax coming in."

She turned and watched the lake, glittering far below, while she waited for the facsimiles to come through the machine. Yes, she thought, things were going well today. The New York affair was being contained—not only contained, but possibly turned to advantage. Jensen had retrieved the papers, but of course she'd known he would do that. The nice thing, the surprise, was Garfield's decision to turn state's evidence. That had come in on the wire just before lunch.

It *would* be Garfield; that figured. He had no prior connection with the underground that Harriet could find—and thus no loyalties. Rittenhouse had obviously gambled on him and lost. Foolish of him. And so typical, she thought with a smirk. Typical of the whole brood of them: still thinking like hippies, assuming they could trust each other just because they'd all worn their hair down to their waists in college. Their greatest weakness, she thought. Thinking they were different from other people. Superior. Smug little bastards.

Atheistic little bastards.

Harriet knew what people were made of. That was why she trusted no one but the Lord.

Unfortunately, Garfield hadn't had very much useful information. But he had identified the third member of the gang: Rosemary Flood.

It had been no trouble to trace her; the Manhattan phone book gave her address as 99 Claremont Avenue, which was a dorm at Union Seminary. Again no prior connection with the underground. A girlfriend, then, doubtless. She must have run out on them after the burglary. There was true love for you.

But just to be on the safe side, Harriet had traced the girl's car and found a picture of her in an old Union newsletter—nasty-looking picture, too; obviously a criminal type—and sent both photo and car description to all the regional offices, where the agents would pick them up in the morning.

After all, the Lord helped those who helped themselves.

"Here you are, Harriet." Ralph appeared, holding out a thick handful of photocopies.

"Oh, thanks," Harriet said. "Tell Jensen to hold on."

While Jensen held on, Harriet gave the papers a quick going-over. Then she gave them a slow going-over.

An expression of displeasure crossed her face.

"What the hell," she said into the phone. "This is just a lot of memos. Where's the important stuff?"

"Gee, that's all they had," Jensen said. "You mean there's more?"

"You bet there is," said Harriet.

· · ·

You bet there was.

By sunset I was reading it in a motel room on the outskirts of Columbus, Ohio.

I was reading all about Harriet, and Bliss Publications and its traveling salesmen in the blue Buicks, and the Christian Innkeepers of America, and Rev. Anderson's Vacation Bible School, and what they called "Conversion Management."

And it was blowing my mind.

CHAPTER 9

OMETHING WAS RINGING.

"What?" I said. "What? What?"

It was my alarm clock going off, that was what.

"Huh?" I said.

Alarm clock. Your alarm clock, Mather. The one you bought in Pennsylvania.

"Uh," I said.

Come on. Up. Up. It tolls for thee.

I sat up. After a while I turned on the light and turned off the alarm. It was two o'clock in the morning.

I looked stupidly around me. A TV set, flowered curtains, blank walls, an air conditioner. On the floor, an army surplus backpack. I had all my clothes on—even my shoes.

"Right," I said slowly, as it began to trickle into my brain. Tuesday. Ohio. Motel. Columbus.

Why on earth had I set it for two o'clock in the morning?

Because the FBI always comes to get you at three, dummy. You remember that. When your defenses are down.

"Oh, right," I said, with a yawn. That was it. Of course. Folklore from the sixties. I'd never known whether it was true or not, but when I'd gone to sleep yesterday, soon after dinner, I'd figured it couldn't hurt. Everything else had turned out to be true; why not that, too?

Staff in hand, and all that. Sandals on feet. Bitter herbs.

How prudent of me, I thought. My father would be proud.

Yes, and the army surplus backpack belonged to Rosie. I'd found it in the trunk of the Volkswagen yesterday, half full

of Rosie's clothes. I had put the papers into it, too, and the
cash, clever lass, to keep any more gas station attendants from
getting a look at them.

Oh, yes, the papers.

"Oh, *right*," I said.

And I got out of bed in a hurry, washed my face, picked
up my stuff, and stumbled out the door.

Yes, the papers. Those awful red-stamped papers.

God help us, I thought a while later, as I crossed the state
line into Indiana. I'd been right all along. It *was* the gangsters'
hideout. The gangsters' house—and it had plenty of mansions,
too. Rosie and Ash had been amateurs indeed. Up against the
big boys.

And now look who's carrying the ball, I thought. A *real*
amateur.

"You and your acts of faith," I muttered to myself.

Yesterday had been a breeze. It had actually been fun. I'd
been so astonished, and so happy, to find myself doing this
outrageous thing—and, what was more, to find myself getting
away with it. I'd driven all the way across Pennsylvania and
halfway across Ohio, yesterday, without a single mishap, as
though the world had been influenced by my state of mind.
I'd charged all my gas on Rosie's credit card, with nobody
batting an eye; I'd bought a toothbrush in one town, under-
wear in another, the alarm clock in a third, and coffee and
cigarettes everywhere, all without the slightest trouble. I was
even starting to get used to Kools. Weirdest of all, I'd passed
two cops toward the end of the day—not one but two—both
of them lurking in their No-U-Turn places on the median,
waiting for speeders. Surely they'd had some kind of a bulletin on Rosie by then—the break-in had been on the radio
since that morning—but somehow they managed not to notice me.

More things in heaven and earth. I'd felt so expansive, I'd
begun wondering if I hadn't had it wrong all along. Maybe
there was some reason for hope in the world after all. Typical

theologian; something nice happens to you and right away you start trying to make a whole philosophy out of it. Driving along yesterday, I'd thought about the famous Bible smugglers of Eastern Europe and how fond the Christians were of saying that God miraculously averted the eyes of the Commie border guards when those saintly folks went through. I'd always thought that that was a lot of horseshit—they just happened to be good smugglers, was all—but yesterday I'd been tempted to wonder if it mightn't be true. Well, conceivable, at least. Conceivable that, in spite of the weight of the evidence, God might be running the show after all, in His own mysterious way.

Sure, I thought this morning. And you've got a friend at Chase Manhattan.

Because today was Tuesday. Today was Cold Feet Day; the novelty of my little adventure had worn off, diminishing as my knowledge of the opposition increased. Now that I'd read those damned papers, I had a feeling it was Harriet Masters running the show.

And it wasn't only the papers. I'd watched the six o'clock news in my motel room last night, and that hadn't helped any, either. A short, perfunctory report about the break-in itself—they'd breezed right past the important part, the fact that it was Anderson's office. Nobody seemed at all curious about that. The only thing that made it newsworthy was that Ash and Garf's share of the stuff (said to have been "cash") had upped and disappeared from the police department's evidence room. Vanished mysteriously; they had a film clip of the cop who'd been supposed to be in charge, swearing up and down that he'd never left his post.

That was news. Although the local anchorman—who looked like a soap opera actor—had nothing to say about who might have stolen the evidence back, or why.

I knew it must have been done by the boys in the blue Buicks—in which case, they were sure to have noticed that they'd only recovered half of it. In which case they would be looking for me today.

But there were only thirty of them, though. That was what the papers said; sixty agents, two to a car, to cover the whole country. Even if they dropped everything to look for me—which I hoped was unlikely—the odds were pretty good that they wouldn't find me. Not right away, anyhow.

Still, if they did find me, there weren't going to be any nice polite Miranda warnings. No phone call. None of that soft-on-crime nonsense. Just a free ride to the brainwashing factory.

"Christ," I said.

And the worst part of it was, they were already winning. Half the cars on the road yesterday had had "Honk If You Love Jesus" bumper stickers. "God, Guns and Guts Built America," for pity's sake—sharing the same bumper space, more often than not, with such messages as "Go Blue" and "See Rock City." It was depressing. Now that I was out of the safety of the seminary, where religion wasn't talked about as though you could master it in an afternoon, I was beginning to realize how bad it was out here. Rosie was right; they *were* everywhere. A guy like Rev. Anderson could take them wherever he wanted, and they, never dreaming that they were being took, would raise their hands and praise Jesus and think it was swell.

And someday—quite soon, if I was reading the papers right—he'd begin taking care of everybody who didn't happen to think it was swell.

He wasn't the opposition; *we* were.

Whoever "we" was.

For the moment, "we" appeared to be me.

Driving along in the dark, following the lonely little beam of my headlights.

Well, I was just going to have to do the best I could.

I went past Indianapolis—it was closed—and then I was out in the farmland again. Everybody was asleep at that hour, even the farmers. Even the truckers.

For a while I had the moon to keep me company, but then it went to bed, too.

I thought about going straight to the top and calling up Dan Rather from a phone booth somewhere. A pleasant idea, but I couldn't see how it could work; surely he had a couple of hundred secretaries to protect him from every nut who might call to announce that she'd solved the kidnappings. So that was out.

I decided, eventually, that I'd be able to get to St. Louis around noon, and there I would go to the *Post-Dispatch* office and throw myself on their mercy. I didn't know much about the *Post-Dispatch*, but at least I'd heard of it. I figured it was a big enough paper to be able to do something about my information, but small enough that I might stand a chance of being listened to.

That seemed to be a plausible plan, and I chewed on it all the rest of the way across Indiana, composing a speech to give to the *Post-Dispatch*'s receptionist that might persuade him, or her, to call a reporter instead of a cop.

But I never got a chance to try it out, because, just after I'd passed Terre Haute, the old Volkswagen's engine began to go "clunk."

It went "clunk" at first sporadically, and then regularly, and at last emphatically; and before I'd gone five miles past the Illinois border, the poor old car gave up the ghost.

Hell and damnation, I thought. And Rosie had just had it tuned up, too.

I coasted it over onto the shoulder, got out, opened the hood in back, and gazed inside. Nothing was spurting or smoking or flaming in there, but beyond that I had no idea what to look for. There's illiteracy for you; give me a text in Aramaic and I might be able to make some sense of it, but I didn't know a carburetor from a hole in the ground. For all I knew, the engine could have been upside down.

I sighed.

However, whatever was wrong with it, it wasn't going to

be cured by my staring at it. Besides, I didn't have time to stare; the sky was gray now, and the sun would be up in a minute; before long there would be traffic, and people staring at *me*. Cops, too, sooner or later. Maybe even a blue Buick. Which was not part of the plan.

So I closed the hood and got Rosie's pocketbook out of the car, and her backpack with the clothes and toothbrush and clock and bundles of money and papers inside it. I took the keys—and the registration, too, for good measure—make them go to the trouble of tracing the plates, at least—and set off pretty briskly down the highway.

By the time I heard the truck coming behind me, I'd put fifteen minutes' worth of good Manhattan-style walking, which would pass for sprinting anywhere else, between me and the Volkswagen. I turned around to look, and frowned; the car was still in sight. It might as well be a lighthouse, I thought, out here in the middle of the flat fields. The truck's driver would have to be blind not to notice it, and an idiot not to guess that it was where I'd come from. Much as I wanted to get out of there, I guessed I'd better not ask for a ride just yet; if the driver's radio happened to be working, I'd be sunk.

So I faced forward again and kept walking, and didn't stick out my thumb.

But the truck slowed down. I could hear it snorting as the driver downshifted.

I turned and shook my head and tried to wave it on, but it was stopping for me anyway. I cursed myself; I should have been bright enough to get rid of the Volkswagen long ago. Should have ditched it in Columbus and taken the bus. How could I have been such a dope?

"A fine crook *you* make," I told myself.

The truck pulled past me onto the shoulder. It was a monster—one of those great big semis, and a fancy one, complete with pinstripes and chrome-plated stacks. "Kenwood," said the cab.

And what the trailer said, in red, white and blue, all be-decked with stars and stripes, was "REV. ANDERSON'S GOSPEL CRUSADE."

"Oh, my God," I groaned, as the thing rolled to a stop. Anything but this. Of all the vehicles on all the highways in all the world, *this* one had to be *here*. It wasn't fair. I should never have taken Rosie's car in the first place, I thought. Shouldn't have answered the phone. Shouldn't even have gone to seminary.

I walked slowly toward it, shaking my head and waving some more. But it didn't do any good. By the time I got there, the driver had set the brake and shoved over and opened the passenger door and was yelling at me over the rumble of the engine.

The driver was a woman. She wore an old, battered straw Stetson hat, and braids, and dark glasses, and a red plaid hunt-ing jacket and jeans.

"Hurry up," she yelled down at me. "We haven't got much time."

"It's okay. Really," I said. "Thanks, but I'm just going up to the next exit." Which I hoped wasn't far away.

And then she said, "Got the papers?"

"Papers?" I faltered. Who was this, one of the Harvest Workers? One of Harriet's agents?

"Yeah—you've got 'em, haven't you?"

"Uhh . . ." I said, taking a step backward. "Uh, listen, thanks anyway, huh?" I was going to have to make a run for it. Across the fields, maybe.

"No, wait a minute!" she said then. "Wait—I'm on your side!" And with that, she snatched off the Stetson and the glasses.

Even without them, what a perfect disguise she had: a com-pletely, utterly ordinary face. Medium brown eyes, medium brown hair, average nose, average mouth—it was easy to see why nobody had ever turned her in, in all these years; nobody had ever noticed her. And never would, either, unless she bumped right into them.

Rosie had shown me a picture, barely two weeks ago, in one of Ash's old clippings about the prayer breakfast. She still looked like the picture, but I wouldn't have recognized her myself if she hadn't been so dramatic about it.

"Louise Macdonald!" I squeaked. "But you— But—" I said, taking another look at the message on the truck.

Louise Macdonald grinned. "So I stole it," she said. "Now get in here, will you? And quit making those funny noises."

CHAPTER 10

WELL! ROSIE! THIS SURE IS A SURPRISE," LOUISE Macdonald said. There was a little bit of a Western twang in her voice. "What the hell are you doing way out here? You're supposed to be in Pennsylvania, aren't you?"

"I—Pennsylvania?" I said, having no idea what to say. "But I'm not—"

She'd been about to pull out into the road, but when she heard me, she stopped again. "Not what?" she said.

"Not Rosie. I'm—uh—I'm Olivia Mather."

She stared over at me.

"I'm Rosie's roommate," I said, starting to blither. "I mean, I—well, see, they blew the getaway, and Rosie was—well, she was—"

She was still staring at me. She really looked surprised now.

"See, I thought— Well, I kind of took her car, and her wallet and stuff; and then I found the papers in there, and . . ." I quit trying. I realized how stupid it must sound. Let's face it, it *was* stupid.

"Olivia *Mather?*" she said at last. "You mean P.K.? Are you Sam's daughter?"

"Sam?" I squeaked. "Well, yeah, I—"

"Well, for heaven's sake!" Louise said, and burst out laughing. "Am I ever glad to meet *you!*"

"You are?"

"Sure as hell am!" she said. "Put her there—why, Sam's the whole reason I'm here at all!"

. . .

My father smiled when he blew up his train full of bombs, one fine spring day back in '72; and back home in Massachusetts we sat watching him on the TV set, and my mother said, "That's for us," and I thought to myself, Oh, great, oh, swell, oh, Jesus, who the hell's going to figure that out? Nobody was going to get the message; just another crackpot blowing up a train, wrong number; the evening news is over, that's the way it is, and here's "The Price Is Right." Why is this man smiling? Is this his idea of victory?

But even while I was sitting there with my eyes beginning to sting, wondering why he'd bothered, and already feeling ashamed of him because didn't he understand explosions were a dime a dozen, didn't he see he'd have to blow up the whole planet before anybody would pay attention, didn't he *know* nobody out there was going to leap to his feet then and there and say, "By God, that does it!"—meanwhile, only a few miles away, in a house they'd rented together in the cruddy part of Cambridge, eight people were in fact leaping to their feet.

Little Did I Know.

"By God," they all cried at once, "it's Sam Mather!"

"Did he do that?"

" 'Course he did, look at him grinning."

"Well, I'll be damned!"

"You tell 'em, Sam!"

"Preach it!"

They were all first-year students at Harvard Divinity School: Zeke, and Beth, and George and Ellen, and Nathan, and Ed, and Muffy. And of course Louise Macdonald.

None of them had been crooks up until that night; they were all nice normal well-behaved middle-class white kids, good Christian folks studying for the ministry.

They all knew my father from the marches and the rallies; they'd spent a lot of Sunday mornings that year in the balcony of his church, too. And when they saw what he did to the train, they got to talking about things.

The usual Bible student things. The Bible and the war, and God and Caesar, and God and Mammon, and the army chaplains praying for victory, and Billy Graham going to prayer breakfasts at the Nixon White House; and what Amos and Hosea said about cheating the poor; and Lenny Bruce's old routine about what if Jesus suddenly showed up in the cathedral with His usual band of lepers and whores and bad guys in tow, and what the archbishops would do about that; and so on; and then somebody mentioned a clergyman they knew, over in Lexington, who'd just bought himself a new BMW, and they got to talking about *him*.

And one thing led to another, and pretty soon it came up that Ed, the oldest of the group, who had been a TV repairman before he went to Harvard Div, happened to know how to hot-wire the ignitions of cars; and it also came up that Louise had spent her afternoons after high school, back in Wyoming, working for the town locksmith, who happened to be her uncle, and she'd gotten good enough to be able to pick locks; and Ed said he bet Louise couldn't steal that BMW and Louise said she bet she could; but, she said, she'd only do it if Ed would hot-wire some old jalopy and drive it over to Lexington and leave it in the BMW's place.

And so that was what they did; and, adding insult to injury, they left the clergyman a little note, tucked under the windshield wiper of the rusty old heap Ed had found, reminding him about the Rich Young Man who went away sorrowful, for he had great possessions.

And they signed the note, "With love, the Soldiers of Jeremiah."

"You did?" I said to Louise Macdonald.

"Sure," Louise Macdonald said to me.

"Really?" I said.

"Well, hell, we had to do something," she told me cheerily. "It was either that or blow up the world, and we didn't think that was what your dad had in mind, somehow."

My dad. Louise Macdonald did *that* because of my dad.

"Far out," I said.

"And we were sober, too," she said. "Hadn't had a thing to drink but coffee."

They kept it small and simple at first. It was a pastime, a way of blowing off steam once in a while after the hours of jail work and hospital work and Bible study, the daily grind of wondering why the wicked prospered. A way of relaxing. Here a stolen car; there a set of silver Communion vessels, stolen from a sacristy and replaced with a bottle of Ripple in a paper bag. From another church, in another suburb, they stole all the hymnals one Saturday night and hid them in a burned-out building in Roxbury, and sent the vestry committee a little treasure map telling them where to look.

They weren't exactly the scourge of Boston—nor, as far as they knew, did any of their victims do anything that could be described as seeing the joke—but at least it gave them something to do besides sitting around and moping.

They went along like that all through Harvard Div, while America was slogging its way through Watergate, the Resignation, the Pardon, and the fall of Saigon. By the time they got finished with their degrees, the System had been declared to be in working order again. Differences had been patched up, deferred dreams crusted and sugared over, and suddenly people all over the place were getting Born Again, praise the Lord, and feeling good once more—and Rev. Anderson, having just dug the first shovelful of dirt for the foundation of his new Crusade Center, was sending out invitations for a Senate prayer breakfast, to be held on July Fourth, Bicentennial Day.

Beth read about it on the society page, a week before commencement. "July Fourth," she snorted. "That's poetic."

"Look, it says Quackenbush is going to be there," said George and Ellen, reading over her shoulder.

"That rat? He born again?" said Muffy, cooking breakfast.

"Looks like it. And Rundel and Hackett, too."

"And Mumford! Jeez, what a crowd!"

"Bet they've got a lot to pray about."

"Who's this Anderson, anyhow?" said Beth.

"Beats me."

"Let me look," said Louise, coming over to look at the picture. "Huh," she said, raising an eyebrow. "I wonder if it's the same guy—yeah, sure it is. He used to have a TV show out West when I was little. Real low-budget stuff. Looked like a home movie. Sure has come up in the world."

They gathered around the picture of the well-dressed man digging in the earth.

"Must have run into a streak of good luck."

"Maybe Jesus loves him," said Nathan.

And they all looked at each other, and drawled, "Uh-huh."

So after commencement they packed up their diplomas and went down to Washington; and on the Fourth, just as Senator Quackenbush was launching into a prayer of thanksgiving for freedom, democracy, and the highest standard of living in the world, seven of the Soldiers charged in with buckets of fresh pigs' blood, which they poured out liberally on all and sundry, while the eighth, Ed, stationed in the basement, tripped all the circuit breakers.

In the darkness and confusion, naturally, they had no trouble getting away. But they decided to do the decent thing: they sent a note to the Washington *Post*, and signed their names.

And so they went underground.

"Sure there's an underground," Louise said, when she noticed me gawking at her. "What did you think? We all just upped and died or something?"

Good grief! I thought, surprised. Was that what I'd thought?

"Naw!" I said.

Of course it was.

It was exactly what I'd thought, all these years. Until . . . Until when? Now? Right that minute, when I realized I'd been sitting there gawking at Louise Macdonald all the way across the state of Illinois, like a dummy, and that there wasn't any reason to gawk at her, because what did I think, they'd just upped and died?

(What the hell did you think, P.K.! Did you think he didn't choose that moment to blow up his train, when he knew everything was already over and dead and buried? God damn, girl! You think he didn't know that; you think he didn't know that's when you begin?)

"Naw!" I said again, and grinned. "What the hell would I think a thing like that for?"

So they rented a house in Bethesda, under assumed names, and got jobs in college bars and cheap restaurants around the Washington area. They made the rounds of the activist churches and read the bulletin boards and alternative newspapers. As they got into circulation, they began to find some kindred souls—people back from Vista, back from the communes, back from Vietnam or Canada or jail. Yarns got swapped, beers got bought, friends got introduced, and before too long they'd gotten enough people together to start thinking about crime again.

"We did a lot of jawing about how we ought to go about it," Louise told me. "We knew we didn't want to be the Weathermen all over again; that's just necrophilia. I mean, we'd love to screw the big corporations—who wouldn't? but we thought maybe we could be halfway creative about it while we were at it. So, we thought, why don't we just take their money and spread it around where it'll do some good? Throw a little Robin Hood in there. And so we split up into a lot of small groups and set up a kind of a network around the country, and that's what we do."

"Good grief," I said, shaking my head.

"Pretty corny, huh?"

"Disgusting."

"Well, it's not all that big a deal," she said merrily. "A little burglary, a little embezzling, what have you. We can only do maybe a couple of mil a year, among all of us."

"Million?"

"Yeah. Much more than that and they start thinking you're a crime wave. Start calling out the racket squads and stuff. Makes it too hard. But if you keep the losses small, they can just write 'em off. Everybody's happy."

"Ah," I said. Naturally. "Who do you spend it on, then?"

"Oh, the usual things," she said. "There's a sweat-equity group in Detroit, and a guy in Brooklyn who started his own prep school when his kids started flunking out. A couple of old ladies in Chicago who run a big vegetable garden in an empty lot—they're a couple of real organizers, too. They've got their whole neighborhood in on it. And there's a few soup kitchens, and an Agent Orange group, and things like that."

She glanced into her rear-view mirror and pulled out to pass a slow-moving station wagon. "So, anyway, we did that full-time until a year or so ago," she said. "We'd gotten so busy with it, we'd almost forgotten old Rev. Anderson. But then Zeke found this farm out in Colorado and went out there to start his retreat center—he always was more of a mystic than anything else; couldn't keep his mind on his work—and damned if he didn't land in the same county where this Vacation Bible School was. He said it was just a broken-down old place when he moved in, just a few shacks and some weeds. But then all of a sudden there was a whole lot of construction going on, he said. They put up a big fence around the whole thing, and a hedge—full-grown trees, so you couldn't see in from the road—and then they started putting up a lot of buildings in there behind it all. Big production. Must have cost a bundle. And Zeke said he'd heard this place belonged to Anderson, and what did we know about it?

"Well, we didn't know anything about it back then, except that back in Washington nobody could believe what a big shot he was getting to be. You know that part of it—showing up at all the parties, and hanging around the Hill, and all."

"Uh-huh," I said.

"So we kind of elected ourselves to keep an eye on him," she said. "And so Muffy brushed up on her shorthand, and dyed her hair, and went up to New York and got a job in his office.

" 'Course, at that point it was nothing but nosiness," she went on. "Or cussedness, maybe. We thought we might find a little dirt somewhere, which would be fun to leak to the press; or, if not, then maybe we could get our paws on a little extra cash. But then the kidnappings started, and Muffy started hearing some weird conversations, and seeing some funny people going in and out; and then she heard about the safe."

"Which was where Ash came in," I said.

"Yeah," she said, making a face. "Good old Ash, huh? So then, right around the same time, we got Nathan into the Crusade Center; they had an opening in their shipping department.

"Now, mostly, all they do is plain old trucking. Nothing but books—back and forth between Arlington and the Bliss plant outside of Chicago, and a string of warehouses here and there. Nathan couldn't get a thing on them. But then finally he gets a memo about this one," she said, thumping the dashboard. "This one's not on the regular schedule, and it's going straight out to the Vacation Bible School. And they're all pussyfooting around, and acting strange, and talking about the 'special shipment.' "

She looked over at me and smiled. "Which is where I came in," she said. "We were pretty sure that that's where they were taking the preachers, so we thought we'd try to find out what they're sending to 'em. It's bound to be interesting. Nathan says the chief of security came down personally and locked the trailer up and took the key away with him."

"Lordy!" I said. "That's pretty brazen."

"We thought so, too," said Louise. "I mean, how could we resist a temptation like that?"

"So you—"

"So Nathan sent the regular driver on vacation for a couple of weeks, and here I am."

"So what about it?" she said, around twelve-thirty, as we approached St. Louis. We could just catch glimpses of the Arch among the buildings downtown, just across the Mississippi.

"What about what?" I said.

"Well, the *Post-Dispatch* building is right over there," she said. "So you can either take your chances with me, or I can drop you off and you can hog those papers all to yourself."

I looked over at the city. "Oh, I don't know," I said. "They've probably all gone out to lunch by now, wouldn't you think?"

"Yeah," she said. "Probably have."

CHAPTER 11

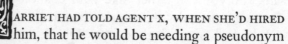ARRIET HAD TOLD AGENT X, WHEN SHE'D HIRED him, that he would be needing a pseudonym (what was it she'd called it? A nom de something), and that as far as she was concerned he could pick any name he liked, so he'd picked "X."

She'd narrowed her eyes at him. "Now, Johnny," she'd said, in the same tone his mother had always used, half coaxing, half menacing, so that he'd never been quite sure which half she'd really meant. "Now, Johnny," she'd said. "You'll be posing as a sales rep from Bliss Publications. Would you care to guess how many people are going to open up to a book salesman who says his name is 'X'?"

But she'd promised. And X, who had been born Johnny Tribble and had suffered for it all his life, stuck to his guns. So they compromised and spelled it "Eckes."

But *he* thought of it as X.

Privately. In the mirror, in the morning, while shaving. "Go get 'em, X," he'd whisper to himself, with a rakish grin.

After his prayers, of course.

X's life had completely turned around when he'd gone to work for Harriet. Changing his name seemed to go with it, just like the Apostles changing theirs. He felt it had canceled out, and made up for, his previous life as Johnny Tribble. Wiped out the years growing up, hanging around on street corners, lonely and bored and itchy, in Tin, South Dakota, a dusty, drab, poky town where nothing ever happened, and never *had* happened, either, except somebody discovering tin there once, but the vein had run out after about two weeks. It had wiped out the hitch he'd done in the army, too; he'd enlisted the minute he'd turned eighteen, hoping and praying that he'd be in time to fight in Vietnam, but it had fallen while he was still in Basic, and so he'd spent his two years, bored and itchy again, doing guard duty at Fort Benning. And finally it had wiped out the years since then, which he'd spent on the police force back home in Tin County.

He'd enjoyed it for a while—the uniform, the badge, the pistol on his hip, and people calling him Officer Tribble instead of plain Johnny. People had looked up to him; he'd looked up to himself. He didn't take any lip from anybody; anybody sassed him, he'd pour their beer in their lap or slam them up against the wall.

He'd had great plans for himself in those early days; he was going to rise through the ranks and transform the Tin County force into the toughest law enforcement machine this side of the Cheyenne. Federal funds, SWAT teams, the whole bit. He would sit home at night with the TV on, exercising with his weights—fifty curls right, fifty curls left—while vicious criminals paraded before his eyes on the cop shows. Cocaine kings, spies, assassins, jewel thieves, Mafia hitmen. And as he sat watching them a surge of excitement would go through his mind at the thought of putting those people's butts in jail where they belonged. And throwing away the key. Teach them some respect for authority. They'd better not try coming to Tin County, he'd thought, because he'd sure as heck be ready for them.

But they never did. And gradually he began to realize they never would.

And so, as the years slid by, he'd slowly simmered down, and had just about resigned himself to the prospect of driving his cruiser around the back roads of Tin County, forever, where the most dangerous criminals he would ever meet up with would be drunken teenagers out joyriding in their fathers' pickups.

But then, when he'd been least expecting it, he'd seen Harriet's want ad. That had been a year ago last January. He'd gone up to Pierre to see his cousin Mickey in the hospital, the time Mickey's girlfriend had thrown that frying pan at him; and he'd happened to pick up a copy of *Christian Challenge*, which the missionaries always left lying around in the waiting room, and he'd come across the ad in the back of it.

"Men wanted," it said, "with police or intelligence experience, for undercover work. A sensitive, dynamic project, requiring discipline, maturity, and above all a strong Christian commitment."

It was only a little ad, but it had seemed to jump right off the page at him. It was exactly what he'd been waiting for all his life.

And when he found out, as he did in due course, that Harriet was really working for Rev. Anderson, he'd practically dropped his teeth, he was so excited. It had been Rev. Anderson who had brought him to know the Lord in the first place—back when he was still out West, before he got famous. The Gospel Crusade had held a big meeting over in Rapid City, with a basketball game between the School of Mines and a Christian team, and X—he was still Tribble then, of course—had gone over, mostly just to see the game, but when he heard those Christian athletes witnessing during halftime, and then when the Reverend preached, why, it was all so overwhelming that the Spirit just came over him right there in the bleachers. It was about the best sermon he'd ever heard. The Reverend had the whole crowd in the palm of his hand; people were screaming and fainting and throwing pocketbooks and all kinds of things.

Darned if the Christians hadn't won the game, too.

He'd never dreamed that things would come full circle that way, but they sure did; and now he was Agent X. Secret agent in the service of the Reverend himself. Finally, for once in his life, he was doing something that really counted. He was helping win America to Christ.

And Heaven knew it needed to be done, and quick, before it was too late. Already America was in the grip of godless atheists, bleeding-heart liberals, and pansies—any half-wit could see that—and if Christians didn't stand up on their hind legs and fight back, the whole country would go straight down the tubes before anybody even knew what had hit them. It would be just like Nazi Germany, or Iran—only worse, because this time it would be the End, the one the Bible spoke of.

That was why the operation was so important. "Conversion Management," Harriet called it. She'd explained to X how traditional methods of Christian evangelism just weren't effective enough in today's world. Working traditionally, she'd said, Rev. Anderson *seemed* like he was doing fine, but actually he wasn't. He was bringing thousands to the Lord every day, true, but when you thought of the size of the country, that left millions—millions!—he wasn't reaching, and couldn't hope to reach. And the problem was, of course, that those millions weren't just sitting on their hands out there; they were busy undoing Christ's work as fast as the Reverend, or any other preacher, could do it.

" 'The harvest is plenteous, but the workers are few,' " she'd told X. "But just imagine what those few could do if they only had some modern tools. And that's what we're going to do for them, Johnny," she'd said, with a wonderful, joyful light in her eyes. "We're going to take away their sickles and pitchforks and give them a tractor and a combine."

X didn't exactly understand how Conversion Management worked; Harriet had told him a lot of things about variables and psychology and mental sets and motivations and something called "subliminal messaging." Most of it was over his head—but that was all right with him. She wasn't paying him to understand it, after all, but just to get recruits. He was sure

Harriet knew what she was doing. She was a heck of a smart gal—in fact, by far the smartest gal he'd ever met. "Technology," she'd told him. "That's all it is. It's been around for quite a while; all we're doing is concentrating it, and beefing it up a bit, and putting it to work for the Lord. That's practically the only new thing about it."

X thought it was about the most exciting thing in the world. And he was proud to be a part of it.

The territory she'd assigned him to was all of Missouri and the southern half of Illinois. Pretty country, he thought; much prettier than South Dakota. At least something *grew* down here. He made the rounds in his new blue Buick—a powerful car, with all the extras; it even had air bags (Harriet said nothing was too good for her boys), and a state-of-the-art radiophone, an 8500, to call in with. Sent a scrambled signal, so nobody could listen in, which was very important in this line of work. Pretty fancy. They sure didn't have anything like it back in Tin County.

The books practically sold themselves, of course; it was a perfect front. From Danville to St. Louis to Kansas City and back again, it seemed like everybody wanted them. X could see why; he'd read a good many of them himself, and every one was more inspiring than the last. They sold like hotcakes in the bookstores; on top of that, a big new market was opening up in the motels (that had been Harriet's idea, too), where they seemed to be filling a real need for traveling people. Traveling Christians especially, who didn't want to watch the filth you got on TV these days.

So the bookstore managers and the motelkeepers were always happy to see X—and to take a few minutes to sit down and chew the fat a little bit. From there it was easy to steer them into giving him the information he needed, about church activities on the local level. He got all kinds of tips and leads that way, just as Harriet said he would; and so, by now, after a year or so on the job, he'd put together a list of eligible preachers as long as your arm.

Whom he called on. Regularly. And who bought sermon outlines, and Sunday school curriculums, and cassette programs, by the ton, it seemed like. X could hardly believe how much they bought. It was as if they didn't have a single thought of their own, at all, and had to have it all spoon-fed to them. Which was the whole point; they were exactly the type that Harriet wanted for recruits. They were spiritually dead. X could see it in their eyes, feel it in their dead-fish handshakes (you could always tell a real Christian by the way he shook hands). They didn't know the Lord—heck, they wouldn't know Him if He was sitting in their lap. It really made X's blood boil, sometimes, to think how people like that could dare call themselves Christians. And, worse, how they could set themselves up as leaders of other Christians. That was the shame of it: they were leading others astray. Straight down the garden path. A pernicious influence, Harriet called them, and X agreed with her totally.

Those preachers were the prime candidates for Conversion Management; they were ripe for the harvest. And in fact X was beginning to find it hard to contain himself, when calling on one or another of them—hard to keep from whipping out his tranquilizer pistol and grabbing the guy right on the spot. He could hardly wait. . . . But Harriet said no, it had to proceed on schedule, in an orderly way.

As of course it did have to; X understood that one false move could jeopardize the entire operation. Secrecy and security were paramount. And discipline. X knew it very well. Yet, still, he was beginning to feel . . .

Itchy.

He hadn't felt that way at all—or hadn't known he did— until the last three weeks. Three weeks was how long his new assistant, Abel Baker, had been with him.

What a name, X thought. Just showed you what kind of a mind the kid had, to have picked a name like that for himself. Kid, yes; though he was as big as X was, he looked about fourteen years old. His ears stuck out, and his chin wasn't any too prominent, either, and he had a tenor voice that sort of squeaked, like a little dog's voice. Actually, that was what he reminded X of: a little yapping dog.

X had never worked with a partner before. He liked his privacy; he'd always been a sort of lone wolf. What kind of a lone wolf would have this little critter trailing around behind him all the time? It made him nervous.

Oh, he supposed the kid was doing the best he could. He was eager to learn the job, it was true; and he was learning fast, and the clients seemed to take to him. But the trouble with him was, he was too eager. He wanted everything to happen right this minute, right *now*. As long as they were with a client, it was all right; but the minute the two of them were back in the car, Abel would start yapping at him.

And what he'd say was, "When are we going to make a *score*?"

Every darned time.

"Well, that's what we're here for, isn't it?" he'd say.

"One a week," X would have to remind him. "One a week is all they can handle at the Bible School, you know that. It's got to be orderly."

And then Abel would start to pout.

"Look, Abel, there's thirty territories in the country! Figure it out. We can't get 'em all in ours," X would say.

"Yeah, but you'd think we'd get *one*."

"We will," X would say. "It's Harriet's decision, not ours. You just have to be patient, that's all; she'll give us a green light as soon as she's ready." And unaccountably, as he said this, he'd find himself feeling depressed.

"Harriet's a heck of a smart gal," he'd tell Abel, a little lamely. "She knows what she's doing."

Abel would say, "Hmph," under his breath, as if he didn't believe a word of it.

Complain, complain, complain. X had never met anybody so irritating. "It's the territory," Abel would say. "Everybody's so *out* of it around here. There's no action."

"What's wrong with St. Louis?" X would say. "What's wrong with Kansas City?"

Abel would turn away and look out the window. "Big deal," he'd sniff. "Now you take L.A., for instance. There's a *city* for you."

X was mightly glad he was a Christian, so he had the strength to put up with all of this. If he weren't, he was sure he'd have lost his temper long since.

But after three weeks of it, day in and day out, it was beginning to get to him.

"When are we going to make a score," indeed. The little pipsqueak.

This morning X was driving the Buick, with Abel slumped in the passenger seat, along I-70, heading west out of St. Louis. They had made three calls so far: two bookstores first, and then Rev. Wilmot down in Webster Groves, who had ordered yet another carload of sermon outlines from the summer catalogue. And Wilmot had given them a new lead: a friend of his, a Rev. Swackhammer out in Jeff City.

Ordinarily, X would have called it a morning well spent. Any friend of Wilmot's was bound to belong on the recruiting list. If X were alone, he'd have been thinking about Swackhammer, and planning to phone him from his next stop, which was a Christian Innkeepers restaurant/truckstop out in Wentzville. He'd have been thinking what he was going to say to the guy, and so on, and generally feeling absorbed in things. . . . But not with Abel there. Couldn't think at all with Abel in the car; Abel just sat over there, looking wistful, keeping up his stream of complaints.

This morning Abel's problem was boredom.

"Three weeks on the job and already you're bored. Spare me," X said.

"Well," Abel whined, "it's just not turning out like I expected, that's all."

What could you do with a guy like that?

X tried to reason with him. "Sure, I know," he said. "The

actual nuts and bolts of it don't seem all that exciting. You're always going to have a slow day once in a while. But you have to keep the long view in mind, Abel. Think of the whole operation!" he said. "We're part of a team effort. We're winning America to Christ; what could be more exciting than that?"

Abel didn't say anything; he just gave him a stony stare. X ignored it, and stuck his chin out and kept his eyes on the road.

That was what you had to keep in mind, he thought to himself. The long view. The grave peril the nation was in, and the chance to save it; that made the actual nuts and bolts very exciting indeed.

Most of the time.

Well, sometimes.

"I mean, it's just like detective work," he said uncomfortably. "That's mostly routine, too, when you get right down to it. Why, even old Sam Spade spent a lot of his time sitting in cars looking at a doorway all night long. Ever think about that?"

"But it takes up *all* our time!" said Abel, sounding squeakier than ever. "My gosh, I'd never have signed up if I thought I wasn't going to be anything but a crummy *book* salesman!"

"For crying out loud! It's just a front, that's all," X said. "The guys in the CIA do the same thing. Everybody's got to have a *front*, don't they?"

Abel slouched down even further in his seat and crossed his arms over his chest. "I'd like to catch me some of them radicals," he muttered after a while. "Like that Flood girl, the one that took the payroll. Bet we'd get a big bonus for her, boy."

X was stung. "You haven't heard a word I've said, have you!"

" 'Course," Abel said, "I can't see why any of 'em would come through *here*."

"Oh, simmer down, can't you!" X said, more loudly than

he'd intended. He took a deep breath. "Just . . . just simmer down," he said.

Honest to gosh, he thought. Him and his John Wayne fan-
tasies. Wanting to come out with guns blazing. Kids these
days, he thought. It was shocking. No discipline, no maturity, no—

And he blushed, as he realized that that was exactly how
he felt. Here they were, stuck out here in Missouri, and nothing was ever going to happen; they would just keep driving
around and around, from one hick town to another, forever,
and . . .

It was the most awful feeling. It made him feel all tight
and clenched-up inside. He tried to fight it off, to remind
himself of the long view, but it didn't work. The feeling
wouldn't go away, and by the time they got to Wentzville,
he was completely distracted. He could hardly keep his mind
on the call they made at the restaurant/truckstop; Abel had
to do all the talking, making the pitch and showing the man-
ager their samples, while X kept staring off into space. He
even forgot to telephone Rev. Swackhammer. All he could
do was tag along with Abel, feeling numb, as they got up
from the meeting and picked up some coffee to go. He wasn't
even looking where he was going; on his way out the door
he practically crashed right into Louise Macdonald, who was
coming in.

"Oops. Sorry," he mumbled.

"No problem," she said.

She went on in.

He went on out.

He blinked.

His mind had to spin its wheels for a minute before it
got any traction. When it finally did, it shot forward as
though jet-propelled. He grabbed Abel by the elbow and
hustled him toward the parking lot as fast as he could. "Did
you see her!" he hissed. "I could swear that was Louise Macdonald!"

Abel's eyes bugged out. "Where? You're kidding," he said.

"Going in when we— No, don't turn around!" said X. "The one in the cowboy hat."

"Who was the other one?" Abel said.

"With the sunglasses?"

"Yeah, the brunette."

The two of them stopped and gawked at each other.

"Flood!" they both said at once.

"Let's go get 'em!" Abel said eagerly.

"No, wait a minute," X said, thinking fast. "Wouldn't want to make a scene in there. Too risky. Uhh . . . don't we have some mugshots in the car?"

"Yeah, I think so."

"Better double-check 'em. Wouldn't want to be wrong."

They scuttled out to the car, and got in, and began rummaging through the extra stuff they kept in the back seat. X was wide awake now, no doubt about that. He felt like his pulse must be about five hundred.

"Here's Flood!"

"Here's Macdonald!"

Both were photocopies from Harriet's files. X took a good look at Macdonald. The shot was several years old—it looked like a college yearbook picture or something—but it was her, all right.

"That's her, all right," he said, nodding several times. "How about Flood? What do you think?"

"Well, I don't know. Those sunglasses," Abel said.

"Yeah," said X. "Well, we'll get a better look when they come out."

"Boy, she sure looks mad about something," Abel said, looking at Rosie's picture.

"Yeah," X said quietly.

And they sat back to wait.

"Radicals; jeez," Abel breathed, after a while.

X knew exactly what he meant. He remembered himself sitting in front of the TV, back in Tin, and he felt the same old thrill coming over him now. And to think that only a few minutes ago he'd been moaning and groaning! It just went to show you. O ye of little faith.

"So then we'll grab 'em in the parking lot, right?" Abel said.

"Probably," X said. "Yeah, I guess."

Abel thought that over.

"What if they've got guns?" he said.

"Guns!" X chuckled. "Heck, they won't have guns. They don't carry 'em. It's against their religion."

At least, he thought, that was what Harriet said.

They laughed uneasily, keeping an eye on the restaurant.

Just then Louise came out the door, carrying a paper bag full of hamburgers. Followed by me, carrying the coffee, wearing her sunglasses. She'd made me put them on; "After all, Rosie's face was on TV last night," she'd said. "No sense taking any more chances than you have to."

"What do you think? Is it her?" said X. He held up Rosie's picture, covering the eyes with his finger.

Abel nodded. "No doubt about it." He already had his hand on the door handle. "Do we go get 'em now?"

X hesitated. What if they put up a struggle, he was thinking; or what if they did have guns after all? Real bullets, against the tranks he and Abel had—he didn't like it. And, too, the four of them would be sitting ducks out there in front of the restaurant windows; everybody could see them. Somebody might call the cops.

"No," he said, catching Abel's sleeve. "I think I got a better idea. We're gonna tail 'em and see where they go."

"Aw!" Abel said.

Gosh, what a baby, X thought. "Don't worry, kid," he said heartily. "Just think—they might lead us to a dozen of their little pals!"

That cheered Abel up no end. "Hey, yeah!" he said.

X felt good about it, too. In fact, he felt relieved, because he was still wondering about those guns.

They watched us heading across the parking lot with our paper bags. They watched us go past the cars, out to the row of trucks; they watched us climb up into one of the cabs.

"Look at that, they got a truck," Abel said.

"Huh!" X snorted, as if it figured.

They heard the clattering of the diesel engine as Louise revved it up. Then the truck began to move out from behind another one that said, "BUDWEISER."

"Christ," said the message on the truck. "America to Christ." They read the whole message as the trailer emerged: "REV. ANDERSON'S GOSPEL CRUSADE—Winning America to Christ."

"Holy cow!" said Abel. "That's one of *ours!*"

"Get Harriet on the phone," said X, starting the car.

CHAPTER 12

ROSEMARY FLOOD?" HARRIET SAID INTO THE phone. It was so wonderful, she hardly dared believe it. She'd been so worried. Ever since that morning, when the AP wire had come in about the girl's car—found empty at the side of the road, with her gone, and the papers gone as well. Harriet had been praying for a miracle ever since, and now it looked as though the Lord had given her one. "Thank you," she whispered, raising her eyes to the ceiling. "Oh, thank you!"

But Abel Baker was saying something else.

"What?" she said.

"I said, guess who's with her."

There was a pause. "With her?" Harriet said slowly.

"Louise Macdonald!" Abel crowed.

Harriet's mouth flew open. Her smile vanished.

"Together?" she managed to say at last. "Are you sure?"

"Sure we're sure," Abel said. "And guess what else!"

". . . Else?" said Harriet.

And he told her about the truck.

"What!" she said, standing up so abruptly that she knocked her leather chair backward against the windows with a crash. "One of ours!" she cried. "One of ours?" It was It. She knew it. "What's your position?"

"We're westbound on I-70, right around Wentzville," Abel said. "That's Missouri."

"West, you say." Her eyes went to the map on her office wall.

"That's right. 'Bout a half-hour west of—"

"—St. Louis," Harriet said fiercely. Her face had turned an angry red; all thought of miracles had left her mind. She was staring at the map hard enough to burn holes in it: Interstate 70 West led, in a dark green unbroken line, from Arlington through St. Louis to Denver, and past it . . . toward the Bible School. There was only one truck in the whole fleet that should be on that route: It. And it was the one and only truck which Louise Macdonald and Rosemary Flood must *not* be driving.

"All right," she said to Abel, barely controlling her voice. "Now you boys stay right behind them. Keep your distance. But not too far. If you lose them, I can tell you, you're going to wish you hadn't."

"Aw, now," Abel protested. But she didn't even hear him.

Abel frowned at the radiophone as he put it back in the dashboard pocket. "The old mother hen," he grumbled. " 'Now you boys be careful out there in that naughty old world.' "

"Come on, she's not so bad," said X. "Probably just worried, is all. You know how women get."

"Humph," said Abel. "Bet she doesn't think we can take 'em."

X said nothing. He drove westward in silence, and didn't take his eyes off the starred-and-striped backside of the truck.

Inside whose starred-and-striped cab, Louise, at the wheel, was munching thoughtfully on her hamburger, listening to me read the papers.

Confidential. Eyes only. Do not file. It was plain enough why they were labeled that way, and why they had to be locked up in a safe. Everything was in them—beginning with a discussion of "subliminal messaging," its nature and uses; proceeding through the setting up of the organizational machinery; and going on from there to Conversion Management, Phases I, II, and III.

Rosie had been right on the money. They didn't want a prayer tower. Not at all.

They wanted to take over.

I read Louise the theological preface to it all, which sounded like one of Rev. Anderson's sermons, only blunter. How, it asked, could our Lord's commandment to preach His word to every creature, to every nation, be reconciled with democratic ideals? "By their fruits ye shall know them," it said. And what were the fruits of democracy? Immorality and perversion, disguised under the name of so-called civil liberties. Blasphemy, demagoguery, and atheistic lies, disguised under the name of the so-called free marketplace of ideas.

No wonder there were so few real Christians in America, ostensibly a Christian nation, it said. Every American must have heard the Lord's word by now, but it had been overwhelmed and drowned out by this Babel of godless voices. Freedom indeed; and what did it produce? Nothing but snares, temptations, and stumbling blocks thrown in the path of those too weak or unsophisticated to defend themselves.

"This is no freedom," it said. And the Christianity that stood by and allowed it to continue was no Christianity. Christians must take the lead; with Christian leadership, immorality could be rooted out from the land of the Pilgrims' pride, and eventually from the whole world.

So, preaching was not enough; they couldn't wait for people to make a so-called free choice to respond to it. Bolder methods must be tried, to break down the people's stubborn resistance. And God Himself had shown us the way, in the Reverend's favorite proof-text: "I shall put my laws into their minds."

"Interesting logic," Louise observed.

"Isn't it," I said.

"And so—?"

"So here we go," I said. " 'The technological capacity to accomplish this has been available for a number of years. It is quite a simple process; the wonder is that Christians have overlooked it for so long. Known as subliminal messaging, it is nothing more than the broadcasting of auditory messages of such low volume, or visual messages of such short duration, that the subject is not aware, or conscious, of perceiving them. In this way the subject's conscious mind, his resistant will, can be entirely eliminated from the communications process—resulting in the direct implantation of the idea into the memory.

" 'In short, neither the subject's knowledge nor his consent is necessary.' "

"Mmm," Louise said, gazing out at the highway.

" 'Subliminal messaging,' " I went on, " " 'is suitable for any application where television, radio, a public-address system, or so-called Muzak, is present. Since this would include virtually every public building and residence in the United States, the possibilities for our work are almost unlimited.' "

"Ah," said Louise.

I plowed through Harriet's discussion of the history of subliminal messaging—its origin as a theoretical tool in the psychology lab; some early experiments with it in TV advertising; its recent use as a therapy for smokers and dieters; and (this was written up with especial enthusiasm) its use in certain department stores, with an anti-shoplifting message played underneath the background music, where after a month it had reduced the shoplifting rate by more than thirty percent.

"A month?" said Louise. "They're talking about a whole month?"

"Quiet," I said. "Listen." And I read on. " 'These results, of course, show only modest success. Such a track record would be unacceptably low if applied to the Lord's work. There is evidence to suggest, however, that it may be enhanced considerably, and within a dramatically narrowed time frame, by the utilization of other factors in combination with the verbal messaging process. Chief among these other factors would be the use of chemically induced minimization of the brain's natural inhibiting mechanisms. . . .' "

"Chemically induced!" Louise said.

I held up my hand. " 'A number of drugs, readily available, can accomplish this effect, notably certain of the major tranquilizers and the antirepressives.' You know what antirepressives are?" I said.

"Uh-uh."

My mother had told me one time. I must have seen the word in one of her psychology journals. "They're hallucinogens," I said.

Louise swallowed a bite of hamburger. "Like LSD and things," she said.

"Yup."

If Rosie had been hearing all this, I thought, she'd have been yelling by now. She'd have cursed; she'd have made a speech, beginning with the Crusades and the witch trials and ending with Dr. Mengele and the CIA. If she'd been trying to drive at the same time, she'd probably have run off the road. But Louise kept going at a steady fifty-five miles an hour, watching the traffic, glancing now and then into her rear-view mirror, and frowning only a little.

"My," she said.

After a moment, she jerked her thumb over her shoulder, indicating the rear of the truck. "Then that must be what we've got in here," she said. "You reckon?"

"Could be it."

"That'd be real nice," she smiled. "Real nice."

"Macdonald, Andy! Macdonald!" snapped Harriet. "Surely you haven't forgotten the prayer breakfast so soon?"

"Ah, yes . . . of course." Rev. Anderson's golden voice glided through the phone like honey off a spoon. "Why, Harriet," he said, "this is very upsetting news."

"You bet it is," she said crossly. "It means we've been infiltrated. Among other things."

"But I have all my drivers very carefully screened," purred the Reverend. "Are you sure your agents couldn't be mistaken?"

"*Our* agents, dear," she corrected him. "And they don't

make mistakes. I don't pay them to make mistakes. Now, you'd better find out who got her into that truck, and be quick about it. Turn the whole Crusade Center upside down if you have to. Meantime, I'm having my boys stay right behind her."

"Shall I report the theft?"

"Heavens, no. We'll have to handle it internally."

"Very well."

"And, Andy— I don't have to remind you how dangerous this could be."

"No," said the Reverend. "You don't."

Harriet hung up, and the green light winked off inside her cabinet.

She scowled at it.

Yes, the prayer breakfast. She remembered the prayer breakfast very clearly, thank you. It might as well have been yesterday. Though she hadn't been there herself—it wasn't wise for her to be seen in the Reverend's company—she'd gone in the limousine to pick him up afterward and found police cars all over the street; and then the Reverend emerged, pale as a ghost, with blood all over him . . . and Senator Quackenbush, too, and the others. . . . It was the most disgusting sight Harriet had ever seen. And she'd known instantly that it was no mere childish prank, or anything of the kind. It was a threat.

Horrible people! she thought with a shudder. Vicious perverts. Hardened criminals. She had a file of news clippings on them an inch thick—for they left their smarmy little notes behind whenever they struck—and every one of their jobs bore all the signs of careful planning.

From the looseleaf notebooks in her desk, she picked out the one marked "M-N-O," and looked up Louise's picture, scanning the notes written under it, which ended with the remark, "Believed based Washington area; present whereabouts unknown."

Present whereabouts known all too well, she thought, looking at Louise's unremarkable face. All too well known. And the idea made her so furious that she jumped up, lit a cigarette, and begun to pace rapidly up and down the length of her office.

The Special Shipment! It had to be that one, didn't it.

And it had to be X and Abel Baker up against them, too. Good Lord, she thought, the irony! She'd assigned those two to that territory in hopes that nothing much would happen there, and that they'd stay out of trouble. And to have them now tailing Louise, *and* the shipment, *and* Rosemary Flood, *and* the papers—it was too much. Abel would be of no use to anybody, green as he was; and X— well, what could be said about X, except that he'd named himself "X."

She should have fired him then and there.

And why, she'd like to know, couldn't they have nabbed the girls on the spot? Then they'd all be on their merry way to the Bible School by now—in the proper way.

That was something she looked forward to. Not only to getting them and their kind out of the way—that would have to be done in any case, for the good of society—but she was dying to try Conversion Management on them. They would be the acid test, the likes of Macdonald and Flood; if it would work on them, it would work on anyone at all.

But for now all she could do was stay close to the phone, and wait. And worry.

Dammit.

It was going to be a long afternoon.

All across Missouri, rolling along in the truck, I kept on reading the papers. We passed little town after little town, and a lot of subdivision houses looking new and raw and bare; the land in between was hilly and windswept, with rows of stubble poking up through the snow. Cars passed us on the road, full of families with kids and luggage and pillows, setting out on their spring vacations. Some of the kids waved to us, and grinned, and made faces; some of the parents, seeing whose truck it was, honked because they loved Jesus, as advertised on their bumpers.

Louise honked back at them—listening closely to me all the while, and nodding now and then as if she were checking everything off against a list in her head.

I read to her all about the preparations they'd made for Phase I—the experimental phase—of Conversion Management. I read how Harriet, acting on Anderson's behalf, had bought out Bliss Publications a couple of years back. Bliss's board of directors had wanted quite a pile for it, in view of the staggering profits being made in the inspirational-publishing game; she had cheerfully paid what they'd asked, and so they didn't complain when she began replacing their sales force with men of her own choosing. They weren't told about the raincoats and Buicks, of course; as the papers put it, they had no need to know.

"You mean these guys sell Bliss Books, too?" Louise said.

"Sure. That's their cover," I said. "And they sell sermon outlines and Sunday School stuff as well; that's how they get to meet the preachers."

That put an ironic expression on her face, which stayed there for quite a while afterward.

And I read all about how the Bible School out in Colorado had been renovated to accommodate the preachers—how they'd put up the fence and the hedge around the outside, for privacy and security, while, inside, they'd fitted it out with individual cells, with TVs and speaker systems to carry the subliminal messages, and central air conditioning, too.

"Air conditioning! Ain't that nice," Louise mused.

"Yeah, only it's not there to be nice," I said. "It's there for the drugs."

"It is?"

"That's how they give 'em to 'em. They're infusing 'em into the atmosphere."

"Kind of like Legionnaires' disease, huh?" she said.

"You got it."

She gave a low whistle.

"That's how they get around the knowledge-and-consent problem, see," I said.

"Mmm . . ." she said, blowing the horn at some passing Christians. "Now I've got to see if I'm getting this straight. These guys grab you out of your church one day, and slip you the old mickey, and the next thing you know you're in one of these cells, right? With the TV going. And it doesn't matter what it's showing you—could be 'Sesame Street,' could be 'The A Team'—because what's really getting through is this subliminal jazz."

"Right. Which is telling you Jesus wants you for a sunbeam."

"And meanwhile you're getting so stoned out, you don't know what the hell is going on, so you start to believe it."

"That's the idea."

"Mmm," she said again. "What have they got for a staff up there, I wonder?"

"The Harvest Workers," I said. "Hand-picked. Specially trained."

"What—those nice boys and girls?"

"That's the ones."

"All right; so what comes next? Phase II?"

"Yup."

"I'm all ears."

Once they'd perfected their technique at the Bible School, and worked the bugs out of it, the next step was to apply it on a mass scale. Naturally they couldn't kidnap everybody in the whole country; some other way had to be found. Not that they had any ethical objections to kidnapping—at least, if they did, it didn't say so in the papers. No, it was simply not "feasible." It would take too long, and it was too cumbersome. Besides, it required the acquiescence of the FBI, and Senators Rundel, Hackett, Mumford, and Quackenbush had let on that there were limits, in that connection, to even *their* clout.

Louise said, "You mean they're in there? In writing?"

"They sure are," I said.

She looked extremely pleased.

So the answer to their problems, for Phase II, came in the form of a trade association called Christian Innkeepers of America. It was a modest little group when Harriet bought it out: run by a modest little couple named Spradlin, who had a motel in Pontiac, Michigan. They were Born Again folks, it seemed, and they'd wanted some fellowship with others in their profession, so they'd started a little newsletter in which they wrote inspirational messages and "hospitality ideas" and so forth.

Well, Harriet put them in the big time. She gave them a budget and a staff and an office and turned their little newsletter into a full-size, four-color glossy magazine, renamed *Room at the Inn*, packed with all the latest motel management news, including advice on how to attract not only the fast-growing prayer breakfast trade but also conventions and conferences of all sorts. Member motels got wall plaques and stickers for their windows; they got advertising discounts and lots of other goodies, mostly financed with Anderson's money. They also got exclusive rights to sell Bliss Books in their lobbies—a very lucrative sideline, both for them and for Bliss.

All in all, it was such a good deal that motel owners signed up in droves. (Proof of Christianity was not required.) Membership was nearing the one thousand mark, the papers said, and climbing.

And all of those motels had TVs in the rooms, of course, and most of them had central air conditioning.

"And the ones that don't?" said Louise.

"They get a special deal on that, too," I said. "Low-interest loans. For 'beautification projects.'"

But the best deal of all—to members only—was the one they could get with a company called CMA Associates. CMA was a "conference packaging service": it did all the work of setting up, staffing, equipping, and cleaning up after conferences and meetings, more cheaply than the motels could do it themselves. CMA supplied all its own labor, audiovisual equipment, mikes, speakers, extra furniture, whatever might be needed; all the motel people had to do was sit back and watch.

Only, CMA was covertly owned and operated by Rev. Anderson's Gospel Crusade, and staffed by Harvest Workers. They got their training at the Bible School, as part of Phase I; and so, once Conversion Management had been perfected, they would be supplying that, too.

When one of their work crews showed up to run a conference, they'd be carrying subliminal soundtracks with them, which they'd wire into every sound system in the place—the speaker systems in the conference rooms, the Muzak in the restaurant, the house TV cable input. And the drugs went into the air conditioning, in carefully adjusted doses (now being worked out at the School)—not so high as to incapacitate anybody, or to arouse suspicion, but just high enough to loosen their minds up a little.

"Which is how they're going to be anyhow," Louise put in. "Everybody gets a little stewed at a convention; they probably won't even notice."

"And if they do, they'll think they must be coming down with the flu or something."

"And all the time they're getting the still, small voice. Far out," she said. "But what about the motel owners? They can't tell them what they're up to, can they?"

"Hell, no. They're trying to convert them, too," I said.

"Oh, of course." She frowned. "But, wait a minute, now. How can they expect this to work?" she said. "I mean, maybe it'll do something to you while you're there—but unless you've got something the matter with you, you're going to get over it as soon as you get home, right?"

"Right," I said. "I was just coming to that. That's Phase III."

"Oh, it is, is it?"

"Yeah; they have to keep reinforcing the message. Convert

the short-term memory into long-term. Strengthen the old synapses."

"No kidding."

No kidding. Phase III was the expansion-and-consolidation program. CMA Associates would move into the background-music market; only, the tapes they sold would have the sub-liminal messages already dubbed in. They planned to sell to anybody who used canned music—restaurants, hospitals, office buildings, stores, dentists' offices, even easy listening radio sta-tions. And of course they'd undercut all the competitors' prices, because their profit margin was taken care of by Rev. Anderson. Result: in a few years they could saturate the country with the sweet love of Jesus.

"And don't forget all those TV stations he owns already," I added. "That's next. Video."

"And the drugs?" said Louise. "What do they do about them?"

I smiled. "Subsidiary number four. 'ACM, Inc., Heating and Air Conditioning Specialists. Offices Nationwide.' "

She leaned back in her seat, tipped her cowboy hat down to a point just over her eyes, and sighed.

"Well, *shit*," she said.

Harriet paced back and forth in her office, blowing out clouds of smoke. She was really beginning to be very an-noyed. Anderson had called her back a short while ago with his report, which went as follows: The driver who had been scheduled to drive the truck had gone on vacation—though he was not due for a vacation for another six months. Louise Macdonald had been hired in his stead, using the name Anne Hutchinson. Very funny.

The man with responsibility for both the vacation and the replacement driver was called Roger Williams; he worked in the shipping department. He had been there a little more than a year. However, he had called in sick today.

Anderson sent his chief of security to call on Roger Williams at his home, listed in the files as an address in southeast D.C.

The address turned out to be that of St. Elizabeth's, the mental hospital.

Roger Williams was in reality Nathan Elliott, of the Soldiers of Jeremiah. They found that out quickly enough. But they couldn't find *him*.

That was not all. No, of course not. She had been in touch with Wilson, too, in the New York office. He had long since questioned his entire staff about Sunday night's break-in and had come up empty; but today, one member of the staff had called in sick. A secretary. Anne Bradstreet.

A.k.a. Marguerite ("Muffy") Townsend. Soldiers of Jeremiah.

Who also could not be found.

Yes. Harriet was extremely annoyed. They were smarter than she'd thought.

And at the moment there was not a goddamned thing she could do about it. The pieces were all on the board—she had put them there herself—but, though she could see them, she couldn't touch.

Ironically enough.

Harriet was not fond of irony.

She paused, in her pacing, before her highway map. The yellow pin representing X and Abel's whereabouts had progressed, during the afternoon, steadily westward from St. Louis to Columbia—and on and on, hour by hour, leaving a trail of pinholes behind it. Still on course. No change.

"Ralph!" she cried suddenly; and in a moment Ralph's blond head appeared in the doorway.

"Get X on the phone for me," she barked.

She was nervous again. She must talk to him one more time—just to make sure he was still there. Just to check.

"God, those papers are perfect!" Louise was saying, as we rumbled through the evening rush hour in Kansas City.

"Muffy said they'd be good, but this is amazing! We're going to nail 'em, P.K. They're wonderful!"

"Think so?"

"Sure. Everything's there—soup to nuts. And names." She eased her way into the through lanes for Topeka. "All we have to do is stir up a little excitement first," she said. "Kind of pave the way for 'em. Get the press interested. And if it *is* the drugs we've got in here, then that shouldn't be hard at all."

She looked over at me and smiled. "Don't look so worried," she said. "Don't forget, this is my job. I'm good at it."

I guessed she must be; in her line of work, you probably didn't survive as long as she had if you weren't. Still, Rev. Anderson was quite an opponent. With all that money, and power, and organization, and respectability, and pals in Congress—it still seemed to me as though we were taking on somebody roughly the size and weight of General Motors.

But as far as Louise was concerned, the bigger he was, the better. "He's news," she said. "And that's the way you get him. The one thing he's not going to want out of this is headlines, but that's what he's going to get."

So. We would pick a small town, somewhere past Topeka, to open up the truck in. "Small town, big splash," she said. "You want to make the front page, you don't want to have to compete with all the rapes and murders and everything."

We crossed the river into the Kansas side of the city. After a while the traffic began to thin out, and we picked up speed again.

Louise began to chuckle. "Conversion Management," she said. "Wow. You know, I think it's about the screwiest damn thing I ever heard of."

"You're telling me," I said.

"It's hard to believe. Even with the kidnappings," she said, glancing into her mirror again. "In fact, I'm not so sure I'd believe it even now, if there weren't somebody following us."

I had been lighting a cigarette just then; I choked on it.

"They've been back there ever since noon," she went on cheerfully, raising her voice a bit so I could hear her while I wheezed. "I thought maybe they were going to get off in K.C., but they didn't."

"Alcatraz."

"Zanzibar."

"Uhh—Ronkonkoma."

"What's that end with? O or E?"

"A," said X haughtily.

"Acacia, then," said Abel.

"Acacia! That's not a *place*."

"Sure it is!" Abel protested.

X rolled his eyes. The truck had hung out there in front of him for five hours—almost six now. Fifty-five miles an hour, no more, no less, except the brief slowdown through Kansas City. The tension of waiting for Louise to do something was beginning to get his goat. So was the sun in his eyes. So was Abel.

And so was Harriet. She'd been calling him every hour on the hour. Just checking, she said. Just checking.

Sure, he thought. He was beginning to agree with Abel; Harriet must not think they could make the collar.

We'll see about that, he thought.

"An acacia," he informed Abel, "is a tree. It's not a place."

"Oh, yeah?" said Abel, sounding more like a yapping dog than ever. "What kind of a tree is it, then, if you're so smart?"

"How should I know what kind of a tree it is? It's an acacia tree, that's all! Good grief!"

He really had been hoping the truck would turn off in Kansas City. He wondered how women's bladders held out so long. Glancing at his gas gauge, he cursed the Buick's good mileage; it was going to last longer than he was.

But he was distracted from that thought by the buzz of the radiophone.

"X here," he said, picking up the handset.

"This is Harriet." Right on time, X thought irritably. "I just want to know how you boys are doing."

"Just fine," he told her. "We're just trucking along here, having a swell old time. We've been playing Geography."

There was a slight, chilly pause, and then Harriet said crisply, "What is your position?"

"Just passed Kansas City. Heading for Topeka, looks like."

"How's the traffic?"

"Just *fine*, Harriet!"

"And the truck?"

X sighed. "Right out front," he said. "About four hundred yards, just like you told me. They've hardly even changed lanes but once or twice."

"Well," Harriet said. "You stay right with them, now."

X nodded.

"And suppose you stop playing Geography and teach Abel a few things about his job."

"Aw, now—"

"He's going to need it," Harriet snapped, and hung up on him.

The sun glared into X's eyes, low and red on the horizon. X glared back.

CHAPTER 13

BODINE, KANSAS, WAS JUST THE KIND OF TOWN we were looking for: a sleepy-looking place about twenty miles past Topeka, a mile or two down the road from the interstate exit. It had a couple of traffic lights, some stores (closed for the evening), a farmers' co-op, a bank or two, and a few streets' worth of tidy frame houses, in whose front windows we could see the blue glow of TV screens as we went by. At the far end of things stood an A&W, brightly lit up in the gathering dusk; across the street from that was the Bil-Mar, the town's only motel.

"Free TV," said the lighted sign out front. "Hot Showers. Truckers Welcome." It was a one-story, ranch-style building, none too new, with a line of pink neon running under the eaves.

Louise nosed Rev. Anderson's truck into the driveway.

"See 'em yet?" I said.

"Nope. But they'll be along. I expect they're trying to sneak up on us," Louise said. "With any luck, they might even wait until they think we're asleep."

"That'd be nice."

"Out with you, now. Got the card?"

I nodded.

"And smile, for God's sake."

I climbed down from the cab, took a deep breath, and went on into the office. Smiling.

The Bil-Mar wasn't a Christian Innkeepers motel; there was no sticker on the door, and no rack of Bliss Books for sale inside. It must be too small a place, I thought, to do Christian Innkeepers any good. And they probably couldn't afford central air conditioning, even at Anderson's special rates. The office didn't look at all prosperous; except for the desk, and an ice machine and a postcard stand, it was bare.

"Hello?" I called.

Through the open door of an adjoining room came gunshots and adventure music. "Be right with you!" a woman's voice sang. That would be Mar, no doubt. Mary? Martha? Marge?

In a minute, a short, plump, gray-haired woman came bustling out, putting on a cardigan sweater as she came. "Howdy! Hope I didn't keep you waiting any," she said, with a big grin. "Just doing some straightening up in there. Had the plumbers in today, and, my gracious, they made such an awful mess, and I got to picking up after them, and you know how one thing leads to another."

"Yes, ma'am," I said, grinning back at her.

"Well! S'pose you want a room," she said, moving behind the desk. "Will that be single or double?"

"Double. Have you got one around the back?"

"Surely. Surely." She glanced out the window behind her. "I always put the trucks out back, anyhow. Plenty of room to park back there. Put you in number eight. That your husband with you?"

"No, my partner. She's a she."

"Oh, Lord," she chuckled. "You girls today!"

I handed her Louise's MasterCard, which was made out in the name of Anne Hutchinson.

She put on a pair of glasses, which hung from a cord around her neck, and read the name, and looked back and forth from it to me until she was satisfied with us both. "That's twenty-eight fifty," she said. "Ice machine's right behind you, soda machine's out back. Looking for some supper, I'd recommend the Rainbow, right down in town, second light."

"Not the A&W?" I said, giving her another smile, while I

forged Anne Hutchinson's signature on the slip as smoothly as I could.

"Aw!" She waved her hand. "You girls go on down to the Rainbow; they'll fix you a *decent* meal. You look like you could use one."

"Yes, ma'am," I said, taking the key she handed me. Good, I was thinking. Nice friendly talkative lady; not likely to call any cops.

Better still, her TV set wasn't tuned to a news station. So in case Rosie's picture might be being shown, she wouldn't see it.

I smiled at her again on my way out.

Room number eight, out back, was pink and beige, with a pair of pitifully swaybacked beds, a TV, a phone, and a Gideon Bible. Over the beds were two pictures of flowers in vases, attached to the wall with screws. The pictures were identical.

Louise sat down on one of the beds and immediately began rummaging in her backpack. "Have any trouble?" she said.

"Don't think so. You?"

"They're at the A&W."

"They *are?*"

"Not time to worry yet," she said. "They went in to get some food. However"—she handed me a flashlight—"no sense hanging around, eh?"

"Nope!"

"Good." She fished a razor knife out of her pack, and a set of tools tied up in a cloth. "Off we go."

Outside, an elderly couple were unloading their car into number nine. Louise smiled at them and said, "Howdy"; then she turned to me and said, "Didn't you hear something fall over in the truck when we hit that bump?"

"What?" I said. "Oh, yeah; thought I did."

"What do you say we check it before we eat."

"Sure. Get it over with."

We walked, as slowly as we could stand to, across the asphalt to where Louise had parked the truck. As we went, she untied the cloth with the tools in it.

"What are those?" I whispered.

"My picks. Let's have some light here."

I turned the flashlight on and aimed it at the padlock on the trailer's rear doors. As Louise began to fiddle with the lock, I glanced nervously over my shoulder, expecting to see the agents come running around the corner any minute.

"Come on, hold it steady," she said.

"Sorry."

The lock fell open, and she undid the latch and swung the door out. It was even darker in there than it was outside; a warm, dusty smell drifted out at us.

We climbed in, and I shined the flashlight over tier upon tier of cardboard cartons, all alike, all printed with the legend, "Bliss Books."

Hell, I thought. This would take all night.

Louise went at them with her razor knife, slicing them open, taking a peek, shoving them out of the way.

"They *are* books," I moaned.

"Yeah," she said, tossing a couple at me. "But they can't all be."

I held the books up to the light. *Faith and the Single Woman,* I read. *The Christian's Guide to Success.*

She'd started on a second row. She worked fast, but the cartons were piled five or six high, all down the length of the trailer. They sure had gone to a lot of trouble.

"You can't open all of 'em," I said, with another glance out the door.

"Nope—no time." She shoved another box aside. "They've got to be here someplace, dammit."

"Maybe if you try the other end?"

"Smart." She took the flashlight from me and went forward over the top of the pile, and crouched down up there and began slicing; and in no time at all, she said, "Well, well. Looky here. The Opiate of the Masses."

I climbed up and joined her. And there it all was, just as the papers said: little glass vials, a whole lot of them. Chlorpromazine, said their labels. Meprobamate. A few other names I didn't recognize. And good old LSD-25. All nestled in their box, packed carefully in bright green shredded cellophane, the kind they use to pack Easter candy in.

"Sure is plenty of it," I said.

She smiled. "The more the better. And look what's on the box."

Stenciled on the box was not "Bliss Books," but "X.I.A." Christian Innkeepers. It had to be.

"Which means—" I said.

"They already have enough to run the Bible School. So this is for Phase II."

"Maybe they're going to hold it there to be picked up?"

"Doubtless."

"Jeez."

"Yeah. Let's get out of here; it makes me claustrophobic."

We scrambled out of the truck, locked it again, and hurried back to number eight.

Inside the room, we both breathed easier. Louise grinned and shook my hand. "Nice job, P.K.," she said happily.

"Nice job yourself. And now?"

"The fun part. We blow the whistle."

Outside the A&W across the street, Harriet's voice came in loud and clear over the Buick's 8500. "Where the hell are you?" she was saying. "Why haven't you called me?"

Agent X took a bite of his Papa Burger. "We're in Bodine, Kansas," he said. And mighty glad to be at a joint with a men's room, he thought.

"Speak up, man."

He swallowed. "Bodine, Kansas. The Bil-Mar Motel."

"Have you got them?"

"No; they just checked in a few minutes ago. We're across the street."

"Well? What are you waiting for?"

X felt his ears getting red. He didn't appreciate Harriet treating him this way at all. She was showing him up in front of Abel—who, he noticed, was looking highly amused as he sat over there sucking on his root beer.

"Actually," X grumbled, "I thought we'd wait a while. I thought maybe they're being met—you know, by their little friends. Then we could take all of 'em at once."

"Forget the friends," Harriet said. "I want you to go in now."

"Why?" said X, in a wounded voice.

"Because I want them caught!" she snapped. "I want Macdonald caught, and I want those papers! I don't want anybody taking any chances on this."

"But—"

"I said *now*, Johnny! Do you hear me?"

Abel tittered. "John-nee!" he mouthed.

X shot him a hateful glare. With an effort, he said to Harriet, "You're the boss."

"Good boy," Harriet said—suddenly all sweetness again, X noted bitterly, now that she'd humiliated him. "Now, Johnny," she went on, "I don't see this motel on my list, so you'll have to do the FBI bit. Call me the minute you've got them."

"All right, Harriet."

"And, Johnny—be very, very careful."

This sent Abel into fits of laughter. "John-nee!" he shrilled as X hung up the phone. "Be careful, John-nee!"

That did it. That was all X was going to take. He started the engine and slammed the shift into reverse. "Okay, kiddo," he snarled at Abel. "You act like a baby, you get left in the car."

"Huh?" said Abel, shocked into sobriety.

X smiled coldly at him. "You heard me. There's only one *man* around here, and he's going in. You'll be the lookout."

Going to take those darned radicals single-handed, he thought. That ought to show them.

He drove unnecessarily fast across the street and up the Bil-Mar's driveway.

• • •

"Yes? FBI?" Louise said into the phone. "Yes, please—I want to report an interstate shipment of contraband drugs. It's in a truck, a semi, parked at the Bil-Mar Motel in—are you getting this?—in Bodine, Kansas. My name? Surely. Louise Macdonald. Sure, I'll hold."

She looked up at me. "They're tracing it," she said. "Why don't you check on things out front while I'm on the line?"

I did as I was told, trying not to freak out at the thought of the real, actual FBI. She'd not only given them her name, but had gone into the bathroom beforehand and put fingerprints, both hands, very neatly, all over the mirror.

I hoped she knew what she was doing. Mainly, I hoped the TV stations in Topeka would take the bait, too, when she called *them* up. If they weren't interested . . .

But I didn't get a chance to finish that thought. I'd followed the line of pink neon around the end of the motel, and when I peeped around the front corner, I saw that the blue Buick was no longer across the street.

The motel office was only a few yards away from me; it was built out from the front of the building. I had a clear view in through its side window, the one behind the nice lady's back where she stood at the desk. She was there now, talking to a burly man in a raincoat.

In a little nook behind the desk, visible to the nice lady and to me, but not to customers, was a bulletin board. The board was covered with FBI "Wanted" posters.

And the nice lady was taking one down and showing it to the man.

As for him, I'd been wondering whether I would recognize him again from lunchtime. No problem. Those puffy eyes, that little gold cross in the lapel of his suit coat—it was him, all right.

I bolted back to number eight and waved frantically at Louise.

She nodded at me. "Yes, that's right," she said into the phone. "Right across from the A&W. You can't miss it."

She'd turned the TV on. It was showing a picture of
Rosie's Volkswagen by the side of the highway in Illinois,
with a lot of police cars around it. There was a phone number at the bottom of the screen.

"Okay," Louise said. "Yes, and thank *you*."

"They're here!" I gasped as soon as she hung up.

"Blue Buick?"

"In the office."

"Well, then, I guess that's our cue." She shouldered her
backpack and handed mine to me. "Turn up the volume on
that," she said. "Nice and loud. Good. Come on."

We hustled around the building in the opposite direction,
the long way around. "We'll have to hitch," she told me.
"We'll wait until they come around the back, then break for
the road."

"Did you call the TV guys?"

"Nope."

"Damn!"

"Don't *worry!* There's a gas station at the interstate. They'll
have a phone."

We poked our heads around the front corner in time to see
Harriet's agent step out of the office. But halfway out the
door he stopped, looked back, and went in again.

Nice talkative lady. She must have thought of something
else to say to him.

"Where's his partner? In there too?" Louise whispered.

"I didn't see him."

"Maybe in the car."

But no—there was their Buick, parked in the front lot, halfway between us and the office. Empty.

Louise looked at the Buick, and a sly grin spread over her
face. "What are we waiting for?" she whispered, and ran for
it, with me on her heels. As we crouched down in the shadow
of the car, she pulled a set of keys out of her pack and began
trying them in the door lock. "He come out yet?" she said.

I took a peek. "Nope."

"Aha!" she said in a minute. To my amazement, one of her keys worked. She opened the door and scooted across the seat behind the wheel; I got in after her with the packs. The same key started the engine, and she backed up with a screech of tires, flicked on the headlights, and took us roaring down the driveway.

I looked back and saw the agent standing in the lighted office door, waving his arms.

"Whee!" Louise laughed. "Ain't this fun?"

"How the hell did you do that?" I said.

"Trade secret."

"I thought it was only that easy in the movies."

"Nah. The only hard part is getting hold of the keys. It's all in who you know."

She drove us back past Bodine's two traffic lights—slowly now, at a legal speed—and onto the tree-lined road leading back to the interstate. "Just take a minute to make that call," she said. "Once that's done, we're home free, all the way to Zeke's."

"All right, that's about enough," barked a tenor voice behind us. A man's head and shoulders popped up over the seat back.

"Jesus!" I cried.

Louise said nothing, but only looked at him in the mirror. It was Abel Baker. While sulking there in the car, he'd remembered this back-seat trick from TV. What a stroke of genius, he was thinking. Now he'd show old X a thing or two.

"Don't try any funny stuff. I've got a gun," he growled, pulling out his tranquilizer pistol. "Keep your hands where I can see 'em. You—" he nudged my shoulder with the pistol. "On the dashboard."

"Anything you say," Louise said politely. A sign said the interstate was half a mile away. I saw her eyes dart toward the roadside, as though she were looking for something.

"All right," he said. "Now pull over and turn around."

"Where? Right here?" said Louise, setting her jaw. Quite

suddenly she yanked on the steering wheel, pitching us off balance in our seats, and stamped on the accelerator. The car lunged off the road, bucketed across the ditch, and flew straight toward a large tree.

Two of us screamed.

PART III

Thou shalt not steal; an empty feat,
When it's so lucrative to cheat:
Bear not false witness; let the lie
Have time on its own wings to fly:
Thou shalt not covet, but tradition
Approves all forms of competition.

—ARTHUR HUGH CLOUGH

CHAPTER 14

RUNNING THE BIL-MAR MOTEL IN BODINE, Kansas, wasn't any bed of roses, that was for sure. Marge Price could tell you that. Twenty-two units, seven days a week, winter and summer, and not much to show for it but a second mortgage. Before Bill passed, it had been fun. Kind of an adventure, watching the people come and go. Her and Bill, they built the place themselves, you see. Bill did most of the maintenance himself, fixing the air conditioners, hanging pictures and one thing and another, and Marge had done the chambermaiding—you didn't mind that if it was your own place, after all. And of course they'd had the kids to help.

Of course, they'd always taken for granted the kids would take it over someday. But then Little Margie got married and went off to live in Wichita, and Sonny—well, the less said about him, the better. Bored with Bodine, that was Sonny. Wasn't good enough for him. Not that anything ever *had* been. Went and joined up with one of those Chinese religions, was what he did, and shaved his head. That was the gratitude she got. Living in a slum out there in San Francisco, going around half-naked—and on food stamps, too. And you knew what that meant. It meant the taxes *she* paid were going to support *him*. If you please.

So now she had to hire a couple of girls from the high school to come in and do the rooms, and she had to hire union labor to do everything else, which was nearly breaking her, along with the fact that people stole so doggoned much nowadays. She could sort of understand it from those truck drivers—they never had any sense anyhow—but families, with kids! Nice folks!

Tch!

Nowadays Marge had to be there practically all the time—evenings to mind the desk, days to keep track of the girls and deliverymen and so on. They'd cheat you blind if you weren't standing right over them. She hardly ever got out to see her friends; why, sometimes she felt like she knew Jane Pauley, on TV, better than she knew Jane Rogers in town, who she'd grown up with. Used to be best friends, the two of them, all the way through school. Wasn't that something?

But, then, Marge supposed Jane Rogers was too busy being the banker's wife, and driving that pink Cadillac around, and running the Ladies' Auxiliary and the Episcopal Church Bazaar and heaven knew what all, to have time to stop by and spend a minute with *her*.

Well, it wasn't any bed of roses.

She guessed that was why she'd gotten started with the FBI posters. It gave her something to think about besides Bodine. She'd started it one parching hot summer after Bill passed, when there was nothing to do but watch TV and stay indoors and try to keep cool—and nothing on TV but reruns and tornado warnings. Business was awful slow—it was the year they had that Arab oil thing, and nobody was traveling—and she was wondering how she was going to make that mortgage payment.

Well, now, a man came and checked in one night that kind of set her to thinking. Colored man, kind of surly and mean-looking, and she got to thinking he looked practically like one of those armed robbers with their picture in the post office. Oh, not exactly, but almost. She didn't mean it *that* way; he just reminded her of it, was all. And she got to thinking here she was, running a public motel right off the interstate, where all kinds of people came through; and she'd never thought about it before, but some of them might be crooks. In fact, the more she thought about it, the more it stood to reason. Like it or not, there *were* criminals in this world, and maybe the reason they could run around loose so much was that people like herself weren't keeping their eyes peeled.

And of course there was the reward money.

She didn't expect it was very likely, of course, in a little one-horse town like Bodine; but you never knew, did you?

So, the next day, she went down and talked to Viv Johnson at the post office (nice girl, Viv. Lost her boy in Lebanon, didn't you know; terrible thing; although Marge told her at least he'd died for his country, which was a darn sight better than her Sonny was ever going to do)—and Viv said sure, she could get her on the mailing list; and so she put up this bulletin board in the Bil-Mar office, right behind the desk, and when the posters started coming in, she put them up on there.

Well, to make a long story short, she never did catch any crooks. For a while there she went through all those posters every afternoon before folks started coming in, and then she'd study all their faces real careful, you know, and watch to see if they did anything peculiar. Oh, she had a couple of scares; she'd take one look at somebody and just *know* she recognized him, and the minute he left the office she'd grab hold of that poster and look at it again. One time she'd even had her hand on the phone, she was so sure. But there was always a scar she'd forgotten about, that was on the picture but not on the real face; or the nose was a little different, or the jawline. So there was only a resemblance—just like with that colored fellow who started it all. Why, the chambermaid had told her the next morning how that fellow had left his room just as clean as you please; didn't take anything, not even the soap. He'd even made up his bed, bless his heart.

Just went to show you how wrong you could be about people. And wouldn't Marge have been embarrassed if she'd blown the whistle on a nice man like that!

So after a while she slacked off some, until nowadays she didn't hardly think about the posters but once a day or so—

which was exactly what Viv Johnson told her she'd do after a while. Viv said when she first went to work at the post office, she'd take a good hard look at those things every time she got a coffee break, almost, and then every stranger she saw at the Safeway seemed like it must be some terrorist or forger or something, and she was all ready to turn 'em all in and strike it rich; but finally she laughed at herself and said it was silly and forgot about it.

So then you could just imagine how surprised Marge was when this FBI man turned up out of the blue and started asking a lot of questions about Louise Macdonald and Rosemary Flood. Why, it was the strangest sensation! It was something she'd thought about happening for the longest time, only she'd never really believed it would *happen*. Anyhow, this FBI man said Louise Macdonald and Rosemary Flood were staying right there at the Bil-Mar and he wanted to go arrest them.

"Louise Macdonald?" Marge said. "Rosemary Flood?" Radical types, both of them. Reds. Wanted for burglaries back East. She remembered. Especially the Flood girl—she'd only just gotten the poster on her that morning, so it was fresh in her mind. "But they haven't been *here*," she said.

"Sure they have. You couldn't have missed them; it was less than twenty minutes ago. Driving a big truck," he said.

"Oh, yes," Marge said. "Dark-haired girl. Kinda skinny." Nice girl, too, she thought. Just as sweet as she could be. Said "ma'am." You didn't hear that very often these days, that was for sure.

"That's the one," he said. "That's Flood."

"Can't be. She didn't look a thing like her," Marge said; and to prove it to him, she reached around and got the poster off her board. "Look here," she said. "It's the same facial type, and the same coloring, but that's about all. Everything else was completely different."

Well, the man got real mad, and acted like he didn't believe her at all. It was all she could do to convince him that it wasn't the same girl, only a resemblance. But she knew what she'd seen; she had a good eye for faces, and she was positive.

"I've got a duty to my guests, after all," she told him. "I can't have a lot of false arrests going on."

He thought about that a minute, and pulled on his nose, and then he said, "But you didn't see the other one?"

And wouldn't you know, in all the excitement Marge had clean forgotten that the dark-haired girl said she was traveling with her partner, who was waiting in the truck.

Could you imagine? Forgetting a thing like that?

"That's Macdonald!" the FBI man said. "It's got to be! Wait—what name did this girl sign?"

Marge looked up the credit card slip. "Here it is," she said. "Anne Hutchinson."

And he said, "Now I know it's Macdonald. That's the name she used when she stole that truck she's driving."

Stole it! Well, that was enough for Marge any day. Those girls had been playing her for a fool the whole time. "They're in number eight," she told him. "You better go on back there and see to it."

And he was halfway out the door, he was in such a rush, before she remembered he'd need the master key. She always kept that in her room, not the office, since she didn't want to have to be watching it every minute—so she called him back while she went and fetched it for him.

"I hope you don't have to shoot anybody," she said.

"I hope so, too," he said. "But if I do, don't worry," he said; "the FBI will pay for any damage. Just send 'em the bill."

Right then they heard a screech of tires out in the parking lot. The agent looked out front and started hollering; it seemed his partner had gone and driven off someplace without him, in that blue Buick they'd come in.

"Isn't that a little unusual?" Marge said.

"You're darned right it is," he said. He was pretty hot under the collar. But then he calmed down after a minute and said it had been an unusual day all around, and he supposed he'd better go on around back.

Marge didn't think anything of it until later.

X glared up and down the road in front of the motel, but he could see no sign of the car. He'd never been so mad in his life. That little pipsqueak! he thought. Driving off at a time like this! Didn't Abel realize this was serious business?

He turned on his heel and stalked off, heading for number eight around the back, thinking black thoughts about what he would do to Abel. Everybody was against him, even the motel lady. Shoot, he thought. Who'd have thought you could walk into a place and say you were the FBI and get a lot of argument?

He spied the truck, dark and quiet, out in the middle of the rear parking lot; and there, under the pink neon, was number eight, lights on, curtains drawn over the window. And behind the curtains . . .

His heart began to race; he was tingling all over. He drew his tranquilizer pistol and sneaked up to the door. Carefully he slid the master key into the lock. He could hear the TV going inside the room. He took a deep breath.

He was ready.

"Freeze! FBI!" he screamed, bursting into the room, wildly waving the gun, ready to blast anybody who made a move. He wasn't scared at all; he was completely in command of the situation.

Only, nobody was there.

"What?" he asked, looking around in bewilderment.

"You work hard," the TV told him. "You need Right Guard."

X kicked open the bathroom door, but nobody was in there either.

"What?" he whimpered. This couldn't be happening! Was he in the wrong room? No—there was the eight on the door. He got down on his knees and looked under the beds. Nobody there, either.

"But—?" he said. Why weren't they here? They were supposed to be here! After he'd tailed them all day long, never once letting them out of his sight; and he was sure—positive—they'd never seen him; and after all that, it was just his luck to get stuck with some crazy old biddy who happened to collect FBI posters. Darn the old fool, anyway! Couldn't she just hand over the key, nice, like a normal person? No! *She* had to stand around arguing over who was or was not Rosemary Flood until X thought he'd lose his mind—so that by the time he'd been able to get away from her, they'd disappeared.

"But *how?*" he wailed. He got up off his knees and began to wander around the room, trying desperately to draw some conclusion from all this.

And then it all came clear to him. Catching his reflection in the bathroom mirror, he saw that he'd forgotten to take off the gold cross in his lapel.

That was it, he thought, horror-struck. The old bat in the office must have seen it. That was why she'd stalled him so long; she knew who he was right away. Somehow she'd tipped off the girls—she must be in league with them, of course; that was why they'd chosen this place to start with—and then they'd lured Abel away; and she was probably calling the cops right now; and *they* would be coming to get *him!*

He'd walked straight into a trap! Of course!

In a panic, he tore the cross from his lapel. Mustn't throw it away; it would be evidence. He shoved it into his pocket. He took out a handkerchief and rubbed his fingerprints off the doorknob, and the master key, too, for good measure; then he rushed out of the room.

The truck, he thought. Take *it!* Get away! Salvage that, at least. . . . But how was he supposed to drive it without the key? Darned girls had the key!

They'd thought of everything!

He hesitated on the edge of the parking lot, turning first one way and then the other; and then suddenly, in a wave of hysteria, he remembered Harriet.

Harriet was going to kill him.

She'd said she would, if he lost the girls. And she would, too. She was just the type.

Every man for himself! thought X.

And he fled.

I thought I heard somebody yelling. I was pinned into my seat, immobilized all the way up to my face by something large and balloonlike, like an enormous beach ball. I struggled with it, and it began to collapse, making a sighing noise.

"Dammit," Louise said.

I couldn't tell where her voice was coming from; she didn't seem to be in the car.

"You okay?" she said to me.

"I don't know," I said. "I guess so."

"Get the packs. And stop yelling."

On the seat beside me was a man's shoe. The windshield was shattered. Ahead of me, about two feet in front of the dashboard, I saw what they mean by the expression, "wrapped around a tree." I could have reached out and touched it if I'd wanted to. I didn't want to.

"Was I yelling?" I said.

"You're still yelling."

"I am?"

"Shhhh!"

I cleared the balloony thing off my lap, and some bits of broken glass with it, and climbed unsteadily out of the car.

In the darkness, some distance away, Abel Baker lay crumpled on the ground. Louise crouched over him, cursing.

"Get me the flashlight," she said. "It's in my pack. Right on top, I think."

I hauled our backpacks out of the car. Hers seemed very heavy, probably because it was full of tools; it clunked when it hit the ground. After a little fumbling, I got the flashlight out of it. I went over there and shined it down, as Louise turned Abel over on his back.

He was all bloody; his mouth hung open in a kind of smile,

and one of his front teeth was missing. So was one of his shoes. He didn't look old enough to be out of high school.

I wasn't feeling any too solid to begin with—only a minute ago, seeing that tree coming toward me, I had been sure that I was going to die, and I was still trying to get control of the fact that I hadn't. The sight of Abel, lying right about where I should have been, made me feel faint.

Louise looked about as bad as I felt. "He wasn't supposed to go flying out," she muttered. "I thought the damned things would be big enough to stop him." She opened one of Abel's eyes and peered into it, and laid a hand on his throat. "They don't bother to put 'em in back, you know—the air bags. Now go look in the—"

"Air bags," I said, dazed.

"Yeah, now go get something to keep him warm," she said. "See if his coat's in the car. He had it on at lunch."

I stood there staring at Abel. The little gold cross on his lapel caught the light and gleamed.

"Go on, hurry up, will you?" Louise snapped.

I blinked at her. "He's not dead?"

"No. Not so hot, but not dead."

"Oh, thank God!"

"But he will be, if you don't move it."

I managed to get myself moving. The raincoat was on the floor in the back of the car, under a couple of suitcases; I took it over to Louise, who tucked it gently around Abel.

As she did so, a car came by on the road, slowing down to get a good look at the wreck.

"Hey! Over here!" Louise yelled, but the driver either didn't hear her or didn't care. He sped up again, and by the time we could get out to the roadside, he was gone.

The next one we were ready for. It didn't look as though it was going to stop, either; we had to block its path to get it to.

"Try to look scared," Louise said to me.

That wasn't hard.

It was a Cadillac. Pink. We ran over to the driver's side as the driver, a middle-aged woman, rolled her window down a few inches.

"Please, ma'am," Louise said breathlessly, "can you go back to town and call an ambulance? The driver's hurt pretty bad."

"My goodness! Did you see it happen?" the woman said, craning her neck to see the Buick.

"Oh, yes; it was awful. We were walking along, right back there, and he just came along and swerved right off the road. Just like that."

"That's terrible! Was he drunk?"

"I don't know," Louise said. "But he needs a doctor right away."

"Well, I—"

"I'd ask you to take him yourself," Louise said, looking at the Caddy's leather upholstery, "but he's kind of bleeding a lot."

"Oh, dear, but I'll be late for my—"

"*Please*, ma'am!"

The woman seemed to collect herself. "Why, what's the matter with me? Of course I will," she said. "Do you girls need a ride?"

"Oh, no, thanks. Don't worry about us."

"I'll be as quick as I can," said the woman, rolling her window up. She did a sloppy three-point turn and sped off back toward town.

We watched her go. Then we both turned and looked back at Abel. We could hardly see him without the Cadillac's headlights; it was too dark.

It didn't matter. We saw him anyway.

"Oh, God, come on," Louise said after a minute. "We've still got to make that phone call."

We picked up our backpacks and ran the other way, toward the interstate.

Marge stayed in her room a while; if there was going to be any shooting, she was darned if she was going to get herself caught in a crossfire. She waited almost an hour, she guessed, thinking about how that Macdonald girl, and whoever her partner was, had taken advantage of her good nature. And then, while she was waiting, she saw one of those newsbreaks on TV about how they'd found this Rosemary Flood's car in Illinois; and she began to wonder if she mightn't have been mistaken about that, too. She'd seemed like such a nice girl, Marge thought, and she really didn't look a bit like her. At least, Marge didn't *think* she did.

Finally, when she couldn't stand the suspense any more, she went around back to number eight to see what was up.

Well! There was the door standing wide open, with her master key right in the lock, so that anybody who wanted to could have paraded on in, and nobody around at all—not the agent, not the girls either. They'd left all the lights on, and the TV, too, for gosh sakes.

Marge thought maybe the girls had gotten away from him somehow and he was out chasing them. Or else maybe they'd lured him off in the bushes somewheres and knocked him out. Or killed him—if they really were hardened criminals, of course, they wouldn't turn a hair at that.

Well, now, she wasn't about to start traipsing around the place in the dark looking for dead bodies, and maybe get ambushed herself, or taken hostage, or anything like that, so she called the police. And they came along (though it took them three forevers)—one of them was Rae Martin's boy; nice boy, used to work in the drugstore; the other one she didn't know. The two of them looked all around the place, but they didn't find anything. They were mighty excited that Louise Macdonald was somewheres around, and maybe Rosemary Flood, and the FBI, too, so they hung around in the office a while to see if anything would happen. Marge made them some coffee, and they had a real nice chat.

And then the real FBI showed up.

Oh, and weren't they something, though! A pair of great big, tall, strapping fellows, and just as cool and professional and courteous as they could be. They showed Marge their badges and said how they'd come to have a look at that stolen truck. Said they'd gotten a tip that it had some kind of contraband in it. They had a warrant and everything.

"Oh, yes," Marge said—she had to crane her neck way up to talk to them, they were both so tall. "Your Agent Smith was just here a while ago, looking for the drivers," she said.

Those two agents looked at each other, and looked back down at Marge, and one of them's eyebrows went up and the other's went down, and they said, both together, "What Agent Smith?"

So then the Martin boy and the other cop both started telling them the whole story; they would hardly let Marge get a word in edgewise; and every now and then the agents turned to Marge and said, "Is that true, ma'am?"—they called her "ma'am," too, bless their hearts—and she said yes, it was the gospel truth. And when they heard Louise Macdonald's name, they both said, "Uh-*huh*."

So then the cops and the agents all went outside and searched the place all over again. They told her they had to search all the rooms, too, since this Agent Smith had had his hands on the master key. Marge thought that was a terrible thing—it was the first time all night she'd thought about her other guests, she'd been so excited by all the commotion. But, instead of being offended, all the guests were about as thrilled as they could be, and half of them came by the office to find out what was going on, and hung around drinking coffee with her until all hours!

They never did find either the girls or this Agent Smith, but they found a whole lot of fingerprints in number eight. All over the bathroom mirror; said they looked like they'd been put there on purpose. And in that truck they found all these drugs—LSD, they said, and enough tranquilizers to open up a mental hospital. Marge almost had a heart attack. And then they called their headquarters and found out there wasn't any Agent Smith anywhere within three states.

Right about then, three or four other cops came around to

get in on the excitement—which made about the whole Bodine police force, as far as Marge could figure. These new boys said they'd just come back from taking a fellow to the hospital who'd had a one-car accident right down the road from the Bil-Mar. Ran right up a tree. He was pretty well banged up, of course, and the car was a total loss. One of them said what a shame it was about the car. "It was one of them new Buicks," he said. "Brand spankin' new. The way them things cost, it was mine, I sure wouldn't run it up no tree!"

And all the cops laughed; but Marge said, "A new Buick—that was it, that was the kind of car this Smith fellow had. Light blue."

"Hey, that's what color this one was," the cop said. "Now ain't that funny." And so the Martin boy said it must have been Smith's partner, the one that drove away.

Things began to die down a little after a spell, and the guests began to go back to their rooms—but, didn't you know, just then the reporters came charging in. All lathered up, and all yelling at once about how they got a phone call from Louise Macdonald—and that handsome Chuck Daniels, from Channel Thirteen, in real life, right there in the middle of them. He was a lot shorter than she'd expected, but, oh, wasn't he the darlingest thing you ever did see! And all the guests came back, seeing as how they all wanted to get on TV. Marge had about run out of coffee by that time, so somebody went across to the A&W and brought back a whole case of pop, and it was almost like a big Hollywood party, with the lights and the TV cameras there. Marge told them the whole story all over again.

"Is that right, Mrs. Price?" Chuck Daniels said. He was standing that close to her.

"Oh, pshaw, you can call me Marge," she said.

She just had herself a field day. Why, it was the biggest thing that had happened in Bodine in she didn't know how long.

She didn't think she would ever get over it.

CHAPTER 15

AT THREE O'CLOCK IN THE MORNING WE WERE cruising toward the Colorado border in a gigantic Oldsmobile driven by a life insurance man from Wichita. He was our seventh ride since Bodine, or maybe our eighth; I'd lost track long since. He was telling Louise, who sat beside him in the front seat, that he was on his way out to Aspen for a sales conference; Louise, chuckling, said that Aspen sure was a good place for it.

"You can say that again!" the man said. "I never been to the Rockies before. Been over 'em a million times, but I never been in 'em. That's why I figured I'd drive. I get so sick of flying, and you know you can't see a thing out of those damned planes anyhow."

"Oh, you're in for the time of your life," said Louise, letting the throttle out on her Western twang. "Hear that, Sally?" she said over her shoulder to me. "Says he's never been in the Rockies. Me and Sally, we grew up in Wyoming," she told the man. "Used to go up in the mountains all the time with Uncle Danny. Why, it makes me homesick just to think of it."

The life insurance man was a big, overweight, garrulous guy, somewhere in his forties, I guessed. Dangling from his rear-view mirror was a square of plastic bearing a cross, a flower, and the legend, "Easy Does It"—that, and a pair of foam-rubber dice. He seemed to have all the bases covered. He'd told us, when he picked us up, how glad he was to have our company, because he hated driving all night with nothing to listen to but the radio. He'd much rather talk to a couple of nice girls like us.

It was a good thing he felt that way, because the radio, turned down low, was trying to tell him what we'd done and what we looked like and that the FBI would pay handsomely to know where we were. We'd made the news at eleven, and midnight, and one and two; each time, we'd been in a different car, and each time, Louise, seated in front, had been talking her head off to the driver, so as to drown it out.

"Gosh, we used to fish and hike, and camp out, and all kinds of stuff," she said. "Hey, Sal, remember those trout we got up at Fremont that time? What do you say, is it God's country out there, or ain't it?"

"Oh, yeah," I said, though I'd never been to the Rockies either; and I started to say something else, to help keep things going, but I yawned in the middle of it.

"Poor old Sal. She's just pooped," Louise told the man. "Working nights at that Pizza Hut and tryin' to get through midterms at the same time— You ever work the night shift? Boy, it really takes it out of you, doesn't it?"

I *was* pooped. I didn't know how Louise did it. There she sat, in one car after another, acting as though she were having a fine old time, spinning a new cock-and-bull story for every driver we rode with (we were pizza waitresses, telephone operators, cashiers in a 7-Eleven; we were going to meet our boyfriends, who also worked the night shift, in Abilene, Salina, Fort Hays, Goodland—keeping the rides short, so as not to have anybody getting to know us too well)—and managing to seem just as fresh and alert as she'd been at noon.

But as for me, much as I tried, I couldn't keep my eyes open. I'd had plenty of practice pulling all-nighters in school, of course, but reading books was one thing, and crashing cars and throwing secret agents through windshields was another. I was still shaking; and telling myself that it had been self-defense, that we'd done the only thing we could do, didn't do me much good. Abel must be still alive—if he weren't, the ra-

dio would certainly have said so—but that didn't make me
feel any better, either. I kept thinking of him lying there in
all that blood, one shoe off and one shoe on—lying there instead of me.

(Does this mean P.K.'s a criminal?)

(Naw, you dumbbell.)

I couldn't get rid of him.

So I fell asleep instead. I'd sit there in the back seats of all
those cars, trying to pay attention to what Louise was saying
to the drivers, but by and by her words would all run together, and I'd sag against our backpacks, and my head would
nod, and one eye would close, and then the other. As sleep
went, it wasn't much; I kept rerunning the crash all night
long, and every time the car hit a bump I'd wake up with a
tremendous flinch, imagining that we were skidding out of
control, with trees dead ahead in our path, or FBI roadblocks,
or God knows what.

But it would only be Louise, still chattering away.

Which she was doing now. "Oh, really? You're a fisher-
man, too, are you?" she said brightly, pouring the life insurance man some coffee from his thermos bottle. "What a small
world it is, huh? Where do you fish around Wichita—they've
got some good-sized reservoirs down that way, don't they?"

Scheherazade would have been proud of her, I thought.
She'd gotten us through another news broadcast; the insurance man was launching happily into a disquisition about bass
and crappies and perch and whatnot, and the radio had gone
back to its country western crooning, and we were reasonably
safe for another hour.

I leaned back and tried to relax and stop worrying. That
was what Louise kept telling me, out there in the dark, on the
roadsides, between rides—not to worry, and especially not to
act worried. None of these people were ever going to connect us, a couple of pizza waitresses, with the dangerous criminals on the news; and if they should, they'd be bound to
dither a while, making up their minds whether they wanted to

get involved or not. And if they did decide to get involved, we'd be long gone by the time they could get off the highway and find a telephone. We'd make it all right. At the rate we were going, we'd be safe and sound at Zeke's place by noon tomorrow—with the evidence in hand. Rev. Anderson's name would be humming through the airwaves all over the country; we'd be able to hand over Rosie's papers to any reporter we liked. It was Anderson who had to worry now.

The radio went on crooning. I looked at my watch and yawned. Zeke's place, I thought, as my eyelids began to droop. Safe house, way up in the mountains; it sounded lovely. If we could just get there in one piece, I would sleep for a week.

I was half aware of Louise giggling, far away, at something the insurance man must have said; then I nodded out. And I went through the crash all over again, complete with the crunch of metal and the sound of glass breaking, only this time when I looked down on the ground at the figure who had been tossed out of the car, it wasn't Abel Baker.

It was Rosie.

I must have said something in my sleep, because Louise reached back and poked me—hard. "How's that, Sal? Hold the anchovies?" she said. "No sweat, kid. We'll take care of it for you."

"Haw!" said the life insurance man.

Rosie, in fact, was also in a car heading for the Colorado border, at that ungodly hour of the morning. She was a hundred and fifty miles north of us, in Nebraska, on Interstate 80. It was only two o'clock where she was, because of the wanderings of the time-zone line; but Rosie didn't know what time it was, anyway. She was what's known in some circles as heavily sedated, and in others as out cold, in the back seat of a blue Buick.

It had happened early in the evening, around the time we'd been driving away from the Bil-Mar Motel. It was the luck of the draw, maybe, or God's will, or Murphy's Law—whatever you like to call it. She had turned off I-80 at one of the Omaha exits, looking for dinner, and had happened to pick a place that belonged to Christian Innkeepers.

Which happened to be being visited by two of Harriet's men who called themselves Junior and Skip. They were making late calls that night in hopes of topping their own record, set last month, for the highest sales volume in the Midwest. Maybe that would impress Harriet enough, they thought, to move her to assign the next preacher to them.

Rosie had no way of knowing what the Christian Innkeepers' Association was, since she hadn't had a chance to read the papers before I'd stolen them from her. There was a sticker on the door of the restaurant, right next to the MasterCard and Visa stickers; but since she didn't know to look for it, she didn't see it.

And there were so many blue Buicks in the parking lot that she'd stopped counting.

She would just as soon not have stopped at all, she was in such a hurry to go find Zeke. She was planning to drive all night; but the Plymouth needed gas first, and she needed food and coffee and a bathroom. She thought it would be all right, though. It was the height of the dinner hour; the restaurant was crowded; safety in numbers, she thought. And besides, she wasn't Rosie Flood. She was *me*. With a billfold full of cards to prove it, in case anybody asked.

But Junior and Skip didn't ask. They knew radicals always carried fake I.D.'s anyhow. They simply loomed up on either side of her, as she was coming out of the women's room, and murmured, "Why don't you come outside with us."

"What's this all about?" she growled at them.

"You know what it's about," they said.

"Hey! Take your fucking hands off me!" she yelled. But they'd already picked her up two inches off the floor, one of them at each elbow, and were hustling her out through the restaurant.

She was wrong about safety in numbers, too. There must

have been a hundred people on the take-out line, and another hundred milling around in the lobby; but they took one look at Junior and Skip, at their muscles and their haircuts and their raincoats, and at Rosie kicking and writhing in their grip, and naturally they assumed there was an arrest in progress. The people in front stood back to clear them a path, while the ones in back stood on tiptoe to get a better view.

"Out of the way, please; thank you; stand back, please," said Junior.

"No!" screamed Rosie. "They're not cops! Somebody help me! They're kidnappers!"

But the crowd saw the ratty old army coat she was dressed in, and stood back a little farther; and in no time the three of them were moving out through the door.

As they went out, Skip nodded to Junior, and they relaxed their grasp just enough to allow Rosie to wrench herself away. As she ran into the parking lot, Junior brought his tranquilizer pistol up with both hands, took aim, and shot her in the back.

"Ow! Shit!" Rosie said, but she didn't fall down. It must not be a bullet, she thought, if she could still run; although, after a moment, her feet began to get very heavy, and the asphalt seemed to get very deep and soft.

It was tough going. Miles and miles and miles to the Plymouth; every step was a struggle, as though she were wading through mud. She made it at last, sobbing for air, and got out her—or my—or somebody's—keys, and tried to unlock the door. But she couldn't seem to get coordinated enough to do it. Leaning against the side of the car, she sawed the key back and forth in the air, until it began to strike her funny. The whole thing was funny: the restaurant, the crowd, and Omaha, for God's sake. She laughed a little. What on earth was she doing in Omaha?

After a while she gave up with the key and sat down next to the car and began to study its front left hubcap very, very carefully.

Two men in raincoats, whom she no longer recognized, came over and got her.

"Omaha!" Harriet shouted into the phone.

She was still in her office at the time. She'd stayed on, long after Ralph had gone home, expecting to hear from X at any moment, but there had been nothing. Silence. Six-thirty. Seven o'clock. Seven-thirty. She had smoked half a pack of cigarettes, pacing up and down the office, and then back and forth, and finally around in circles—glaring at the map on the wall all the time, as though it, at least, might have told her something. But the yellow pin she had stuck into it at Bodine had stayed where it was, and the phone hadn't rung.

Every time she'd heard the Associated Press machine start typing, she'd leapt for it, with her heart in her mouth—but it was only a car bombing in Belfast or a border raid in Nicaragua. Nothing about X.

And now this.

She gnashed her teeth and emitted small strangling noises while Junior told her about the fake I.D.'s, all very skillfully done, under the name of "Olivia Mather," and the perfect resemblance between the prisoner and the picture Harriet had sent out, and (the clincher) the fact that the prisoner had known right away that he and Skip were not policemen. It was definitely Flood, he said; no doubt about that at all. She'd been driving a Plymouth, he reported—which was no surprise to Harriet; obviously she would have gotten hold of another car, having ditched her own—however, unfortunately, the papers weren't in it.

"We figure she must have handed them off to somebody else," Junior said. "You know, maybe when she switched cars. Sorry we couldn't get 'em for you, but at least we got *her*."

A great many thoughts rushed violently through Harriet's mind. She opened her mouth and closed it several times. Finally she said, "You know where to take her. Better get on with it."

And she slammed the phone into its cradle.

Omaha. Then Flood had never been in Bodine.

She took a moment to collect herself. Then she tried to call X and Abel, fully intending to give them a tongue-lashing such as they had never heard before—but the line was dead. She slammed the phone down again, stubbed out her cigarette, snapped off the lights, and went home, fuming all the way to Winnetka.

She sat, seething, through the ten o'clock news, which told her that a woman purporting to be Louise Macdonald, the fugitive, had called up the FBI from Bodine, Kansas, informing them of the truck with the drugs in it. There were pictures of the truck, lit up by floodlights, with the Reverend's name clearly visible. There were pictures of the motel owner. There were pictures of the room, where fingerprints had been found, but no trace of Louise herself.

Nor of her companion—whose identity, Harriet reflected bitterly, could now be marked down as unknown.

Olivia Mather, indeed. Anne Hutchinson. Of all the impudent—! How dare they? Did they think this was all a big joke?

There was no mention of X and Abel on the news, or any information about precisely how they had managed to bungle the job, but it was quite plain that they had.

Harriet had figured that out, of course, long before ten o'clock. Accordingly, she had already drafted some remarks for the Reverend to make to the press, to the effect that there were no drugs in the truck when it left the Crusade Center, and that he'd had no idea the truck was stolen until notified by police, and furthermore that Louise Macdonald had always been out to get him for reasons known only to her anti-God, anti-moral, anti-American self, so that it was clear to Rev. Anderson that she had planted the drugs in a vicious effort to discredit him and to destroy his work, but that our Lord had warned us that we would be reviled and persecuted for His sake, and so Rev. Anderson was praying for her and wished to urge all his fellow Christians to do likewise.

And (in case he should be asked) that, no, he saw no link-age between the stolen truck and the burglary in New York, unless they were both, perhaps, part of a far-reaching conspiracy against him; but of course that would be for the law enforcement people to determine.

"And be sure," she'd told him over the phone—which, like the one in her office, was hooked up to an 8500 console—"Be sure to be just as sweet and helpful as you can be."

"Of course I will," Anderson had said.

"Of course you will. And another thing, Andy: I'd suggest you touch base with Quackenbush as soon as possible. I think a small contribution would be in order."

"I'm ahead of you, for once," he said. "I'm meeting him for breakfast tomorrow."

"Wonderful. Give him my love."

"Harriet? We—we'll get through this all right, won't we?"

She'd smiled. "Of course we will, dear. Remember, the Lord knows our every need, even before we ask. Now you just concentrate on being sweet and helpful, and I'll worry about the rest."

And now, at three o'clock in the morning, she was sitting in bed, wide awake, leafing absently through the Bible on her lap while she worried about the rest. She still hadn't heard from X and Abel, the fools. She *was* going to kill them—if Louise Macdonald, and whoever it was she was traveling with, hadn't already done it for her.

Which was still not going to get those papers back.

She couldn't sleep; she was far too angry for that. Macdonald still at large, she thought, and this other one; and Muffy and Nathan, too. Flood was out of the way now, yes—but all the rest of them had slipped through her fingers. Insufferable! And how many more of them were floating around loose? The whole gang? Ready to strike again, very likely—but where? And how?

The present damage seemed to have been contained. For the moment. And with God's help, and with continued pressure on the Bureau . . . and if Andy did a good job of stone-walling the press . . . But she detested being on the defensive like this. Always a step behind the adversary; it was so frustrating that she could hardly bear it. She wished there were some positive step she could take, some bold counterstroke. If only she could anticipate the gang's next move and be there waiting for it!

She gazed down at her Bible. Our every need, she thought. Oh, if only He would send her a sign!

And that was what He did. As He had done so often before in Harriet's life, He used the telephone. Often as it had happened, over the years, she still had not quite gotten used to it; and so, when the phone rang, she picked it up with a trembling hand, sure that a fresh disaster was upon her.

It was Skip, calling her from western Nebraska.

"Hope I didn't wake you," he said, "but I thought you should know. We tried giving the Flood girl that new stuff for her second shot—you know, the pentothal?—and she . . ."

Died, Harriet thought. The way things were going, she'd died on them.

". . . Talked," said Skip.

Harriet let out a long, slow sigh.

"She didn't say much, and she didn't make a whole lot of sense," Skip told her. "But she said something about Corinth; we're not too sure, but it sounded like she might have been on her way out there. That's right up near the Bible School, isn't it?"

"Yes," Harriet breathed.

"And she gave us a name, too. She said, 'Zeke.'"

Harriet's thoughts began to race. "Yes, yes?" she said.

"No last name," Skip said. "But we thought it might mean something to you."

She was sitting bolt upright now, her eyes shining. "Yes?" she said. "Yes, I think—yes!" It definitely rang a bell. Her Colorado agents had mentioned someone by that name, in one of their reports, some months back. A hippie type who'd bought a—a farm? A commune? No—a retreat center. Thought to be Zen, or Quaker, or some such. Her agents hadn't had any hard information, but they'd thought Zeke and his group looked suspicious, and bore watching.

"Yes, of course!" she said, making the connection she'd failed to make at the time. At the time, she'd simply put the report aside, having found no one in her files named Zeke. But now—!

"Thank you, Skip," she said. "Thanks very much."

It was Zychowicz; of course! Edward Bellamy Zychowicz, one of the original Soldiers. Incredible that she'd missed it the first time.

Was blind, but now I see, she thought. And she uttered a prayer of thanksgiving to the Lord, her strength and her salvation.

She punched out the number of the Bible School and had one of the senior Harvest Workers, whose name was Derek, rousted out of bed. She spent ten minutes giving him his instructions.

There, now, she thought, as she hung up the phone. That ought to tidy things up a bit.

And she snuggled under the covers and went soundly to sleep.

CHAPTER 16

AT MIDMORNING ON WEDNESDAY, DETECTIVE Sergeant Robert Fleischmann, Kansas State Police, Topeka HQ, screwed a carbonless quadruplicate form into his typewriter and, typing with two fingers, began to fill in the blanks.

"BAKER, Abel," he typed. "NMI."

> Male. Caucasian. Date of Birth 8/10/58.
> Ht: 6-1. Wt: 195.
> Eyes: BL. Hair: BR.
> Scars and Other Identifying Marks: None.
> Soc. Sec. No.: 121-83-9351.
> Residence: 388 Oak St., St. Louis, MO.
> MO. Operators Lic. (Class A) No. B2900351-
> 5MP271-BA4.
> Violations: None.

Fleischmann frowned a little as he typed, partly out of habit, and partly because, thus far, the only accurate thing on the form was the physical description. St. Louis Information had no listing for an Abel Baker, or an A. Baker, or an A.-anything-else Baker. The woman who had answered the phone at 388 Oak Street that morning said her name was Baker, all right, but there wasn't any white man in her house, and nobody who was Abel, black or white.

Which had amused her, but hadn't particularly amused Fleischmann.

As for the social security number and the driver's license,

they were both duly registered to Abel Baker, 388 Oak Street, but they were both exactly three weeks old.

> Occupation: Sales Representative.
> Employer: Bliss Publications, Inc., P.O. Box
> 97707A, Chicago, IL.
> Employee I.D. No.: 921.

Bliss Publications was a real enough company, he'd found, with headquarters in Schaumburg, Illinois. Headquarters, which of course didn't know anything, had put him on hold for ten minutes—complete with Muzak—only to switch him over to one Ralph Simpkins in their sales office, who said he was sorry, it was company policy not to give information about employees over the phone, he'd have to submit a written request. The little weasel.

So much for the guy's wallet. There was nothing else in it that could be traced—no checkbook, no credit cards, not even a laundry ticket. Just seventy-four dollars, cash, in old bills.

Preliminary fingerprint check showed no arrest record—not in Kansas, anyway. He had put in a request for a further check, Federal and military and so on, but it would take a while.

Present Whereabouts: Rogers Mem. Hosp., Bodine, KS. Condition: Stable, unconscious; skull fracture, assorted other injuries. Whoever he was, he was under police guard, as of this morning, per Fleischmann's instructions. He would have a few questions to answer when he came to, all right.

Fleischmann leaned back in his chair, ran a hand through his gray hair, and sighed. Terrific timing, he thought. Just his luck to get a Chinese fire drill like this one dumped in his lap, three days before vacation. Two weeks of peace and quiet, and sanity, in his old buddy Connolly's cabin—just him and Edie and Connolly and Doreen.

Sanity, he thought. Imagine that.

Connolly, at least, had had the brains to get out of Kansas and join the Colorado force, where he could be near those mountains all year around, the bum.

Well, maybe Baker would come out of his coma before Friday, and save everybody a lot of trouble.

Not that he would be likely to say much when he did. On the face of it, he looked like he had quite a lot not to say.

Which brought him to the car (Buick Sdn., '86, 2 dr., lt. blue), equipped with, of all things, air bags. Registered to John T. Eckes, at a St. Louis address as phony as Baker's; present whereabouts of *him* unknown. Eckes would be Baker's partner, if Marge Price at the Bil-Mar Motel was right—the guy who'd told her he was an FBI agent.

Which in turn brought in all this stuff about Louise Macdonald, and this girl who either was or wasn't Rosemary Flood, and the stolen truck, and the phone calls—but that wasn't Fleischmann's problem. It was the Feds' problem, thank God. All Fleischmann had to do was find out who the hell this Baker was.

Time of Accident: Approx. 7:30 P.M.
Location: N-bound on Cty. Rte. 13, approx. ½ mi.
S. of I-70 interchange.
No. of Vehicles Involved: 1.
Remarks: Vehicle left pavement on E. side of road-
way, struck tree.

It was the accident, of course, that had gotten Fleischmann called into it. No skid marks to speak of, no booze in Baker's system, and way too early last night for a typical asleep-at-the wheel case. And then those fancy air bags, which were, after all, supposed to work; if they had, then Baker wouldn't have gone through the windshield like that. Which made it a fair prospect for a non-accident. Which would implicate the two Caucasian females who had flagged Jane Rogers down at the site, and who had promptly disappeared. No positive I.D. on them (it was dark, and good old Mrs. Rogers had been driving without her glasses), but it was a pretty safe guess—given everything else—that they'd just come from the Bil-Mar.

Of course, it was possible that there had been more than

one pair of Caucasian females running around loose last night. He was going to rule that out, though, as being entirely too preposterous.

At least for the time being.

What he really wished he knew was why they couldn't have picked someplace else to run around loose. New Zealand, for instance.

Visions of snowdrifts and evergreens danced in his head. And beer and steaks and firesides.

And receded again.

"Charges Filed," said the next heading on his quadruplicate form; and here so many tempting possibilities occurred to Fleischmann (few of which, unfortunately, were in the penal code) that he had to get up from his desk in order to keep himself from writing all of them in the space provided.

He poked his head out the door of his office and looked out over the busy squad room. "Hey, Gene," he called to the man who occupied the nearest desk. "Where the hell's that report on the car?"

Gene looked up from behind a mountain of paperwork. "The Baker car?" he said. "I dunno; it hasn't come up yet."

Fleischmann scowled. "What are those jokers doing down there? It's almost ten o'clock."

"Want me to call 'em?" Gene said.

"Nope," said Fleischmann. "I'll go down myself. Do me good to kick a little ass this morning."

He marched off toward the elevators, but Gene called after him, "I wouldn't go that way if I were you, sergeant."

"Why not?" Fleischmann said, pushing through the swinging doors. He saw at least a dozen reporters, who all saw him at the same time and scrambled to their feet, mikes at the ready.

He turned his back on them and headed back into the squad room.

"Why don't somebody give 'em a lollipop and send 'em home," he grumbled at Gene on his way toward the back stairs.

"They all want to know if we've found Macdonald yet," Gene said.

"What do they think, she's gonna waltz in here and give 'em an interview? Sheesh."

Bunch of dimwits, he thought, as he went downstairs. Called themselves a free press. Terrific.

And as for the guys down in the lab, if they thought they were going to keep him waiting around all day, they'd have to think a little harder. Not today. Prima donnas—they knew everything had to wait for them, so naturally they always took twice as long as necessary. Watched too much TV, that was their problem.

He found them sitting around on crates in the garage, taking a coffee break. "Oh, hi, Bob," the four of them said, cheerily, in unison. "Have some coffee."

They were all dressed in starched white lab coats, with their names embroidered on the breast pockets. Way too much TV, Fleischmann thought with a frown. "What's the story here?" he said irritably. "This a holiday, or what?"

The lab guys simpered at him. "Surprise," they said. "We're all finished." And four thumbs jerked in the direction of the Buick across the room.

"Dave was just about to type up the report."

"Yeah," said Dave, with a shit-eating grin.

Fleischmann didn't have time for a lot of foolishness. "Let's have a look," he said, heading for the car. "And I'll take that coffee."

The car's trunk was open and empty, and its interior stripped, with all the contents lined up on a counter along the garage wall. The front end of the car was demolished; windshield smashed. "Impact speed?" Fleischmann said, looking it over.

"Maybe forty."

"Air bags deployed?"

"Yup."

"No defects?"

"Nope."

"So he wasn't driving."

"Not unless he could drive from the back seat," said Dave. "Looks like that's where he was. Back seat, center."

"Okay." Green light on the two Caucasian females.

One of the lab guys handed Fleischmann a Styrofoam cup of coffee, which he accepted with a nod, though he was still looking at the car. "Fingerprints?" he said.

"They're up in Computer. Most of 'em looked pretty smudgy."

"Better none of 'em come from any Bodine cops."

They all smiled sourly at that. Fleischmann moved over to the counter to inspect the stuff they'd taken out of the car.

First, there were two suitcases, with a couple of changes of clothes apiece. "From the trunk," said Dave. "Different sizes. Different brands in the shaving kits."

Fleischmann nodded. The partner. Check.

"We got hair samples and all that; we'll call you on 'em," one of the others said.

"Good."

Next to the suitcases were two salesmen's sample cases full of Bliss Publications. Fleischmann wasn't very surprised to see the name Bliss again, but he was surprised at the publications themselves. Sunday school programs. Sermon outlines. And piles of paperback books. *Is Jesus Your Quarterback?* he read, flipping through them. *God's Talent Scouts. The Menace in Our Schools. Golden Moments and Tranquil Reflections.*

He made a number of mental notes, mostly having to do with the kind of people who posed as Bible salesmen. "No address book?" he said.

"Didn't find any."

"Damn." Then the partner must have it. Fleischmann wouldn't have minded having a look at it. "What's all this?" he said, moving on to another pile.

"That's the rest from inside the car," Dave said. "It was all loose, mostly on the floor."

Amid the pile—the usual car trash, including some wadded-up litter from an A&W, and also including a man's shoe—were a couple of letter-sized pieces of paper. Fleischmann smoothed these out and found that they were Xerox copies. Photos of two Caucasian females, with handwritten captions underneath. The females were Macdonald and Flood.

Fleischmann sucked his teeth.

"And look at these," said Dave, shaking a dozen small, sharp objects out of an envelope. "You don't see these every day."

No, you didn't. They were tranquilizer darts. "Shit!" said Fleischmann. "Where's his gun?"

Dave shook his head.

"I want it. Send somebody back to look for it, and tell 'em not to come back here without it. And what have we here?"

At the end of the counter lay what was left of the radio-telephone, all squashed and twisted. "Jeez, it's a big one," Fleischmann said. "Powerful, huh?"

In a hushed voice, Dave said, "It's an 8500, Bob."

"An 8500! Are you kidding?"

"Nope. Scrambler, debugger, and everything. And powerful, yeah—they had to have an auxiliary battery to run it on."

"But you have to have permits up the ass for these things!"

"Worse," Dave said. "Top-level security clearance. The damn things are so sophisticated, they don't want the Russians to get 'em. Or that's what they say, anyhow."

"How top is top?"

"It's top," Dave said. "Don't worry, we looked it up."

Fleischmann sipped his coffee and gazed at the mangled 8500, with the lab guys gathered around him, thinking about top-level security clearance—what it took to get it on the one hand, or, on the other, what it took to get an 8500 system without it.

He reckoned he could guess which hand it was on, too.

This Baker was turning into one mighty smelly young man.

"Well," he said. "Let me take some of this stuff with me." He picked up the two Xeroxes and a handful of the ridiculous paperbacks. "And run that report up"—he cast a sharp glance at Dave—"the minute you get it done, hear me?"

He took his time getting back up the stairs, pondering, as he went, first the picture of Louise and then the one of Rosie, with the biographical sketches written underneath, covering their schooling, their travels, their criminal careers—Louise's long, Rosie's very short.

So the partner, Eckes, had told Marge Price one thing that was true, at least: he and Baker were hunting for these two.

So the only question was why, and who was paying the bills.

To which the logical answer was, either somebody at Bliss Publications, or somebody using Bliss as a front.

For which this Rev. Anderson was a likely candidate. Why not? It was his truck. And it wasn't the first time the girls had picked on him.

Could it be Anderson? It could. If he was worth half of what Falwell and Oral Roberts and those types were worth, that would make him about half as rich as Croesus. He could certainly afford Baker and Eckes, and Bliss, too, if he'd wanted to own it.

God's Talent Scouts. Fleischmann shook his head. Loonies, he thought. Bunch of Jesus freaks chasing each other around. It gave him a pain.

Although, he thought, you wouldn't go to all that trouble and expense just to chase down the likes of Macdonald and Flood, would you. All that elaborate setup. Even if you were loony. Even if you thought they were the scourge of Christianity—why didn't you just hire a private eye instead?

Well, then, it had to be the drugs. What the hell else could it be?

By the time he got back to his office, he'd satisfied himself that that was it. Sure, Anderson had claimed the girls had planted the drugs; that would be plausible enough if it had been a thimbleful, and not, as Fleischmann had heard, a stash with a street value of maybe two or three million. And then there was the fact that Anderson hadn't gotten around to reporting the truck stolen. Claimed he didn't know. More likely, he hadn't wanted the authorities involved—because his own people, viz., Baker and Eckes, were supposed to be taking care of it.

The girls, and that gang they ran with, must have gotten wind of the shipment somehow. Fine—but Baker and Eckes were in place long before that.

Which made them one pair among many—riding herd on the shipments, or making contacts, or making sales, taking orders, God knew what. Whatever it was, considering the amounts of money involved, an 8500 for their cars wouldn't be too much to ask. Since any nine-year-old could tap into a radiophone conversation, naturally you'd want to scramble it if you had the means.

Yes, and Anderson had a lot of big-shot pals in Washington; he'd be likely to know the kind of people who could have gotten him the 8500s. In return for a cut of the profits. Well, why not.

All right, Fleischmann thought, drumming his fingers on his desk. He could leave the big shots to the Feds—that was a blessing, anyway. What he would have to do, first off, was to pin Baker on Bliss Publications—have to get some subpoenas going—and then pin Bliss on Rev. Anderson. Anderson would have set up a whole string of intermediaries and street names between himself and Bliss, by way of concealing his connection with it; it was going to take a hell of a lot of work to run it all down.

And him with his vacation coming up.

Well, then, he'd better get to it.

A few minutes later he had calls in to the courthouse, Rogers Memorial Hospital, the reference librarian at the city library, and a number of other places. He'd pushed aside the litter on his desk to make room for a fresh legal pad, which he was rapidly filling up with notes, whistling softly through his teeth all the while. He was just about to call upstairs to Narcotics, to see what he could find out about the LSD market these days, when his office door opened and Lieutenant Hazeltine walked in.

Without knocking, as usual.

Hazeltine was the brass's boy. He never came to see you without a message from On High; and the message was never anything you wanted to hear. Your office was going to be painted, it would take a month, you'd be operating out of a broom closet in the basement. You were being assigned to guard the Governor's dog for two weeks. A new efficiency program, you'd have to go back and do all your reports again in quintuplicate this time, on pink forms instead of yellow. That kind of thing. But even Fleischmann wasn't prepared for this one, because what Hazeltine said, after he'd shut the door, sat down, crossed his legs, and lit a cigarette, was, "I have to put you on another case."

"What!" said Fleischmann. "Why?"

Hazeltine shrugged. "Brass," he said—which was what he always said. "We got a holdup this morning; didn't you hear the sirens?"

Fleischmann hadn't. He must have been down in the lab.

"Mercantile Trust. Over on West Sixth. Big one," said Hazeltine. "They think it's the same guys that pulled those other ones."

"Well, hell, Perkins is on that. He can handle it all right."

"Yeah, but they want somebody else. More bodies. They want the citizens to see how hard we're workin' on it."

"Oh, brother," Fleischmann said. "Look, do me a favor. Get Quarles or somebody on it, huh? I'm just getting going good on this Baker thing."

"What, that car accident?"

"Yeah, only it's turning into a lot more than that." And he told Hazeltine about the fake I.D. and the 8500 and the rest of it.

A flicker of enthusiasm passed across Hazeltine's face, but then his bureaucratic responsibilities got the better of him, and it went away. He went back to looking like the miserable little pill he was. "Sounds good, Bob," he said, "but the brass tells me they've just got to have you. Sorry, but my hands are tied on this one."

Fleischmann let out a grumble of protest.

"Besides," Hazeltine said, brightening, "that's the Feds' case anyhow. We can't be having a lot of duplication; you know how they bitch about that."

Fleischmann knew. He also knew how, earlier that morning, he'd been looking forward to dumping the whole thing on the Feds and saving himself the grief. But now—well, hell, he'd gotten sort of interested in it now. Served him right, he supposed.

"You can write it up in the morning and we'll shoot it right over to the Bureau," Hazeltine was telling him. "Oh, and be sure and use those new IU-44 forms. You got some of those?"

"Reams of 'em," Fleischmann said.

Hazeltine had stood up, signaling an end to the discussion. "Sorry," he said again, and glanced at his watch. "Oh, jeez, Bob, you're supposed to be over there already. Perkins is waiting for you."

"All right, all right." Fleischmann reached for his raincoat.

He stalked out through the squad room, a couple of paces ahead of Hazeltine, and slapped the swinging doors open. Immediately the reporters mobbed him, all yammering questions about Louise Macdonald. Fleischmann plowed his way through them, saying, "You want to ask Lieutenant Hazeltine here; he knows all about that," and gesturing to the rear, just as Hazeltine followed him through the doors; and the reporters all went and mobbed *him*, while Fleischmann got on the elevator and pushed the button for the ground floor.

Robbed, he thought on his way down. Damn brass anyway. Leave it to them to get all hot and bothered about public relations right this minute. Not that he had a leg to stand on; it *was* the Feds' jurisdiction, after all. Face it, it was interstate from one end of it to the other. He'd just wanted the satisfaction of working it out. Get the prelims tied up nice and neat; put it all on their crappy IU-44s, if that made 'em happy, but do it properly, do it right. Pure selfishness.

And of course he wouldn't have minded getting part of the

credit for it, either; a drug bust that size would look pretty good on his record.

But there was no use arguing with the brass. When they decided they wanted something up there, it stuck, no matter how stupid their reason was. In fact, the stupider it was, the more it stuck.

"Cripes," he muttered, thinking sardonic thoughts about the Chain of Command, but having no idea that the chain, in this particular case, went all the way back to Washington.

CHAPTER 17

WELL, ACTUALLY, ALL THE WAY BACK TO
Arlington. As Senator Quackenbush had
pointed out, it would have been foolhardy for him and Rev.
Anderson to be seen together that morning, and there was nowhere in Washington where they could have met without being instantly recognized; and so they had settled on Rev. Anderson's office at the Crusade Center as their best available
option.

Rev. Anderson was early. He had hardly slept at all last
night, thanks to the reporters besieging his house. He had
spent half an hour with them on his doorstep, telling them everything Harriet had told him to tell them—he thought he'd
handled them rather well, in fact—but they wouldn't go away.
Far from it. They had camped out under his windows all
night long, trampling his grass, telling crude jokes, and throwing their cigarette butts into his azaleas; and when he'd arisen
at five o'clock, having finally given up trying to sleep, there
had been twice as many of them out there as before. They
had tailed his limousine into Washington and lingered outside
the studios while he'd taped his interviews for the morning
news shows, and from the studios they had tailed him to the
Crusade Center.

Where he'd left them loitering on the front lawn, and had
retreated into the building—leaving instructions with his chief
of security to meet the Senator at the shipping entrance, which
was at the rear, and to escort him up the back elevator.

And a few minutes later, at eight o'clock, the Reverend

stood alone in his paneled and carpeted office, among the photographs of himself shaking the hands of Presidents and dignitaries from around the world, and looked sourly down at the reporters from behind the heavy velvet curtains drawn across the window.

Behind him, on his mahogany desk, he had deposited his copy of the morning paper—face down, so as to hide the appalling headline, "Probe LSD in Gospel Shipment."

He scowled out the window at the people who had written that headline.

They were like vultures out there, he thought, waiting to move in and pick him clean.

Well, he wasn't going to let them.

This whole distasteful business was a test. A severe one, to be sure; perhaps the severest he had ever been through; but, he thought, God hath not given us a spirit of fear, but of power. If he and Harriet and the Senator kept faith unto the end, they would certainly prevail.

For, of course, it was God's power, not their own. The Reverend was quite sure of that. He was always careful to ask the question—whose power it was, and whose will—knowing how easily human nature could deceive itself. Even when you were saved, there was always the possibility, however remote, that you could be mistaken or misled; but in his own case, every time he asked, he always got the same answer. It was God's power indeed.

It had always been God's power, from the very beginning. There was simply no other way to account for his life. How else could he have been raised up, in these few brief years, from utter obscurity in the wilderness of Colorado to where he was today, at the helm of the greatest Christian enterprise America had ever known? When Harriet discovered him out there in Denver, he'd been a humble and little-known evangelist, the son of an even humbler evangelist, with none of the things which—by merely human standards—marked a man for greatness. He was handsome, true, but he was not educated, or popular, or wealthy; he'd had nothing to his name but the Vacation Bible School in the mountains—an old and decrepit place, hardly more than a collection of shacks—that, and an equally old and decrepit school bus, decorated with the sign of the Cross, which were all his father had left him when he'd run off for the last time.

He'd grown up in that school bus; he'd eaten and slept in it (for the rear of it had been made over into rough living quarters) almost ever since he could remember. He'd had all his Bible training in it, from his father—when he was sober—and all the rest of his education, too, since they'd never stayed in one place long enough for him to go to school. Every summer the two of them had carried busloads of children up the mountain, where the father taught them their lessons while the son led them in wholesome recreational activities; every fall and winter and spring they had hit the road, wandering all over the prairie states on the camp-meeting circuit.

That was all the life the Reverend had ever known—a shadowy, marginal, threadbare existence—and there he had been, nearly forty years old when Harriet found him, still running the Bible School, and still living in the bus, for lack of anywhere else to lay his head. By that time he had quit the camp meetings—he'd managed to rise above that, at least—and spent most of the year in Denver, running his TV program.

It went on at eight o'clock in the morning—opposite "Captain Kangaroo," which doomed it to a pathetically small audience share—and, at that, it was only aired over three local stations, the one in Denver and two others in Wyoming. The Reverend had kept videotapes of it (which he watched now and then, in his private screening room at the Crusade Center, by way of reminding himself of his humble origins), and in retrospect it was plain what a shabby little production it had been. Its lighting was garish, its sets tacky, its music tinny. It was excruciating to look back on it. His interview guests, sincere Christians though they were, were awkward and inarticulate; they came across on tape like absolute hicks.

And so, sad to say, did he.

He'd been all too aware of it, even at the time. It had caused him no end of grief to realize that his show was the poor puny thing it was, because, deep within his soul, he knew the Lord had much greater things in mind for him. Ever since boyhood, he'd dreamed of becoming a great and mighty evangelist. While other boys dreamed of becoming pilots or football stars, he'd pictured himself in a splendid pulpit, with a hundred-voice choir at his back. Vast crowds would hang on his every word; he would win souls to Christ everywhere he went, from one end of this great nation to the other.

He was sure that God had put that dream into his childish soul Himself—who else could have put it there? And who else could have made it grow, as in time it did, into a grown man's all-consuming passion? Who else could have shown him the true meaning of the age he was living in (as, over the years, he saw his country lose half of Europe, China, Korea, Cuba, and Vietnam; as he saw the freest government in the world infiltrated by godless Communists; as he saw schoolchildren forbidden to offer even a simple prayer to the Almighty; as he saw the entire nation slowly degenerate into a stinking cesspool of crime and perversion). Who but God Himself could have shown him that America's only hope lay not in worldly solutions but in a total revolution; a revolution of the inner man; a Christian revolution?

To say he was eager to start this revolution would have been to put it too mildly. He burned for it. He ached for it. He hungered and thirsted after it. He preached it every day on his TV show (plaid suits and all, tinny music and all) as if his life depended on it—which it did.

And yet, when he went home at night to his school bus parked in its trailer camp, and thought about his day's accomplishments; when he sat there thinking of the squalid reality of his life, and how abysmally short of the dream it fell . . . how, in spite of his prayers, his tears, his toil, he was reaching not all of America, not even half of it, but only small portions of two sparsely populated states . . . not even enough to show up on the Nielsens . . . There were times, he had to admit, when he came perilously close to doubting.

So it had to have been God's will that brought Harriet to him. Who would have thought that this pretty girl would have the mind of a genius? But that she did—yes, and the soul of a saint. The Lord had called her, just as He'd called the Reverend, to the same great dream of a Christian nation, an America governed by His laws alone.

But, unlike the Reverend, she had both political experience and a fine education. She knew how to get things done. She had discovered a way to translate the dream into reality, a method as bold and daring as the dream itself. She had the full backing of Senator Quackenbush and a few other perceptive Christian leaders; and for nearly two years she had been scouring the country for the right man to help bring it about.

And the Lord led her to Denver, where she watched the Reverend's poor little TV show at eight o'clock one Tuesday morning. She was at the studio—out of breath, radiant, joyous—by the time the klieg lights went off.

"I've seen all kinds of evangelists, all across this country," she'd told him. "I've seen the famous and the not-so-famous, rich, poor, black, white, purple—and, quite frankly, all of them have disappointed me. But you—!" She'd sighed happily. "I just knew it, the minute I saw you, Reverend! All you need is a decent suit of— What I mean is, you're not like the rest of them. Not a bit. You really believe what you're saying, don't you—you really want to do His will!"

The Reverend had blushed hotly. He'd been praised—and tempted—by beautiful women before, but never like this.

"I just know the Lord wants to do great things through you. Really great things," she'd said. "That He wants to raise you up and make a real Christian leader out of you, and that— oh, you'll think this is so crazy—"

He'd protested that he would never.

"Well—I think He wants me to help."

A lesser man than the Reverend would have thought she *was* crazy—a man, that is, who was still blinded by the sinful values of this world. But the Reverend saw her with the eyes of faith—saw her as (he had no doubt) the Lord saw her. And when she told him her story, at a corner table in the quiet restaurant where she'd taken him to lunch, and told him who her backers were, and fixed him with those penetrating blue eyes of hers, he realized that she meant every word.

And when she told him exactly what she had in mind, he was thunderstruck. A way literally to manage the conversion process, to bypass the sinful and stubborn will and put God's love and God's laws directly into people's minds, as easily and efficiently (as Harriet put it) as an intravenous injection—now *that* was revolutionary!

"Praise the Lord," he'd whispered, after a long and thoughtful silence. His eyes brimmed with tears as he thought of all the times, while doing his show, when he'd wished for something (had he but known *what*!) more than mere words, when he'd wished he could reach right out through the living room screen to grab his viewers and hug them, or shake them, he didn't know which; and as he remembered how the Lord had sent prophet after prophet, and finally His only begotten Son, to deliver His Word to mankind, but mankind had turned a deaf ear; how different it would have been—how utterly, wonderfully different—if only they'd had the technology!

"Can it be true?" he'd asked Harriet. "Can this actually be done—now? In our lifetime?"

She'd smiled tenderly at him. "Let's find out, shall we?"

Like the sons of Zebedee on the beach, he hadn't stopped to think twice.

And after that, it all seemed a blur, it had happened so fast. Harriet got him a tailor, a voice coach, a technical staff; she made him stop using Grecian Formula ("God gave you

that white hair!" she'd said; "It gives you an air of authority!"); and it was as if the Lord, having finally gotten them
together, didn't intend to waste another minute, for suddenly
the Reverend's show took off. Letters and donations poured
in; he was syndicated to four states, then six, then ten; his
popularity grew by leaps and bounds; the Harvest Workers
were started, and soon had chapters everywhere; and before
he knew it, the Gospel Crusade Center was built, and he'd
arrived in triumph in the Nation's Capital.

All of which was only a prelude; the best had been yet to
come. In the ensuing years, just as the Lord continued to
prosper the Reverend openly, He'd also prospered Harriet in
secret, while she'd made the preparations for Conversion Management. It had been a monumental task—buying the subsidiary companies, selecting and training the staff, renovating the
Bible School, and a thousand other things—but nothing was
too hard for the Lord. Even the most sensitive steps in the
operation had gone off without a hitch—the Senators (true
Christian patriots, all of them) had taken care of the FBI,
allowing the preachers, when the time came, to be recruited
right on schedule. It was truly miraculous; thirteen of them,
like clockwork, without a single mishap—and the experimental
results were coming in, Harriet said, exactly according to
projections—until, as of this morning, Phase I was within three
short weeks of completion.

Or would be, except for Louise Macdonald.

Only three weeks! That wretched, wretched woman! The
Reverend had indeed prayed for Louise's soul this morning,
just as he'd said he would; it was his duty as a Christian, even
though she hardly deserved it. He'd prayed for her the first
time around, too, when she'd made fools of him and the Senators at the prayer breakfast—though that had been a trivial
matter, no real harm done. (A little humbling now and then
never did anyone any harm—and besides, the attack had actually enhanced their images around Washington.) But now—
now the harm was real, and the danger immense! In three

short weeks, Phase I, the only really tricky phase, would be over. The ministers would all be returned to their homes as swiftly and secretly—and safely, he might add; he had personally insisted on that—as they'd been taken from them; and the FBI, its obligation fulfilled, would be able to turn its attention to more important matters, allowing the kidnapping cases to fade quietly into oblivion.

Once those last bridges had been crossed—almost, the Reverend liked to think, like crossing the Red Sea—they would all be home free. In three weeks the real work of Conversion Management could begin. For, once it progressed into Phases II and III, out into the motels and public buildings of the nation, there would be no way to detect it, and hence no stopping it. The word of the Lord would spread like wildfire; every day it would be written upon more American hearts, and more, and still more. Millions would be saved—saved, and united, and *mobilized*—and then, by God, you'd begin to see some changes made!

But that dazzling future, so near at hand, might be snatched away in an instant—all because of Louise, and a truck, and a few vials of chemicals. If the rest of the story got out, everything could be lost. The public would be up in arms; they'd call it brainwashing, or worse; how could they fail to, slaves to sin that they were? They would condemn the very means of their freedom—on a mere quibble—just as the Jews had condemned the Savior of mankind for healing on a Sunday. Let the truth be known when the time was ripe—yea, and shout it from the rooftops!—but for now, it must remain secret.

Out on the front lawn, outside the Reverend's window, the groundskeepers were raising the flags on the row of flagpoles, sending them fluttering up, one after the other, into the blue sky. Always an inspiring sight; even the reporters stopped to watch. The Reverend watched, too, lost in thought, until the intercom on his desk began to buzz.

It was his chief of security announcing that Senator Quackenbush was on his way up.

"Fine," the Reverend said. "Tell Helms to bring in the coffee, will you?"

He straightened, sniffed, and composed himself to meet that stout-hearted Christian, a man deeply committed to Conversion Management and all that it would mean for America— indeed, the Reverend hoped, America's future President—and let out a yelp of surprise as the Senator strode in through the door, wearing an absurd pair of lime-green sunglasses and a curly, bright orange wig.

"Like it?" grinned the Senator. "Swiped it from Mrs. Q. Don't guess anybody'd ever recognize me in this getup, eh? Why, what's the matter, Reverend—you look terrible this morning!"

"Oh, well, I've been—"

"Up all night, I bet, haven't you? Well, cheer up, son. First time for everybody," the Senator said, taking off his disguise and smoothing his hair. He was a big, jolly man, with a ruddy face and sharp little eyes that didn't miss much. "We all have days like this once in a while; comes with the territory," he said. "You'll get through it all right. Harriet and I have been up all night, too—and I think we've got the cat pretty well back in the bag by now."

They sat down as Helms, the Reverend's secretary, came in with the coffee and a platter of sweet rolls. When he had gone out, the Senator, discreetly pocketing the thick white envelope which the Reverend laid on the desk for him, said he certainly didn't think three more weeks was too much to ask for.

"Of course, it's a serious problem," he said, helping himself to a roll or two. "The boys at the Bureau had their noses pushed out of joint a little bit. They thought you should have called 'em right away about the truck, instead of trying to handle it internally. But they're good sports; I had a nice long chat with 'em, and kind of let 'em see our side of it, and they're going to stick with us. After all," he added, "they're in this about as deep as we are."

Rev. Anderson didn't like to hear it expressed in quite

that way—the Senator could be rather vulgar sometimes, he thought—but under the circumstances he was willing to let it pass. "How about the Kansas police?" he said. "They're involved in it, too, now. I understand they've put a detective on it. It could be extremely dangerous if he—"

The Senator waved his napkin. "That's no trouble, Reverend," he said through a mouthful of sweet roll. "We'll just get him taken back off it, that's all."

"Really? Can you do that?"

"Well, I can't, personally—but our friend Hackett can. He's from Kansas, you recall."

"Of course!" the Reverend said. "Praise the Lord, I'd forgotten." Geography had never meant much to him; once he knew a man was in Christ, he never asked where he'd come from.

"Sure," said the Senator. "I'll get on the horn to him soon's I get to the office. I'm sure somebody out in Topeka must owe him a favor or two."

"It's as simple as that?"

"Don't see why not." The Senator licked his fingers. "See, Reverend, you've just got to have a little faith, that's all. Though," he said, with a sly grin, "it never hurt anybody to be wise as serpents, either."

The Reverend smiled back, but his eye caught the newspaper on his desk and his smile faded. "What really frightens me is the publicity," he said. "Those reporters crawling all over the place. I did the best I could, but—well, you've seen the headlines."

" 'Course I have. But that's not going to last. Your stuff's on the TV right now—I caught some of it before I left the house—and I must say, Reverend, you did a bang-up job. Couldn't have done better myself. This evening, they'll all be carrying that instead; and then tomorrow, or the day after, they'll have forgotten all about it."

Could that be true? Rev. Anderson hardly dared believe it. "How can you be so sure of that?" he said.

"Well, when you've worked with the media for as long as I have, you know how short their attention span is, for one thing," said the Senator. "They don't really give a damn about digging for the truth. All that Woodward and Bernstein stuff—that's just a lot of hooey. Oh, sure, they can make things pretty rough for you for a couple of days, but they hardly ever follow up on anything. That's one," he said. "And two, let's face it—when you get right down to it, this thing really isn't a crime story at all. It's a religious story. The media always drops that stuff in a hurry, because they don't understand it. Anything short of the Pope—phfft! Three-day wonder."

"But I'm nationally famous," the Reverend said, a little peevishly.

"Of course you are, Reverend! I was just about to say that," the Senator said. "But what I'm trying to get across to you is, you're a nationally famous . . . *preacher*. That makes all the difference in the world. It's a stumbling block to the wise, don't you see? Just like the Scripture tells us. The minute they hear the Lord's name, all their brains go right out the window! They'll put you in the same pigeonhole with all the other preachers who ever got mixed up in a scandal. They think it's trivia. Crackpot stuff. It ain't news. They can't imagine it could ever turn into an important story, because they can't imagine how the Lord could be important—and that protects you, see? You're—why, you're invisible! You're free to do anything you want, right under their noses!"

"Oh," said the Reverend, utterly confused.

"But I tell you what. Just in case I'm wrong," the Senator said, draining his cup of coffee. "Just in case, why, I'm fixing to grab a few headlines myself this afternoon. We've got this crime bill we've been working on, you know, and the President has really been dragging his feet on it. Tell you the truth, Reverend, I'm starting to think maybe he's gone a little soft on crime. Well, maybe it's time somebody got up on his hind legs and said so."

He leaned forward. "Now, I'd been thinking I'd wait until next week, when I was going to release my staff's annual survey on the prison system. But under the circumstances"—here a man who hadn't been saved might have patted his breast pocket, but the Senator restrained himself—"I thought I'd push the whole thing up to today. It ought to bump you out of the spotlight long enough for this little business to blow over. What do you say to that?"

The Reverend had finally caught on. He rose from his chair, his face wreathed in smiles. "I say, Amen!" he said, wrapping his arms around the Senator in a manly embrace. "God bless you, brother! What would I ever do without you?"

And he escorted him down to the shipping entrance and sent him off, disguised again, into the early morning sunshine.

CHAPTER 18

THERE WASN'T ANY MORNING SUNSHINE IN
Colorado—only a sky full of heavy clouds
and a cold, steady, drizzling rain. The roads were slick and
traffic was slow; it was lousy weather for hitchhiking. It
took Louise and me all morning to get across the flat part of
the state. We spent eternities standing around on the entrance
ramps in the rain, gazing moodily at the bleak, wet landscape,
while the cattle in the feed lots—waiting for their turn to be
trucked off to the slaughterhouse—gazed moodily back at us,
and the traffic passed us by.

We made it to Denver somehow, and past it as far as Route
40, where we turned north. But the pace didn't pick up any
in the mountains. Forty was a slow, winding road; we crept
past mining town after mining town, each one smaller and
more poverty-stricken than the last; and by the time we
dragged ourselves out of the last pickup truck at Corinth, it
was late in the afternoon.

Corinth was even sadder-looking than most of its neighbors. There wasn't much to it but a gas station, a couple of
saloons, and a ragged row of houses, clinging to a hillside, that
looked as though you could push them over with one hand.
The newest thing in town was the regional high school, and
even it looked to be twenty years old.

There was no reason to linger. Zeke's place was two or
three miles away, up a side road, out of town. We loaded
our packs onto our backs and started walking.

We were cold and wet and disgruntled. Even Louise looked

weary by this time, and neither of us had anything pleasant to say, so we trudged along in silence with our heads down. Rain dripped from the brim of Louise's Stetson, and from the edges of the morning's Denver *Post*, now quite soggy, which I was using for a hat.

The *Post* had a nice big story on our evening at the Bil-Mar, complete with pictures; it made pretty juicy copy, what with a well-known fugitive, a fake FBI man or possibly two, LSD, and Rev. Anderson combined. "No Trace of Driver," it said.

> Louise Macdonald, who has been wanted by the FBI since 1976, allegedly made the phone call to FBI headquarters in Topeka. Sources close to the investigation indicated that fingerprints matching those of Macdonald were found at the motel.
>
> MYSTERY WOMAN AT SCENE
>
> Meanwhile, witnesses stated that an unknown female accomplice had been seen with Macdonald, both at the motel and at the site of the auto crash.
>
> While her identity could not be confirmed, clues recovered at the crash site revealed a link between Macdonald and Rosemary Flood, the divinity school student wanted in connection with the burglary of Rev. Anderson's New York office over the weekend.

It didn't mention any links to Olivia ("P.K.") Mather, daughter of the notorious Sam Mather, the mad train bomber; they hadn't sorted that out yet at the *Post*. They didn't have to, as far as I was concerned. I had no need to see my name in print; I already knew how deeply I was mixed up in it. I could write the stories myself. Jailbird's Daughter Turns to Crime. "Can't Believe It"—Classmates. I was in it up to my chromosomes. It ran in the family. It ran in the species, all the way back to Father Cain.

Still, I'd been delighted, and so had Louise, when we'd bought the paper that morning. Good for them, we'd thought.

We'd made our big splash. Now all we'd have to do was make a phone call, from the safety of Zeke's house, and hand over the documents. Maybe even to the *Post* itself; they had a local interest, since Denver was where Anderson had gotten his start. We would give them an exclusive. As protected sources, naturally.

Only it hadn't turned out that way. Every news report we heard on the radio—when we were lucky enough to be in a car—was worse than the last. At seven o'clock (Mountain Time) we heard Anderson's syrupy voice explaining how Louise, poor deluded soul, must have planted those terrible drugs in his truck in some misguided effort to defame him, his ministry, and the living God. That wasn't so bad; naturally we'd expected the man to defend himself. But at nine o'clock they played his statement again, unchallenged. They tacked on a short summary of Louise's career but, oddly, no new information.

Then, at noon, they'd rewritten the story with a whimsical lead-in ("Nothing much ever happens in Bodine, Kansas . . ."), moved it to the "light news" slot at the end of the broadcast, and treated it as a goofy practical joke played by one lunatic fringe upon another.

And by two o'clock they'd wiped the whole thing off the air to make room for Senator Quackenbush's remarks about the President. Just like that.

We didn't know what the hell was going on. Payoffs? Blackmail? Simple coincidence, plain old rotten luck? Or did the press actually believe what the Reverend had told them?

We'd had plenty of time to talk it over while standing on roadsides all day long, and by the time we got to Corinth we had about exhausted the subject, and ourselves. The only conclusion we'd come to was that, whatever the reason for it was, we'd be lucky to get a filler on page 39 tomorrow morning.

So we walked.

The road twisted its way up through a narrow valley with

a creek rushing along at the bottom of it, a dark ribbon in the snow. Great tall fir trees loomed all around us, and huge outcrops of rock that were all slick and black and alive with trickling water; way up overhead, the tops of the mountains appeared and disappeared again among the clouds. It was even prettier than Louise had told the life insurance man. Of course it was all wasted on us as we plodded along, thinking black thoughts about what passed for journalism these days. But after a while we couldn't help but look around a little, and after another while it began to cross our minds that not only was it gorgeous up here but we didn't have to hitchhike any more, and nobody was chasing us, and soon we'd be warm and dry with Zeke and his friends to help us feel sorry for ourselves. And we began walking a little faster, and a little faster, and before I knew it we came around a bend in the road and Louise said, "There it is!"

The valley opened out in front of us into a wide, shallow bowl, just wide and flat enough to accommodate a smallish farm. There was a rambling farmhouse, sheltered by trees, with solar panels on its roof; there was a windmill, too, and a barn and a cluster of sheds. Beyond them lay the snow-covered fields, sloping out to the edges of the bowl. There was a fringe of evergreens out there, and then the mountains rose up again. Two fat horses stood around in the middle distance; the sight of them brought the grin back to Louise's face.

"That's Luther and Calvin," she told me.

"Oh, no," I groaned.

"Oh, yes. They plow with them. And also they need the manure; the soil's pretty crummy up this high. Zeke won't use fertilizer; says it gets into the water table and poisons it. And besides, he doesn't want to support the chemical companies. It's so organic around here, it's hilarious."

The lights were on in the house. We practically ran the rest of the way, with Louise telling me what a sweet old-fashioned nature boy Zeke was, a regular St. Francis, and how I was going to love him. Everybody did, she said; he always had a full house. People came up here to hide out for a few days and wound up staying for weeks, just for the privilege of pitching Zeke's hay and canning his tomatoes.

"They make honey, too," she said. "Look, you can see the beehives out at the edge of the field there."

And she was so busy talking about Zeke, and pointing out things, and counting the cars and trucks in the driveway and trying to guess whose they were, that she failed to notice there wasn't any smoke coming out of the chimney. On a raw, wet afternoon like this.

"Yoo-hoo!" she sang, as we clumped across the porch. She pounded on the door; waited; listened. Chickens clucked behind the house, but that was the only sound we heard.

"Hey, Zeke!" she called.

Nothing.

"That's funny," she said, and tried the door, and found it unlocked. We went inside, and stopped, and stared.

Louise turned white.

There had been a battle in there.

It was a big room, serving as living and dining room both, and it must have been comfortable once—a nice old shabby sofa, some cozy-looking chairs, a fireplace, a rug on the floor—but the whole place had been destroyed. Chairs were tipped over, curtains ripped from windows, books and belongings knocked off tables, tables smashed to pieces.

About the only thing still standing was the big dining table at the far end of the room. That would have been where Zeke's people were when they'd been broken in on. Just sitting down to breakfast—it was clear it was breakfast because that was what the floor was covered with: bacon, eggs, toast, and dark stains that looked like coffee, along with a lot of broken china and silverware. Some of it was near the table; a lot more of it was splattered at our feet, where they'd evidently thrown it, dishes and all, at the intruders.

Who had evidently won, and had taken Zeke and his friends with them when they left.

Because there sure wasn't anybody there now.

I stood in the doorway with my mouth hanging open for a long time, too appalled to think or feel or do anything. The silence was awful. The sight of Louise was even worse; she had really leaned into it, and she just stood there, sagging against the door and staring. I didn't want to look at her, so I turned away and began to wander uselessly around the room, picking things up and putting them down again, counting the chairs around the table (there were seven of them), reading the spines of books scattered among the wreckage (heavy on the Rodale Press). I looked at those, and I looked at a trail on the rug that might have been made by a body being dragged out, and when I got sick of that I went into the kitchen for a while.

In the kitchen I turned off the stove; there was a coffee pot on it, still simmering, turned to mud but not dried up yet. And I decided that the grease in the frying pan probably hadn't been there for more than a day. It was an old black cast-iron pan, good and heavy; it occurred to me that it would have made a perfectly good weapon. So would the pot of coffee. So would the carving knives on the knife rack, come to that, but nobody had thought to come in here and use them. Maybe their minds didn't run that way. Or maybe they would have if they'd had time.

Back in the living room, by the fireplace, the fire tools still hung from their hooks. Nobody had touched them.

I wandered over there, trying not to step in anything on the way, and picked up the poker and poked at the ashes with it. They were still hot. A wisp of smoke curled up out of them.

So it had been this morning, then, and not before. While we were on the plains somewhere, getting rained on, wishing we were here.

I'd never seen one of their darts before, but it was easy to tell that that was what it was. I was looking at a desk in the corner, wondering whether it had been trashed during the fight or whether they'd ransacked it afterward, and I came across the dart stuck into the paneling nearby. It was just a little thing, not more than an inch long, a miniature needle with four tiny plastic fins.

I turned it over in my fingers, marveling at it.

Not peace but a sword, I thought.

So here we were, then. We'd come full circle. Bodies all over the place.

And there we'd been, feeling sorry for ourselves, standing around on the highway ramps in the rain, on our way here. Late.

Hours late.

So then all this had been for us. Hadn't it.

Of course it had. They'd never have expected us to do a bush-league thing like hitchhiking. Why on earth would we do that, when Louise was a car thief? We'd have stolen a car in Bodine, wouldn't we, and driven all night without stopping, in which case we'd have been here already. In plenty of time for breakfast.

So then the women who *were* at breakfast—there must have been at least two of them, and they must have thought they were us. And when they figured out that they weren't us, they'd be back.

After dark, most likely. And it was getting dark now.

I turned around, suddenly wanting to go away from there. Very far away.

Louise was still standing in the doorway, staring into space.

"Hey," I said, touching her on the elbow. "What do you say we get out of here."

At first I thought she hadn't heard me at all. Then she turned her head and gave me a straight look, as if she'd heard me, all right, but it was the stupidest idea she'd ever heard in her life.

Then, without a word, she swung around and bolted up the stairs.

"Louise?" I said. "Hey?"

No answer. She was already out of sight. I went up after her and found her flying madly around from one bedroom to another, until she came to one I guessed she knew was Zeke's.

The bedrooms had all been searched; the intruders had been up here, too, and had turned them all upside down looking for something. Probably the papers they thought we'd brought with us. Louise was looking for something, too, though; she was rushing around Zeke's room, cursing under her breath, turning it all upside down all over again, looking in his closet, in his boots, under his bed, everywhere.

"Get some sleeping bags," she said over her shoulder. "And a heater—they must have a space heater around here someplace. Dry out these clothes."

I gaped at her. "We're not staying!"

"In the barn, they won't look in the barn," she said, tossing books out of Zeke's bookcases.

"What!" I said. "Aw, Louise, come on, we've got to get away from here, this is nuts!"

"Fine, g'bye, I'll say I never saw you." She was pawing around under the dresser.

I let out a strangled cry, and threw my hands up in the air—and stalked off down the hall to look for a heater. I didn't know what else to do. Anything, as long as it was quick.

"Okay, suppose we go down to Denver and call the cops," she called after me. "That what you want to do?"

There was a heater in the bathroom. I yanked its plug out of the wall.

"So, great," she said. "The cops give us to the FBI—come on, damn it all, where'd you put it?—so the FBI puts us under the jail, and then, gee whiz, whaddya know, they can't find the papers."

I snatched a couple of sleeping bags off a couple of beds. "So what the hell are we supposed to do instead?" I said.

"Well I'm going to tell you as soon as I— Oh, for God's sake!" she cried. "It's in his Bible!"

She showed me. It was on crisp onionskin paper, carefully Scotch-taped across a double spread in the middle of Jeremiah—taped in, so it wouldn't fall out if a stranger fanned the pages looking for it, but in Jeremiah so that a fellow Soldier would know where to look: a lovingly drawn, detailed map of the Vacation Bible School.

The paper crackled when she moved it. It sounded like something falling out of a frying pan into a fire.

I looked at it, and then I looked at her, and then I looked at it again.

I didn't say anything. My mouth had gone dry.

"Come on," she said.

I knew what was coming. Bodies all over the place; cluttered with bodies from one end to the other. Who's next? Take a number; line forms to the right.

So I went with her.

We thundered down the stairs, Bible, heater, and sleeping bags in hand. "Back door, back door," Louise said, and we threaded our way through the mess in the living room and past the breakfast table.

The kitchen was where the phone was. Louise picked up the receiver and listened to it, then screwed off the mouthpiece and examined the works—for bugs, I guessed—and screwed it back on again, and did the same with the earpiece. She dialed a number—ten digits, long distance—and let it ring once, and hung up. She stood there a while, timing the interval by her watch, and dialed again, and listened, and snapped, "Yeah, this is a network message from Louise. 'Activate Plan Z.' Got that? Good. You're damn right."

We stayed long enough to gather up some food to take with us, and then we dashed for the barn.

It didn't take them long to come back. We had just had time to get the space heater working, sweep the floor around it, change our clothes, and string up a line to dry our wet stuff on. We were sitting there in the gloom, listening to the drizzle on the roof, and trying to eat the food we'd scrounged, when we thought we heard, and then were sure we heard, the purr of a motor out on the road. It was coming down the valley, from the direction away from town. Naturally it was coming fast.

We snapped the heater off—even its feeble little glow might be visible through the barn's windows—and stumbled frantically around in the darkness, dismantling our little campsite and hiding everything in corners; then we groped our way up the ladder to the hayloft. We opened the loft door an inch or two and peeped out.

They had put out their headlights before they came around the last curve. As they got nearer we could see they were in a van—the better to cart bodies around in. They swung into the driveway with the van's doors already open, and four of them jumped out and ran over to the house, bending over as if they expected to be met with a hail of bullets. They kicked open the front door and burst inside.

A few minutes later they came back out again. After a quick conference, they fanned out and began to scout around. They looked under the porch; they went around the back of the house; they inspected the chicken coop and the sheds and peered into the windows of all the parked cars. Then they converged on the barn.

We ducked.

We heard the barn door being rolled open. A flashlight beam played all around the interior, high and low, even hitting the hay bales we were hiding behind. We ducked down even further—I tried to guess what kind of a jump it would be from the loft door, and whether or not we'd break our legs when we hit the ground—and then there was a yell from outside, and three quick cracks, and, a long moment afterward, a heavy thud.

The flashlight beam went away. There were footsteps, and then silence, and then laughter.

"Shit! It's a horse!" said one of them.

"What'd you do?"

"He tranked a horse, look at this!"

Louise leaned back and closed her eyes.

Down below, the four of them stood muttering together for a few moments, as if they weren't sure what to do next. Finally they decided that a quick exit would be the best solution, and they moved away.

"Wait'll we tell Derek you bagged a horse," one of them snickered.

"Haw!"

"You better not!"

Then we could see them again, under the loft door, giggling and shoving one another. And they got back into their van, turning the headlights on this time, and went back the way they came.

I let out a long, slow sigh.

It was Luther they'd shot. He must have come around the corner of the barn to see what was going on, or maybe hoping to be fed. The tranks had been designed for people, not horses, so by the time we got down from the hayloft—still shaking—he'd gotten back on his feet again. He was wobbling around, looking very puzzled, while Calvin hovered nearby.

We praised them to the skies, and led them both into their stalls, and loaded them down with more oats and apples than they could have eaten in a week.

"Gawd," Louise said.

After we'd done that, we set up our campsite one more time, and collapsed into our sleeping bags.

I think Louise went straight to sleep. I couldn't. I lay awake for a long time, listening to the horses munch their oats, and listening to it rain.

CHAPTER 19

ROSIE ROLLED OVER, OPENED ONE BLEARY EYE, and found herself in a dark, windowless room with a color TV set. She heard country western music—the complaining whine of pedal steel guitars and a woman's voice whining along with them. It was a heavy, plonking waltz with about three chords in it.

> You stood by me (branggg-a-dang dang)
> When I was lone—lee (brang-a-dang, brang-a-dang)
> Hadn't a friend—in the world (burr-ranggg)
> Except you on—lee (branggg—dang-a-dang) . . .

Rosie had an evil, splitting headache, and her body was sore all over. She felt as if she had drunk several gallons of cheap booze and then fallen down a flight of stairs.

"Gch," she said, and closed the eye.

The song whined on.

> Oh, you shel—tered me (oooh-waahh)
> With yer precious love (oooh-waahh)
> And I wanna say thank you (hush!)
> Thank you (hush!)
> Thank you, Lord! (Brang-a-dang dang *dang*.)

Make that a couple of flights of stairs, Rosie thought, and having to listen to that miserable caterwauling wasn't helping any. God, she felt awful. And the funny thing was, she hardly ever drank; the last time she'd been drunk was when she was seventeen years old. Who turned that shit on, anyway? And what the—

" 'Lord'? "

She sat upright, both eyes open, and glared indignantly at the TV screen, where the woman, in a white chiffon gown and blond bouffant hairdo, was bowing graciously and soulfully over her hand-held microphone.

"What is this?" Rosie said, looking around her. The room really was dark. Not just dark; black. Black as pitch, black as a coal cellar—even by the light of the TV. And except for the TV, it was silent.

Really silent.

Completely silent.

"Praise the Lord, isn't that lovely," said a weaselly-looking man on the TV. "That's our own Dawnella Staggers, friends. She'll be back with us later on, but right now . . ."

Rosie blinked and shook her head, trying to wake up. She felt as if she were still half asleep. Wisps of memory floated through her aching brain; they merged, mingled with wisps of dream, and floated away again.

Funny, she thought—any room ought to reflect at least a little light, a little sound. Not that she'd ever thought about it before. She shaded her eyes from the TV screen and looked around some more, but she still couldn't see anything. It was peculiar. Even the couch she was sitting on was invisible; she could feel that it was covered in some kind of plush—black, probably—but she couldn't see it.

She'd been looking at her own bare feet and legs for some time before she realized that she did see them. They were hers. They were bare. She was wearing a light-colored skirt and a T-shirt.

"My clothes!" They'd taken her clothes! Her jeans, boots, blouse, sweater, army coat! Gone! And her watch, too! She clutched herself all over in a slapstick caricature of panic—and caught herself doing it; and she would have smiled at herself, except that, at the same time, she realized who "they" were and where she had to be.

And how she'd gotten there.

"Oh my God!" she cried. "Did I tell them?"

"Yes, dear friends, it's all right here in this little booklet," said the weaselly-looking man. "You'll find out what to expect in the days to come, when to expect it, and what the Lord is going to do for you. And it's written in simple, clear, easy-to-read language. . . ."

Zeke in Corinth, Rosie thought. Oh, Lord. And the two goons in the raincoats. And herself, trying to run across the parking lot. Had she told? Had they even asked? She couldn't remember.

She thought she remembered lying in the back seat of a car, going somewhere, unable to move. . . . Nah! She'd never have told them! Would she?

"Ah, cram it, willya?" she said to the weaselly-looking man, who was telling her about a handsome pin or tie-tack she would receive, absolutely free, if she ordered his booklet right away.

Well, she thought, if she was going to be cooped up in here, she sure wasn't going to put up with that crap. She got up off the couch and headed for the TV set—and took three steps into the pitch darkness, lost her balance, and fell flat on her face.

"Ow!" she said, more surprised than hurt. What had they done to the floor? Built it on a slant, or what?

It was carpeted. Black again; black on black. On black. Damn! She couldn't see a thing! She sat up and tried to get her bearings, tilting her head (which was throbbing again) from side to side, but it was no good. She couldn't make up her mind which direction the slant was in. Or whether there was a slant at all. Maybe there wasn't; maybe she was imagining it. It was too dark to tell; the TV was her only point of reference, hanging there in the black void like a moon with no horizon. And even the TV didn't seem to want to stay put; it drifted, as she watched it, left, right, up, down, leaving a red smear behind it as it went.

Some moon. With a man in it, a portly fellow (and too young to be portly), wearing a three-piece suit that fitted him like a sausage casing. He was walking restlessly back and forth, with an open Bible in one hand, holding it out from his body while he yammered away. And while he yammered, his other hand had a finger pointing, and he swung the hand over his head and brought the finger arcing down and plunged it right into the V of the open Bible.

Rosie's head swam. Throbbed *and* swam. She sat there on the floor for a while, feeling nauseated. When that had passed, she picked herself up and moved forward again—carefully this time—sliding one toe along in front of her, waving her arms, and cringing a little, as if she expected to run into a pit or a pendulum. As she made her way along, the TV rose and rose above her (it had been at eye level, she could have sworn, from the couch), and its picture, with the man and his Bible in it, flattened into a thin crescent—until finally her fingers touched a carpeted wall.

Ahh! Made it! She leaned on the wall and breathed a sigh of relief—and looked up. She was standing directly under the TV.

"And your Father, who sees in secret, will reward you! It's written down right here," the man said fiercely, plunging with his finger. " 'He that overcometh, and keepeth my works unto the end, to him will I give POWER over the nations; and he shall RULE them with a rod of iron!' "

Rosie reached up at the TV, but it was too high. She jumped at it, fell heavily to the floor, got up, jumped higher, and fell again.

"Bastards," she snarled, and tried another couple of times. No good. She couldn't get at it. It might as well have been a basketball hoop.

"Well, she's up."
"Who? Number twenty-one?"
"Yeah."
"About time, too."
"Mark it down."

Over Rosie's head, upstairs in the monitoring room, three blond young men sat comfortably in swivel chairs. They wore lab coats over their shirts and ties and chino pants. Their room was crowded with electronic equipment, floor to ceiling and wall to wall, all beeping and humming and oscillating in a quiet and discreet way.

They were watching a bank of closed-circuit TV screens, each of which showed the image picked up by an infrared-sensitive camera mounted near the ceiling in one of the Management Units below. The cameras were motorized so that they could track the motions of the occupants: small, solitary human figures, white against a gray background, some of them standing, some sitting, some lying down.

One of the blond men glanced at his watch and wrote down the time on a clipboard. "Eighteen past. My nickel again," he said, and held out his hand while the other two shrugged and paid up. "That's five hours and, uh, thirty-three minutes—yeah, Skip gave her the last shot at quarter to eleven."

"Skip's a nice guy."

"Yeah."

The three of them looked at Rosie for a while; she was leaning against the wall of her unit, looking up at them. She looked a little sick. But then they all did, right after they came to; it seemed to be a standard side effect of the darts.

The one with the clipboard made another note.

"She's talking," said one of his mates.

"Pick it up! Pick it up!"

The one with the clipboard flipped a switch or two, and the room was filled with sound.

"—kin', lousy, stinkin', cocksuckin' sons of bitches! Turn it off! Shit!"

"Whoo-hoo-hoo!" crowed one of the blonds, fanning himself with his hand. "Whew, she's a hot one!"

The other two blushed furiously; one of them flipped the switches off again. They'd never heard such language before this bunch of radicals came in. The seven of them early this morning, and then this one, number twenty-one, a few hours later—every one of them with a gutter-mouth. Absolutely foul. The preachers had sworn a little, too, at first, but not like this; mostly they'd wrung their hands and worried, in the early stages before the process began to take hold. Whereas the radicals yelled. They ripped their couches apart, wetted wads of paper toweling and threw them at the TV sets, and generally acted hostile and aggressive. They chanted and sang and talked to themselves, and then they cursed some more. Most of them had been at it all afternoon; this last one looked as if she would probably start shortly.

Of course, the experiment was supposed to be double-blind; the teams who worked the monitoring room weren't supposed to know who the subjects were or where they came from, or the dosages, or anything like that. They were just there to record results. But of course you could tell by looking at them—with their hippie hair, and the men with their crazy beards and drooping mustaches. (That is, they'd arrived that way. The preachers were all bearded now, too, naturally, but they'd been clean-shaven and well-groomed on arrival.) And, too, the Bible School was a gossip mill, like any isolated community. There wasn't much else to do up there on the mountain. Not that Christians ought to gossip, but they were only human, and there wasn't really any harm in it.

"Hey, did Pete get back from the doctor yet?"

"Yeah—I saw him after lunch. It's broken all right. Got a cast clear up to his shoulder."

"Poor guy."

"Well, what do you expect? Four against seven."

"Yeah, they should've taken some more guys with them."

"Which one of them did it, did he say?"

"Number fifteen, wasn't it?"

"That little shrimp? He broke Petey's arm?"

"Oh, they're mean— Whoop! Look at this guy; he's going to throw another one."

One of the little figures wound up and threw.

"Ah, he'll calm down."

"How long do you bet it takes him?"

"That one? He looks tough. Probably not till tomorrow."

"Nickel says tonight. By ten p.m."

"You're on."

"Derek told me they all knew karate."

"Really?"

"Hiyaaahh! Samurai!" one of them said, slashing the air.

Rosie had to rest for a minute; all that jumping around had made her feel light-headed. She growled at the man with the Bible. She wished she could smash the TV set, not just turn it off. If she'd had a shoe, she'd have thrown it—which was doubtless why they'd taken her shoes away.

"Assholes," she said.

But the man with the Bible only talked louder.

Well, she thought, she'd better find out what she was up against in here.

She spent the next few minutes making her way around the perimeter of the room, keeping one hand on the wall and groping before her with the other. There weren't any pits or pendulums; it was just a room, maybe twelve feet by fifteen, and roughly rectangular roughly, because she was fairly well satisfied, as far as possible in utter darkness, that there wasn't a right angle in it. Everything was just a little off. One wall seemed to lean out, another to lean in—relative to a floor that dipped and rose at odd moments—until she was no longer sure what was level and what wasn't. It made walking a lot of work, even with the wall there to steady her.

Goddamned fun-house, she thought. These people were really sadistic.

She found the door—or at least a door-shaped seam in the carpeting—midway along one wall. It had no hinges and no knob. She found the bathroom, an alcove in the wall opposite the TV, with a toilet and sink in it and a large drain in its floor—in case she should want to stop up the sink, she supposed, and lean on the faucets (they were spring-loaded) until it overflowed, which she didn't see any point in doing. She found the paper towels, though, and wetted a dozen or so and winged them at the TV set—all misses—before she got tired of it.

Meanwhile, the man with the Bible had departed at last, only to be replaced by a Christian ladies' aerobics show—leotarded limbs flying to the beat of a driving, frenetic rock song. The song's lyrics made Rosie stop and stare.

> I'll make a helper (helper!)
> Fit—for—him!
> Gonna make a helper (helper!)
> Fit—for—him!
> (*Thump*-thump-*thump*-thump-*thump*-thump!)
> Fit—for—him!

"Eeeee!" Rosie said. Bodies flopped violently back and forth, pink and yellow and green.

> It's not good for the man to be a-lone (no—no—no!)
> Flesh of my flesh and bone of my bone (uh—uh—uh!)
> So I know what I'm gonna do (ah—ah—ah!)
> A godly man needs a woman too (yeh—yeh—yeh!)
> Gonna make a helper (helper!) . . .

"My God, what a pile!" Rosie yelled over the music. This was a new one on her. Obviously she hadn't been watching enough TV; it was worse than she'd dreamed. "Bring back Dawnella!" she yelled. "Shit! She was better than this!"

And with the music dinning in her ears, she lurched off for another go at the room. She pounded furiously on the walls—which was useless; they were quite solid and quite soundproof. She tried climbing on the toilet and the sink, hoping there might be a heating duct or some opening near the ceiling, but she couldn't reach anything but more carpeted wall. She tried to shove the couch over to the TV set in order to climb on it, but the more she heaved and strained, the less

it moved; all she did was tire herself out. When it finally occurred to her to feel around the couch's feet, she discovered
they were bolted to the floor.

She groped her way back to the sink and tried rapping out
an SOS on its drainpipe (in counterpoint to the thumping
music), but all she had to rap with was her knuckles; they'd
thoughtfully put an elastic waistband in her skirt so that she
wouldn't even have a button to rap on pipes with.

In any case, she didn't get a reply.

When she was done with all that, she wobbled back to the
couch, feeling dizzy and exhausted. She lay there, panting,
and watched the exercise leader thrusting his mike into the
face of an exercisee—a young blonde in a green leotard who,
of course, didn't need to lose any weight. "Oh, yes," the
woman said happily. "I want to be fit for my husband when
he comes home at night. But, more than that, your body is
the Lord's temple, and I believe you should keep it in the very
best shape you can!"

"And I'm sure the Lord is pleased with the way you've
been keeping yours," leered the exercise leader.

"Thank kew!" said the woman, wrinkling her nose ador-
ably.

"Oh, man!" Rosie said in dismay, while the music came
back up.

> *Thump*-thump-*thump*-thump-*thump*-thump!
> Fit—for—him!

And then—she didn't know what happened. She closed her
eyes for a moment, just to rest them, but she must have fallen
asleep again, because the next thing she knew, there was a
different show on the tube.

And a crack of light under the door.

Which widened into a horizontal slot, maybe eight inches
high, dazzlingly bright—and then instantly snapped shut again,
leaving the room, if possible, even darker than before.

She was too startled to move. Maybe this was it, she thought;

they were coming to get her. She braced herself against the couch, tensely watching the place where the slot had been, waiting for the rest of the door to fly open. But it didn't. Nothing happened at all, and then, a moment later, she smelled the food.

"Whew!" she said, relieved. Dinner! She hadn't even been thinking about food, but instantly her mouth began to water and her stomach to growl, and she realized she was famished. She felt as though she hadn't eaten anything in days.

She had a lot of trouble getting over there; her knees were trembly, and she had no sense of balance, since the light under the door had left a bright green stripe across her eyes which kept drifting off in one direction while she was trying to walk in another. But eventually she made it. Sitting down, a trifle heavily, she found a hamburger, French fries, and a pickle, on a paper plate on a little cardboard tray.

No need for silverware—clever bastards. She dug in. It all tasted even better than it smelled.

She wondered if it *had* been days since she'd eaten. It had been, what, Tuesday when they'd grabbed her in Omaha? And it would have taken them all night to get here from there. But she'd been knocked out for no telling how long after that. It might still be Wednesday now, or Thursday, or Friday; bloody hell, she thought, she had no way of knowing. Pick a day, any day. With no wristwatch, and nothing but that relentless Christian stuff on the TV—no sitcoms, no soaps, and especially no news—she had no way of judging time at all.

Damn, she thought. And only last Sunday she'd been in New York, pulling all that beautiful stuff out of Anderson's safe. And racing off to the rendezvous with it, ready to save the world. And, from there, to have come down to this—sitting on the floor in the dark, eating a hamburger she couldn't even see. Like a goddamned rat in a cage. Or a Skinner box. Whatever. Trapped, anyway.

She'd been trying to keep from admitting how thoroughly trapped she was. As long as there had been some corner of the room she hadn't yet explored, there in the blackness, there'd been some hope—we hope for what we see not, she thought sourly. Might have been a chink in the wall, a loose brick under the carpet, just waiting for her to find it. Or something she could pry loose or unscrew or climb on or break. But now that she knew there wasn't, there wasn't much for her to do but admit it.

It gave her the creeps. It was like being in a cave, miles underground—that cold, eerie, stony silence. They might as well have put a flock of bats in there. Maybe a lizard or two.

She shivered, though the room wasn't cold.

She'd never felt so alone.

The TV was quiet at the moment; it was showing a film of a teen-aged boy wandering moodily down a gray, deserted city street. It was winter. He looked dejected; his head was bowed, his hands were jammed into his jacket pockets, and as he poked along he was muttering to himself about how there was nothing to do and nobody to do it with, and no point in doing it anyway.

Rosie sat idly watching this, swallowing the last of her French fries. The soundtrack of the film wasn't very good, she noticed. It was a little heavy on the bass; it had an undertone in it somewhere. And it seemed as though it were almost synchronized with the picture, but not quite.

The boy wandered on and on, the sound of his footsteps seeming to lag a microsecond behind his moving feet. He passed a playground full of kids his age, and a video parlor, ditto; he looked, shrugged, turned away, and kept on going. Evidently he was looking for Something More. Rosie had a feeling she knew what it was, too. Sure enough, a few blocks later he came to a church, with its doors open wide and people going in—all of them, Rosie noted, wearing such beatific expressions on their faces as would shame the Virgin Mary. The boy hung back a while (perhaps momentarily overwhelmed); then, having made his decision, he meekly followed the people inside. End of film, with organ music.

Rosie made a face. What a gooey mess, she thought. All it needed was Bing Crosby and Barry Fitzgerald. Or maybe Bambi and Thumper. Was that the best they could do? Pitiful! Really! If they thought they were going to change anybody's life with a sugary little film like that, they'd better think again.

Better work on their recording technique, if nothing else. The organ music was still playing over the closing credits; the bass undertone was even worse than before.

But never mind that, she thought. That wasn't the best they could do. Not here, anyhow; they hadn't put her in here just so that she could sit and scoff at their TV shows. This was just for starters. They were trying to soften her up in here first, with all this sensory-deprivation shit. Get her all disoriented. Sooner or later, they were going to come in after her, probably take her away to an interrogation cell somewhere, and start in with the heavy stuff.

Well, good for them. Let 'em come. She'd be ready.

Let them do all their tricks. Let them gang up on her and shine the light in her face and browbeat her until they wore themselves out. She knew how it worked: they did that for a while, and then they sang hymns and spoke in tongues and loved you to death, and then they turned around and browbeat you some more. It was all peer pressure, and it was nasty as hell. And if you were young and impressionable, and searching for answers, and you didn't know yet that answers weren't the point—then you could collapse under it very easily.

She knew plenty of people who had. And who had limped into places like Union Seminary, walking wounded, trying to put their lives and minds together again afterward—after they'd been ripped to shreds by one group of these creeps or another. Took them a hell of a long time to do it, too.

"Okay," she said under her breath. "Come on in, fellas. Let's get a move on."

She was looking forward to it. There were going to be

some mighty sore Christian butts before she was through. She'd let them have it with both barrels; they'd be sorry they had ever let her in here.

She hoped they would come soon. Her head was beginning to ache again, and her stomach didn't feel too good, either. She wondered if she were coming down with something.

The TV set had been droning away at her all this time. She'd been thinking so hard, she'd been only dimly aware of it. But now a familiar voice caught her attention; she looked up, and the handsome face of Rev. Anderson loomed into view.

"Well, well, looky here," she said with a snarl. "If it ain't old Laughing Boy himself."

She wished *he* were in here with her. They could have a cozy little chat.

He smiled down at her from a desk surrounded by potted plants. ". . . Introduce my next guests," he was saying. "They're the founders of Americans for Morality in Education, and I know we all want to hear about their fine efforts. Let's give them a warm Christian welcome—Joy and Ernie Goodhue!"

Rosie curled her lip.

There was copious applause, and Joy and Ernie marched on, followed by two children. They all settled themselves in chairs among the lush greenery.

Joy was a formidable woman with a sallow complexion and a narrow, pinched nose; she wore a tailored suit with a red bow at the throat. Ernie looked like a drill sergeant; he had a ramrod-straight back, a florid face, and a flat-top crewcut.

"And their two lovely children," Rev. Anderson said.

"Jason," said Joy, "and Jennifer. Say hello, precious."

The camera turned briefly to the children, perched timidly on the edges of their chairs: a boy of about nine in a cadet's uniform, and a girl of six in a frilly white dress with a pink sash. They looked terrified.

"Oh, great," Rosie said.

Their mother was talking. ". . . Had to pull Jason out of school when we found out what they were teaching him over there," she said with a shocked expression on her face. "Then we found out we weren't the only ones who felt that way. There's a great groundswell of opinion; the school boards just aren't responding to it."

The soundtrack was out of whack on this one, too. Rosie could still hear the undertone, like a very faint echo, down in the bass.

"Children are naturally prone to error," Ernie was saying, while Rev. Anderson nodded approvingly. "They need guidance. Moral authority. And if their teachers won't provide it, the parents have to step in."

It was as if the TV were tuned to two channels at once, Rosie thought—two frequencies, one below the other. She couldn't put her finger on it, exactly; it was as if it wasn't quite sound, but more like a vibration. Subliminal. Maybe that was what was making her head hurt. She was really beginning to feel lousy.

"Pressure the school boards to stop forcing these ideas on our children," said Ernie.

"Permissiveness. Relativism," said Joy. "Stranglehold on our schools."

"Yeah, right, lady," Rosie said—but she was still listening to the soundtrack. The whole thing was getting louder; they seemed to be shouting now, though she could see that they weren't. And the undertone went right along underneath. There; no . . . yes, there it was again. Had she heard it, or was she imagining it?

God, she felt weird. She felt weak, even sitting down; dizzy, quivery. Sick. Was she hallucinating? Was she still drugged? Surely it would have worn off by now, wouldn't it?

"Banished from the classroom!" Joy said loudly.

"Weakening our moral fiber!" Ernie said even more loudly. "The future of the American family unit!"

"Oh, what do you know about it!" Rosie snapped at them,

as the camera cut back to the two cowering children; and suddenly, unaccountably, she burst into tears.

Now she was scared. "Oh, come on!" she wailed. "What is this? Dammit!" What on earth was happening to her? Her whole system was breaking down. She was falling to pieces—and she couldn't. She mustn't. She had to get a hold of herself, before the sons of bitches came through that door.

She swallowed hard, sniffed, blinked, and fought the tears down. She felt sicker than ever. The TV blared in her ears. Drugs? she thought. Side effects?

Her eyes widened. The food! she thought in alarm. It had to be! They must have spiked it—that was the only way they could have done it!

She struggled to her feet and went reeling toward the bathroom. She had to get it out of her system fast. Her legs had turned to rubber, and she could hardly keep her balance at all; she needed to lean quite heavily on the wall in order to make it.

"Joy and Ernie," yelled Rev. Anderson, while Rosie threw up, "can show you how to start a chapter in your community. Write to them at this address."

She hauled herself to the sink, leaned on the spring-loaded faucet, and began gulping water down, handful after frantic handful. The running water was as loud as Niagara Falls; behind her, the voices thundered in the TV.

"Beautifully behaved," roared Rev. Anderson.

"Yes, aren't they," rumbled Ernie.

"Praise the Lord," boomed Joy.

Rosie gasped for breath, feeling worse by the minute, never dreaming that it wasn't the food, it was the air she was breathing, so the water wasn't going to help her at all; and when she had drunk all she could hold, she straightened up and turned around, and saw the TV set, floating in the blackness. It was showing the Goodhue family—the fierce parents, the wretched children—standing together among the palm leaves.

It had acquired a halo.

Not the family; the TV set. The whole set was on fire. Tongues of flame radiated from it in all directions. Flaming swords, in all colors: Oz green, ruby red, sapphire blue.

Rosie's hair stood on end.

Dear God, she thought. Not LSD. Don't let it be LSD.

But it was; and the halo began to grow larger. Thunder and lightning, fire within fire, all shimmering and pulsating in time with her own pulse; it grew, and bloomed, and spread, and billowed, like—like nothing she had ever seen. Or ever wanted to see. It was horrible. With four grinning faces in the center, hideously distorted—stretched, like pulled taffy, into grimaces of pain. They were still talking in there, in that bright little world, but she couldn't distinguish their voices; they all blended together with the undertone, which was growing and spreading too, a deafening cloud of sound, until it filled the whole room—crowding her out, buckling her knees, forcing her to the floor. She had a sense of bone-crushing pressure, as if the very life were being pressed out of her.

And then, from the midst of all that roaring, she heard a voice.

Aren't you tired? it said gently.

It was deep and comfortable and unbelievably soft.

Come on, join us. Be one of us.

We're here to help you.

And Rosie began to howl.

Upstairs in the monitoring room, the three blond men looked at her, checked their watches, and smiled.

PART IV

The promised land always
lies on the other side of a
wilderness.

—HAVELOCK ELLIS

CHAPTER 20

AT 9:32 ON THURSDAY MORNING, THE EARLY business flight from Washington (via O'Hare) came down through a heavy overcast into Stapleton Airport in Denver.

It landed without incident, taxied, and came to a stop at the arrival gate, only ten minutes late.

A hundred and fifty-nine passengers stampeded off the plane. All but six of them were dressed in identical dark suits, and carried identical briefcases and Burberry coats. The other six, who pretended not to know each other, wore old clothes and sturdy hiking boots.

The first of these was a tall, thoughtful man with a pipe and a face full of bushy black beard. The second, a few yards behind him, was a redhead with wide blue eyes; she was dressed in faded jeans and an army field jacket .

Behind her came a square, solid, muscular fellow, wearing a Baltimore Orioles baseball cap, who looked as if he had just gotten off his shift at the factory.

Next came a man and a woman, both in ponytails and bib overalls (he with a drooping mustache, she with a pair of large hoop earrings); and last, a woman who belonged in an L. L. Bean catalogue—pageboy, turned-up nose—wearing painter's pants, a down vest, and a turtleneck with little whales printed on it.

They looked tolerably out of place among the business passengers on the plane, but they kept pace with them and moved right along, hurrying through the arrival gate, pausing briefly to get their bearings, and dashing away down the corridor toward the main part of the terminal, and nobody paid them any attention.

Least of all the three airport security guards in plain clothes who were loitering by the gate, peering out from behind their magazines, as they all went by. The guards weren't looking for people in old clothes that morning; they were there to intercept a noted cocaine dealer who was due in from Bogota, who would naturally be wearing a suit and carrying a briefcase. So they scrutinized every one of the hundred and fifty-three possible candidates, taking especial care to watch for wigs, eyeglasses, putty noses, and the like, and didn't give the other six a second thought.

In the terminal, five of these people wandered casually off in various directions while the sixth, the female of the bib-overalls pair, went to the Avis counter to rent a car, using an American Express card made out in the name of Elizabeth Seton, which wasn't her real name. Her name was Ellen Rinehart, and she had made the American Express card herself in the back room of the small custom printing shop which she and her husband George (that was George in the mustache, strolling toward the baggage claim area) owned in the town of Zion, Pennsylvania.

The Avis clerk didn't look twice at the card (Ellen did excellent work; she'd been making credit cards, drivers' licenses, and all sorts of I.D.'s for the Soldiers of Jeremiah for years now), and soon the paperwork was done, and Ellen took the car keys, thanked the clerk for wishing her a nice day, and proceeded to the parking lot. There her companions reappeared, one by one, back from their errands—George, and Nathan with the beard, and Beth in the army jacket, Ed in the cap, and Muffy in the painter's pants—and they all got into the car and drove unobtrusively out of town.

Just as they were leaving, a nonstop from Miami touched down on the runway. The security guards were there to meet it, although they doubted that the cocaine dealer would be so rash as to take such an obvious route. And they were right; he wasn't on the plane. Two people who were on it were Joanie and Gus, a suntanned, athletic-looking couple in jeans and sweatshirts. They came from Tekoa Park Estates, a suburb of Palm Beach (just south of Tekoa Park and west of Tekoa Gardens); Gus worked in an art gallery, where, in addition to his legitimate business, he did a brisk trade in paintings, diamonds, and Oriental carpets which Joanie stole from houses in the area.

The two of them followed the crowd through the gate, past the guards, and into the terminal. Gus's Visa card said his name was John Knox; he rented a Hertz car on it, with no more trouble than Ellen had had, and in a few minutes he and Joanie were on their way.

There were four more on the next flight: Hector, Pharaoh, and Floyd, who stole truckloads of assorted merchandise from the docks and airports around Los Angeles, and Hector's girl-friend, Dolores, a tiny, dark, energetic woman who ran a soup kitchen in the barrio with part of their profits.

Hector caught the attention of the security guards for a moment, until they realized he was about six inches too short; they let him go by, and shrugged, and moved off toward the next gate.

An hour later, Wally, Dick, and Nadine came in from St. Paul, all three of them wearing horn-rimmed glasses. They were computer programmers at one of the big defense contractors in the Twin Cities, and they were also the reason Ellen's credit cards worked so well; when they weren't embezzling from their employer, they were busy inserting Ellen's account numbers into the credit companies' computer files and making sure they got paid up every month.

Several paces behind them was sweet, round-faced Sister Margaret, also from St. Paul, who taught Christian ethics at a college run by her order, and who spent a good deal of her spare time opening bank accounts, under a variety of corporate names, where she laundered the money her three friends embezzled.

The last ones in, on a flight from Dallas, were four enormous men named Howie, Earl, Dub, and Parker, all of them in nylon windbreakers, warm-up pants, and size 14 running shoes. They towered over the rest of the passengers; they were big enough to have passed for defensive linemen, which in fact was what they were. They had played together at Arkansas A&M in the early seventies, and they would have gone on to the pros, too, if they hadn't set fire to the files at the local draft board at the end of their junior year. When they'd gotten out of jail for that, they'd moved to Joshua, Texas, which was Dub's home town. They still lived there, in a ramshackle house with dogs, cats, parakeets, and immense quantities of dirty laundry; they commuted every day into Dallas and Forth Worth, where they washed the windows of skyscrapers. Except for two or three times a month, when, armed with dollies and official-looking clipboards, they visited the offices they'd seen through the windows and made off with typewriters and copying machines.

They were giggling as they got off the plane because somebody had thought Earl was L. C. Greenwood and had asked him to autograph his in-flight magazine. Still giggling, they lumbered down the corridor and into the terminal, unmindful of the commotion behind them as the security guards converged on a real estate agent from Waxahachie and asked him, politely but firmly, if he wouldn't mind coming with them for a moment—with loud protests from their victim, who had committed plenty of offenses in his career, but dealing coke wasn't among them.

It took the real estate man a good half hour to convince the guards that he was who he said he was, and not the coke dealer he bore such a striking resemblance to; and by that time Howie and Earl and Dub and Parker were long gone.

They went west out of Denver, as Ellen and the others had done, until they came to Route 40. Then they turned north and headed into the mountains.

• • •

And so a couple of hours later there were five rented cars parked under the hayloft in Zeke's barn, wedged in next to Zeke's horse-drawn plow and harrow and a weird contraption that looked like the original McCormick Reaper. The rest of the barn was full of people yelling, hugging, kissing, and carrying on the way people generally do at reunions. Joanie and Gus broke out the trunkful of fried chicken they'd bought on their way up from the airport, and Wally and Sister Margaret passed a case of beer around; and when that was all gone, everybody gathered around the space heater, settling down by twos and threes on hay bales, crates, sacks of feed, and whatever else they could find to sit on, and Louise called the meeting to order.

She talked for about forty minutes, telling them what she and I had been up to in the past couple of days, and what Rosie's papers said, and why she'd asked them all to come. They all listened carefully and didn't interrupt her. A lot of eyebrows went up while she explained how Conversion Management worked, but most of the rest of it they'd either seen on the news, in one form or another, or figured out for themselves. And so nobody was very surprised when she told them about the mess we'd found when we'd gone inside Zeke's house.

And when she got to the part about the tranquilizer dart, they were even less surprised. They all just leaned back, and went a little tight around the mouth, and said, "Mm-hmm."

Nathan was sitting in a corner, sucking meditatively on his pipe. "And they came back last night," he said to Louise after a while. "And they didn't find you."

"That's right," Louise said.

"Which would mean, either you never got here, or—"

"Or else we got here, took a look, and took off again."

"But, either way, you must be holed up somewhere by now," he said.

"Right."

"Certainly not here," Gus put in.

"That would be dumb of us."

Everybody nodded.

"So you're holed up. And you've got the papers," Nathan said. "So what do they think you'll do now?"

"Well, we could go to the cops," Louise said.

"Right," said Nathan. "And they've got that angle taken care of, because it's a federal case."

Muffy said, "So the FBI takes the evidence and that's the last anybody hears of it."

"Right," said Louise.

Nathan said, "So you wouldn't do that."

"No."

"So you go to the press instead," said Beth. "Like you did in Bodine."

"Make a bunch of Xeroxes. Send 'em all over the place."

"Good idea."

"But they've got that taken care of, too," Dolores said in her clipped Spanish accent. "They've got the press thinking you planted the drugs—"

"If they're thinking at all," Hector said.

"No lie," agreed Floyd.

"—Yeah; so if you turn up now with a bunch of papers," Dolores went on, "they're going to wonder even more about those."

"Aw!" said Louise. "What are they going to think—we made 'em up?"

"Sure, why not?"

"Nice people like us."

"But," said George, "even if they do think they're real, they can't just print 'em without checking the facts first."

"Pretty serious charge, kidnapping," Ellen said.

"Think of the libel suits," said George.

"So the first thing the press does is call the cops," said Beth.

"Right," George said.

"So here come the Feds again. Back to square one."

"Right," said Ellen. "Or else, the second thing they do is call Anderson."

"Who tells them, A, the papers are fake," said George, "and, B, if they don't think so, they're welcome to come look around the Bible School any time they want."

"And by the time they can get up there, it's all been cleared out."

"Naturally."

"So, in short . . ."

"Nobody's going to believe any of this unless they see the preachers," said Muffy.

"Sitting in their laps," added Gus.

"With the papers in *their* laps."

"That's about right."

"Which means we'd have to go up there and break 'em out ourselves," Louise said.

There was a pause, and a number of people exchanged glances.

"Have to raise an army first," Wally said casually.

"And even if you could," said Nadine, "they'll be bound to have good tight security up there."

"Sentries. Alarms. All kinds of shit."

"Not to mention people."

"Yeah, those Harvest Workers," said Joanie. "Probably sleep with their boots on."

"So we'd be insane to try it," said Louise.

"Right."

"It'd never work."

"No."

Nathan looked around the room. "Then that's what we do."

"Mm-hmm," everybody said.

Zeke had drawn his map of the Bible School with a heavy black felt-tipped pen. It showed a group of buildings, and a lot of lawn, enclosed within a longish rectangular frame. The frame he'd indicated by a squiggly line, and he'd neatly labeled it, "Hedge/Fence, 10 ft., chain link/b-wire." There was a gate at the front, marked "Elec. Eye," with a gatehouse beside it, just inside the fence, marked "Sentries (2), 24 Hrs."

A driveway led from there, up through the middle of the front lawn, to a parking lot halfway along the rectangle. Next to the parking lot was a single large building, set crosswise, with a door at either end. It was the biggest building on the place, and it was marked, simply, "It."

Behind that, at the far end, was a quadrangle: three dormitories in a row ("Pop. 100"), a dining hall, a chapel, and a handful of other buildings.

The map, still taped into Zeke's Bible, was spread out on a milk crate in the middle of the room, where the light from the space heater, such as it was, could fall on it. All of us moved in close around it, studying it over Louise's shoulder, and murmuring in agreement now and then, while she told us how she thought it should go.

"So we want to go over the fence about here," she said, pointing at the squiggly line.

"Pretty high fence," said Hector. "Be a mess to try to climb it."

"Ladders, then."

"Yeah."

"Put it down, Nadine."

"Got it," said Nadine, who was making up a shopping list.

"Ed, Joanie, you'll take care of the gatehouse and the gate. And we'll want the phones cut."

"Right," said the solid Ed. " 'Course, we'll need some tools. Can't get anything through those X-rays at the airport."

"I've got some with me," Louise told him. "Zeke must have some around here, too; we'll buy you whatever else you need."

"Fine."

"How long do you think it'll take you?"

"Well," Ed said, "if the wires all go through the gatehouse, then it shouldn't be long once we get in there. What do you think, Joanie? Five or ten minutes?"

"Yeah," Joanie said. "Call it ten, to be safe."

"Need any help with the sentries?"

Joanie shrugged. "I don't know; how's your karate these days, Ed?"

"Not too bad," he said. "I've been working out pretty regular."

From the snickers that came from Beth and Muffy, I gathered that that was an understatement.

"Okay, ten minutes," said Louise. "That'll give the rest of us time to get into position."

Gus said, "Now, we're talking about, what, thirteen preachers in there? Plus Zeke and the others—"

"Plus us, of course," said Dolores.

"Going to need some serious vehicles."

"I was thinking about a truck," Louise said.

"Or a bus," said Pharaoh.

"Mmm. Better. More civilized."

"Get one down at the high school," Pharaoh said. "Saw 'em on the way up, just sitting right out there. Remember, Hector?"

"Sure," Hector said. "They ought to be able to spare us one."

"Being for a good cause and all."

"Perfect," Louise said. "That and Zeke's pickup ought to do it."

Wally was frowning at the map. "I don't much like the position of those dorms," he said, pushing his glasses up on his nose. "They're awful close to the main building."

"I know," said Louise. "I don't care for it much myself."

"Not with a hundred people in there."

"Not if they wake up," said Dick.

"Yeah," Louise said. "Then we'll need to figure out something to slow 'em down." She looked up at Howie. "Think you guys could handle that?"

Howie grinned at her. So did Earl and Dub and Parker.

"Okay, and we'll take care of putting their cars out of action," Louise said. "Don't want 'em all to get away after we've gone."

"What are you going to do, slash their tires or something?" said Wally.

"No; they'll drive on the rims if they want to bad enough."

"Distributor caps, then."

"Take too much time," Louise said. "I thought maybe we'd do the old potato trick."

Floyd started to laugh. "Potatoes!" he said. "My Lord, I haven't heard that one since I was eight years old!"

"Works, though."

"Potatoes?" said Nadine.

"Sure. Put 'em up the tailpipe," Floyd said. "Exhaust backs up. You can get the engine started, but you sure can't keep it running."

"Isn't science wonderful?" said Louise.

"Put it down, Nadine!"

Nadine shook her head and wrote it down.

"So that about does it," Louise said. "Get a good night's sleep, get the shopping done in the morning, and we'll go tomorrow night. That suit everybody all right?"

She didn't look at me, which was just as well. I was doing some arithmetic in my head, and no matter which way I added it up it still came out a hundred Harvest Workers and twenty-two of us. We would have the advantage of surprise, it was true; it would be two o'clock in the morning, and they'd be fast asleep. Their defenses would be down, just as the FBI used to say.

Still, all the hardware didn't sound like enough. We ought to shop around for some trumpets, too, and see if we couldn't scare up a Joshua.

Going to need some serious prayers.

CHAPTER 21

ERGEANT FLEISCHMANN'S LAST WEEK BEFORE vacation was certainly ending with a bang. Or a whimper. Or a combination of the two; he hadn't quite made up his mind. Whatever it was, he didn't expect he'd be crying when he and Edie finally got out of town. If they ever did.

Wednesday had been a real winner. After Hazeltine had kicked him off the Baker case, he'd spent the rest of the morning and most of the afternoon over at Mercantile Trust. Supposedly lending Perkins a hand on the robbery, but mostly hanging around with nothing to do. There was no reason on God's earth for him to be there; Perkins was running it and doing just fine; he'd even asked Fleischmann what the idea was. "Beats the hell out of me," Fleischmann had replied. There were already plenty of warm bodies on hand to impress whatever citizens needed impressing. Perkins had four city cops and two state troopers on the scene by the time Fleischmann had gotten there, and they'd long since taken statements from all the witnesses in the bank and were going up and down the street, finding out that, as usual, nobody in the neighborhood had seen a thing.

The holdup had all been recorded on the bank's cameras, so Fleischmann had killed some time looking at the videotapes. Yes, it was the same gang that had pulled several other robberies in recent months: three Caucasian males, well-dressed, forties, solid citizen types. Same M.O. as the other jobs. They'd stood politely in line, passed a note to a teller, gotten three thousand dollars—which was all they'd asked for—and the teller had turned in the silent alarm while counting out the money, but of course before the police could get there the men had knocked over the security guards and walked out.

Fleischmann couldn't have cared less.

He'd gotten back to the station around four o'clock, and there he'd run into Walker and Schneider, the two troopers he'd assigned to guard Baker's room at the hospital. He'd asked them what they were doing back, and they'd told him they'd been relieved by Agents Knoblauch and Slattery of the FBI.

Fleischmann had thought that was pretty odd, but no odder than anything else the Feds ever did. If they wanted to waste a couple of overeducated agents sitting around a hospital room watching a guy sleep, when two troopers could have done it just as well, it wasn't any business of his.

So that was Wednesday.

Thursday, Hazeltine had come around in the morning and collected his report on the Baker case (Fleischmann had spent an hour retyping the damned thing onto his precious IU-44s) and had taken it away with him to messenger over to the Feds—saying once again how sorry he was, but that his hands were tied—and that was that, and Fleischmann had spent the rest of the day trying to get caught up on his paperwork. All crushingly boring, and enough to make him count the hours not only until vacation but until retirement as well.

In between which, he'd had phone calls dribbling in all day about the Baker thing. Typical nonsense—the original APB's had had his name on them, but, though they'd been superseded by the Feds' APB's, naturally nobody had read their teletypes for the day, so they called him instead.

He heard from police departments in Iowa, Texas, Kentucky, and North Carolina, all reporting alleged sightings of Macdonald and Flood. Plus, he heard from three out-of-state reporters who had seen his name on the wire services (twenty-four hours old) and wanted to know the latest.

All of whom he referred to the Feds, who, he was sure, were going to be delighted to talk to them.

One of the calls was from none other than Connolly, in Denver, who called to ask if he and Edie were still coming or what (God, yes), and oh, by the way, he'd gotten a report from a citizen who said he'd given Macdonald and Flood a ride.

"You too?" Fleischmann had said. "What time was this one?"

"Around 0600 yesterday." Which was Wednesday. "Guy says they were hitchhiking. He took 'em into Limon."

"Sorry," Fleischmann had told him. "According to my records, they were in North Carolina at 0600."

Connolly had laughed. "Moving pretty fast, aren't they?"

"Yeah. 'Course, in North Carolina, they had a car. That's how they got to Sioux City by lunchtime."

"Oh, my. Sounds like you're having fun on this one."

"Nah, it's a little late for that. The Feds took it over."

"Since when? Wasn't that your APB?"

"Since yesterday morning. Why don't you read your wires once in a while, Connolly? Christ, you guys are gettin' as lazy as we are. Pretty soon they'll have to close you down and send you all home."

"When? Tell me when!"

"Sooner than you think, buddy."

"Well, pass it on to the Feds for me, will you? Save me another phone call; they're kickin' my ass about my budget around here."

"All right," Fleischmann had said. "Now get the hell off the line so I can get some work done."

And he'd gone grudgingly back to his paperwork. He'd never dreamed he'd gotten so far behind on it. He kept finding more reports that had to be done, or redone, or rerouted, or compiled into quarterly stat sheets, or God knew what, and by the time he got off shift he was so sick and tired of it that he had to take a little drive in order to clear his mind out.

He found himself going west on the interstate, and when he got to the exit for Bodine he found himself getting off. There were two gas stations at the cloverleaf, a Mobil and an Arco; he picked the Mobil.

"Were you working on Tuesday night?" he asked the guy in the office.

"Yeah," the guy said.

"What time did you come on duty?"

"Six. Stay till midnight, every night."

"You have some pay phones outside here."

"Uh-huh."

"Would you have noticed if anybody used those phones Tuesday night?"

"I don't know; who'd you have in mind?"

"This would be two women, both in jeans and jackets. One of 'em had long dark hair. The other one had a cowboy hat on."

The Mobil guy didn't recall seeing anybody like that. But the Arco guy across the road did.

"Yeah, they were on foot," he said. "I thought that was pretty weird. I mean, I thought they'd probably want a can of gas, or else they'd be meeting somebody. You know. Lot of girls pick up guys around here in the evenings. But I saw 'em making a call, and then they went off again."

"Happen to notice which way they went?"

"Well . . ." The guy looked up and down the road for a minute. "Well, yeah, they went off that way."

"Did they go up the ramp? Or under the underpass there?"

"Well, now, I don't make it my busi—"

"Just tell me whether you noticed or not."

"Yeah, they went up the ramp."

"This one here. Westbound."

"Yessir."

Well? Fleischmann had thought. So they went west. So what?

He had no idea so what. That was the way they'd been going in the first place, so it wasn't exactly a revelation. He had no idea why he'd even checked.

He got back into his car and went home to Edie.

That was Thursday. This was Friday now, a rainy, nasty morning—a big slow-moving low coming off the Rockies—and he reminded himself, as he crept through traffic on his way to work, that this was his last day, he had only this one last day to get through, and he arrived to find a memo on his desk informing him that his Blue Cross had been terminated. Of all the Christalmighty things. He stamped off upstairs to Hazeltine's office, without even taking his coat off, and it took him half an hour's ranting and raving to establish that the reason for this idiocy was that he'd signed his last claim form on the wrong line, and another half an hour's ranting and raving to get it straightened out again, and when he came downstairs again he was good and steamed. He'd had a craw full of Hazeltine, enough to last him several years. What a way to go out on vacation. It was going to take him the whole two weeks to get the crap out of his system, and then, for God's sakes, he was going to have to come *back* here.

Phones were ringing and typewriters were clattering in the squad room. He walked rapidly across the room, pausing long enough to splash some coffee into a cup, and as he went past Gene's desk, Gene held the telephone up and said, "Hey, Bob, it's for you."

He marched into his office, set the coffee down, snatched up the phone, and said, "Yeah, what is it?"

And then he said, "Who?"

And then he sat down, scrabbled around for a pencil, and began writing very fast.

CHAPTER 22

AT TEN MINUTES PAST NOON, THE DAY BEFORE this, a Greyhound bus pulled up outside a cafe, which served as a bus depot, on the main street of a small, isolated town in the middle of the Montana prairie, and discharged its lone passenger: a burly man in his late twenties, unshaven and a little puffy around the eyes, wearing a raincoat.

A moment later the bus pulled away again in a cloud of sooty exhaust, leaving the man standing in the street, blinking. He didn't do anything for quite a while—just stood there as though rooted to the spot, slack-faced and expressionless, under the leaden sky, as though he had come to the end of the line and had no wish, or reason, ever to move again.

It was Agent X. Or what was left of him—ex-agent X, his mortal remains. He was much changed since his running exit from the Bil-Mar Motel two days before. Now, in spite of his size and bulk, he looked stooped, worn-out, deflated. His arms (he carried no luggage) hung limply at his sides. His raincoat, with a dog-eared newspaper sticking out of one pocket, was creased and rumpled; his suit looked as if he had been sleeping in it, which he had. He was covered from head to foot in a thin layer of oily grime.

He looked vacantly up and down the street. It was eight blocks long and consisted of two rows of one-story buildings with ziggurat-shaped facades, most of which hadn't been painted within living memory.

One of these buildings said "Sunset Bar" on the outside, in

large, faded block letters; X gazed at it for a long while, and then, finally appearing to have made a decision, he moved toward it. He shuffled along slowly and painfully, like an old man; he went inside, sat down all by himself on a stool at the very end of the bar, and began to drink.

He had traveled so many miles since Tuesday night that it made his head hurt. Kansas, Nebraska, South Dakota, Wyoming—round and round, a route so circuitous that it had confused even him. Sitting cramped-up in the backs of numberless busses, staring out at the desolate, gray-brown, endless prairie. Dust covered with snow covered with dust. It had all run together until he no longer knew where he was. It was all the same—the bleak, windswept prairie towns—and in every town the knots of teen-aged boys with Stetsons on their heads, the brims carefully curled into elaborate patterns, and their fingers jammed into their jeans pockets, lounging hopelessly on sidewalks, with nothing whatever to do.

All the towns exactly like his home town, all the boys exactly like himself. Little Agent X's, little Johnny Tribbles.

Little Abel Bakers, too.

He'd stared out the windows at them, while they sneered back at him, until he couldn't stand it any more.

He'd eaten so many greasy hamburgers, and greasy fried egg sandwiches, and bowls of greasy pea soup, and breathed so much stale, foul, diesel-smelling air, that he couldn't stand any more of that either—all the while playing it over and over again in his mind, trying to figure out where, how, he'd gone wrong. The girls got to the motel; he followed them. They went around to the back; he went around to the back. He opened the door—and they were gone. Vanished on him. Up in smoke, as if they'd never existed at all. Making a complete and utter fool of him—and he'd still felt like a fool, riding around in circles on all those busses—until he'd found the newspaper, lying discarded on an empty seat (when had that been? it must have been Wednesday), and had opened it up and read it. And the headlines had shimmered like heat waves before his eyes. Seared their way into his brain. Telling him what had really happened in Bodine, and how much of a fool he really was—because it wasn't the girls at all, it was the truck, it had been the truck the whole time—causing whole new landscapes to open up in his mind, bleaker, wider, windier than anything he'd ever dreamed of.

Ever.

"Mev'm," he mumbled, taking a deep drink of his fourth double Scotch.

He'd been unable to bring himself to eat anything today. On top of that, he was out of the habit of drinking, not having touched the stuff since he'd been saved. He drank slowly, methodically, and steadily all afternoon, and soon he was plastered, and soon afterward he was soused, and by four-thirty or so he'd drunk enough to give him the courage to call Harriet.

Not that it was courage, exactly. He wasn't sure why he called her. He had no definite plan in mind as he stood in the phone booth, stewed and swaying, clumsily pushing coins into the machine; but what he said to her, when he heard her voice, was, "Why, Harriet?"

"What?" she said. Her voice sounded as though it were coming from a distant planet.

"Wan' know," he slurred. "Jus' wanna know . . . why."

"What are you talking about?" she snapped. "Who is this?"

"Thiss X," he said. "An' I jus'—"

"Where on earth are you calling from?"

"I jus'— Eh?" She was talking so fast that it took him a minute to catch up with her. "From?" he faltered. "Uhh, I don't . . ." He fished in his hip pocket, suddenly having an idea, and pulled out the canceled stub of his bus ticket, and held it up to his nose. He couldn't focus on it. "Jus' second," he said, squirming around in the phone booth, holding the ticket, and his face, up to the glass doors to get some light.

Alien characters swam before his eyes. He squinted at them. "Spring . . . Falls," he read.

"Johnny, are you drunk?" Harriet said.

MT, the ticket said. "Oh. Montana," he said, in some surprise.

"Are you?"

"Mmm?"

"*Drunk?*" she said in a menacing tone.

"Now, Harriet—"

"Well, now, isn't that splendid," she snarled. "First you botch your assignment. Then you desert your duty, *and* your partner, and then I don't hear from you for two entire days, but that's not enough for you, is it? Now you—"

"Harriet—"

"—turn up out of the blue and you're *drunk!* I suppose that explains why you—"

X closed his eyes and leaned against the wall of the phone booth. His head began to spin.

". . . fat lot of good you're doing me *there*. Now for pity's sake will you stay put until I can wire you some money. Don't go anywhere until I can—"

"No money," he mumbled.

"Johnny, you realize this is—"

"No!" he said. "You jus' listen to me a minute! I jus' want you," he said, pointing, "tell me . . . one . . . thing. Why."

"Now you can't expect me to carry on an intelligent discussion when you're in this condi—"

"Why didn' you *tell* us? Huh?"

She paused; and then she said, "Tell you what?"

"Truck," he said. " 'Bout the truck, Harriet."

"Oh, for heaven's sake, Johnny. I can explain *that*."

He heard someone say thickly, "No. You can't."

It seemed to have been him.

There was a silence, so long that he wondered whether he had blacked out for a moment. Then he heard her voice again; it was icy. "You are not now," she told him, "nor have you ever been, associated with this organization. You bear sole responsibility for your actions. Should you be apprehended, the organization will disavow all knowledge of you."

And then she hung up on him.

He stood there for some minutes looking at the receiver in his hand.

He hiccuped.

Then he hung the phone up, opened the door of the booth, tottered back to his bar stool, and resumed drinking.

Time passed. Liquor flowed. The room around him filled with customers (after work) and emptied (for the dinner hour) and filled again. The customers hardly noticed him in their midst. There was nothing to notice; only a seedy-looking stranger sitting all by himself at the end of the bar, his head bowed, his feet hooked over the rung of his stool, and his grimy, funky raincoat hanging down behind, a soiled newspaper folded up in the pocket of it. He said nothing to anybody—just sat there for six more hours, in silence, looking only at the glass in front of him, filled, emptied, filled again. Outwardly he was deathly calm; nobody could guess, looking at him, at the terrible volcanic activity going on in his head—eruptions, meltdowns, earthquakes, floods, all whirling around a single motionless image—a semi-trailer truck that had come to rest in a little town in Kansas, with two hundred cartons of Sunday school books and one carton of LSD.

LSD, he thought. Sweet Lord Jesus, it was LSD the whole time.

So God didn't have anything to do with it.

Never had had anything to do with it.

Had He.

And X had been so glad, all that time, the unbelievable sap, to be a part of something that really mattered, really counted. The kidnappings—LSD—oh, Lord, those poor dumb preachers! What was she doing to them! And him just waiting for his turn to come, so he could get in on the action. Go get 'em, X. Thrown himself into it heart and soul.

And nobody had ever told him.

Though, he thought, if nobody had told him, then he couldn't have been expected to know, could he?

Yes, he could have. Should have. If he'd had any brains at all.

If he'd thought about it for five minutes.

He'd been looking at the wrong thing all the time. Just his little part of it. Single-mindedly. Obediently. And never once looked at the rest.

Oh, it was unbearable. How was he ever going to look himself in the eye again? He was scum. A worm. The lowest of the low. Lower than that, even; and worse off, too, because now she . . .

Knew where . . .

Now she knew where he . . .

"Oh, gosh," he said, suddenly breaking out in a cold sick sweat, and turning green. Gray. Green.

He had put away such an enormous amount of alcohol by that time that he was no longer merely drunk but damn near poisoned. Only a few of his brain cells were still functioning, but even those few were able to recognize that they had to get him out of there absolutely immediately.

Through a heroic effort, those cells managed to push a message down his spinal cord and dislodge his feet, which he couldn't feel at all any more, from the rung of the bar stool, and get them under him, stand him upright, and send him lurching toward the door.

The bar was crowded to capacity just then, it being the height of the evening. It was a cheerful, noisy crowd, and they stood aside good-naturedly, a little amazed at this poor derelict who'd been sitting all night quiet as a mouse and who was now zigzagging his way past them, suddenly come to life, whispering, "Oh, gosh, oh, gosh," and looking as though the hounds of Hell were after him. A few of them even helped him on his way, since he was obviously bombed out of his mind and barely able to walk.

Everything went along fine until he got to the bar's front door. He pushed it open, and a blast of cold air smacked him in the face; and so did the sight he saw on the street.

The sight was a blue Buick parked at the curb, with two men, dressed exactly like himself, only cleaner and soberer, climbing out of it and heading for him.

He blinked at them, just once. Then he slewed around and lurched back into the bar, took an unsteady bead on the first patron he came to, and hauled off and punched him on the ear.

He wasn't too clear on what happened after that. Some kind of a disturbance. He had a vague impression of a few punches, some yelling, a bit of flying glassware, all of which took place at a great distance and with a very faint, furry soundtrack, as though it were all happening under water. He had an even vaguer sensation of sailing gently, gracefully, head first into the back of a police car—but perhaps he dreamed that last part, because he couldn't possibly have been aware of it; his last few brain cells had turned out the lights by that time, and everything had subsided into a soft gray-green fog.

So that was Thursday. There was an interval—blank, dark, quiet, deep—and then he awoke to the sound of somebody yelling, "Rise and shine! Come an' get your coffee. Up and at 'em. Rise and shine, and give God that glory glory."

He opened his eyes and was immediately clobbered by the most blinding light in the universe—it must be the Big Bang—and he clapped his hand over his eyes to protect them from it.

"Ohhhhhhh," he moaned.

"Come on, champ. Got a nice hot cup of coffee for ya this mornin'. Come an' get it before it gets cold."

"Ungghhhh," X said.

"Go on, open your eyes, a little light won't hurt 'em."

With an effort, he got them open again, and squinted painfully around him. He was on a cot in a brightly lit jail cell whose walls were painted a bilious green. An extremely fat man in a khaki uniform was grinning through the bars at him; he wore a Sam Browne belt and an enormous pistol, and an American flag on his tightly stretched shirtsleeve. He had one hand in his back pocket and the other extended through the bars as far as it would go, which wasn't very far, with a Styrofoam cup of coffee in it.

"Had a big night last night, didn't you, champ?" the fat man said cheerily. "Tried to take the whole town apart all by yourself, 's what I heard."

"Nng."

"Quite a shiner you got there. Oughta see poor old Wheatley, haw, he looks even worse'n you do."

X hauled himself into a sitting position. It was nearly too much for him. When he'd recovered, he reached out and shakily accepted the cup of coffee.

"There you go, champ, fix you up in no time," the fat man burbled. "Now you just sit there and enjoy yourself. I'll go over to the cafe in a while and get you a nice big plate of ham an' eggs, how's that sound?"

"Urk," X whispered.

And the fat man waddled away, chuckling to himself, around the corner and into the main part of the police station, where X could hear him telling somebody that he looked like he was going to live after all.

He could see a slice of the room out there—a wall painted the same green as his cell, some checkered linoleum, and parts of two desks, each of which had a pair of feet propped up on it. Nobody seemed to be working very hard; what conversation there was was about doughnuts. There were leisurely footsteps now and then, and doors opening and closing, and a typewriter going about six strokes a minute.

So he'd been in a fight last night, had he? And slugged one of their fellow cops in the process. Terrific. He sat and ached and drank his coffee and tried to remember what he'd done that for.

For a while he couldn't remember anything at all, he was in such bad shape. But eventually, as he sat there, things began to come drifting back. Slowly at first, then a little faster. Then a lot faster, until finally he had all of it: Harriet (oh), the truck (ow!), the preachers (agh!), the whole wretched mess. And his two colleagues in the Buick.

Right, he thought miserably. So that was why.

But—there was something else, too. Something he had to do now, something he—

He whirled around, suddenly agitated, and began flinging the bedclothes off the cot. "Fuh . . . Fuh . . ." he said to himself. Oh, yes, if it wasn't too late.

He found his raincoat wadded up in a corner. Eagerly he snatched it up and dug through its pockets.

Farnsworth? he thought. No, no. Flannery? Fletcher?

The pockets were empty.

"Hey!" he cried, leaping to his feet. "Where's my paper? I had it right here!"

He heard grumbling from the main room, and the type-writer stopped.

"Who took my paper?" he shouted excitedly. "Give it back, it's mine!"

"What the hell's eatin' him?" one of the cops growled.

"I dunno, something about a paper."

"You seen a paper around here?"

X rattled the bars of his cell. "It's gone! I gotta have it, I gotta call the guy!"

There were more grumbles out there, and the noise of a chair squeaking; then the fat man lumbered back into view, brushing powdered sugar off his shirt front. "What's the problem here?" he said.

"Kansas—the guy—Topeka!" X yelled.

The fat man frowned. "You wanna try sayin' that in English?"

"I gotta call him right away!" X said. "I get a phone call, don't I?"

"Well, you—"

"What's he, want to call Topeka?" one of the cops said.

"Kansas?" said another.

"But that's long distance, he can't do that."

"But he's a cop!" X hollered. "Look, I gotta talk to him, it's—"

"Who's a cop?"

"Guy he wants to call," the fat man said over his shoulder.

"In Topeka, for Chrissakes?"

"Yeah, Kansas State Police," X said. "He's a detec—"

"What the hell does he want to do that for?"

"Never heard of anything like—"

"He's in charge of the *case*, that's why!" X roared. Oh, why couldn't he think of the man's name?

"Who is?"

"What case?"

"The Macdonald case, for cryin' out loud!"

The fat man narrowed his eyes. Behind him, in the main room, both pairs of feet came down off the desks, and two faces appeared around the corner—followed a moment later by a third, evidently the typist's.

They all looked at X. They looked at his shiner, his three-day beard, and his filthy clothes.

"This is a joke, right?" one of them said.

"No, it's true!" X cried. "Look in the paper, I was there, the guy's looking for me!"

The cops looked at each other, and at X, and back at each other.

"Well," said the typist, "we woulda gotten an APB on that, wouldn't we?"

"Would we?"

"S'pose we could try checkin' it," said the fat man.

"Might could," the others said.

And they turned on their heels and vanished into the main room.

X could hardly contain himself. He felt . . . why, good heavens, he felt almost happy. He craned his neck after the cops; he couldn't see much but he could hear them blundering around out there, opening drawers, shuffling through stacks of papers.

"What's it under, Interstate?"

"Coupla days old, ain't it?"

"Wait a—"

"What's this stuff here?"

"Fuh . . . Fuh . . ." said X.

"Nah, that's Federal. Try over there."

"Christ, it's a wonder we ever find anything around—"

"Here it is. Under your lunch, haw," the fat man said. "Let's see—'Louise Macdonald, Rosemary D. Flood, John T. Eckes.' "

"Hey, that's him!"

"Right!" X said. "That's what I'm trying to—"

"How come nobody checked this last night?"

"Don't look at me."

"Bet they got tired of lookin' for it."

"Fuh . . ."

"Oh, come on, it's right there in plain—"

"Fleischmann!" X yelled triumphantly from his cell.

"Why, yeah, that's right."

The fat man came over with a huge bunch of keys and swung the cell door open. X felt like kissing him.

And he told Fleischmann everything he knew.

CHAPTER 23

H-HUH," FLEISCHMANN SAID.

"I see.

"Mm-hmm. Spell that for me, will you."

He wrote steadily on his legal pad. Flipped to a fresh page, his third, and wrote some more.

His face was impassive. If anything, he looked slightly annoyed, as though he were being told what it was going to cost him to have a car fixed.

But his mind was doing loop-the-loops.

"All right, Eckes," he said at last. "Let me talk to whoever's in charge out there."

A moment later the fat man came on the line.

"Listen, this guy Eckes is a material witness in a case down here," Fleischmann told him. "Oh, you heard about that, did you. Okay, I'm going to start things moving to get him transferred, but it's going to take some time. Trouble is, I have to be out of town for a few days. You got anything you can hold him on? Well, then, make it protective custody. Right.

"No, there's not anybody else you can contact on it. Here, I'll give you a number you can reach me at if you need to."

And he gave him Connolly's number in Denver.

"Leave a message," he said. "I'll get back to you."

"Right. Oh, uh, thanks."

He hung up the phone.

He sat there for a minute and looked at what he had written on his pad.

"Jesus," he whispered.

Then he got up and went over to the window. He looked down at the street, jingling the change in his pocket, while the traffic lights went from green to red to green again.

No, there was no point in even trying to get Eckes moved down here. Even if he had the authority to do it, which he didn't. The Feds would step in so fast it would make his head swim.

Unless he could get some heavy support from the department.

Right; sure; and who was he going to ask for that? Hazeltine?

Well, then . . .

Go on, he thought. Risk it.

What were they going to do about it, fire him?

Well, that would be too damn bad, wouldn't it.

He picked up his raincoat and his legal pad, turned out the lights, and shut the door behind him.

CHAPTER 24

ED AND HOWIE AND NADINE AND I GOT PICKED for the shopping detail. We went down to Denver bright and early on Friday morning, in two of the rented cars, and we got everything done in a couple of hours.

Most of what we needed we bought at Sears, including two fine fire-escape ladders, the roll-up kind, which would be a lot less trouble to carry than regular ladders. The salesman assured Howie that they were strong enough to hold him, and we all agreed that if they would hold him they would hold anybody.

We hit a couple of other stores, too, and a supermarket. When we were done with that, we drove past the Denver police headquarters and picked out a good spot, not too far away, where we'd be able to leave the school bus, with the preachers on board, for the cops to find.

We were back in Zeke's barn by lunchtime.

Then we had the rest of the day to kill. We talked, and smoked, and went over the plans and the equipment, and tried not to think about anything.

It went very slowly.

Late in the afternoon, the overcast began to lift. A breeze came up in the upper atmosphere and pushed the clouds along on it—big fat wet clouds, moving south over the mountains.

By sunset there were only a few patches of them left, nice and red. And by the time it got dark, even those had gone; the sky was clear and black and full of stars.

At eight o'clock Louise and Pharaoh left for the high school. They came back an hour later, just as the moon was rising—Louise in the car and Pharaoh in a shiny new bus, number 62, all gassed up and ready to go. It was much too big to go into the barn, but it fitted nicely behind it, on the side away from the road.

It was safe enough to go across to the house under cover of darkness, so Muffy and Sister Margaret went over and boiled a vat of water and brought it back to the barn and made coffee.

At ten o'clock we were all eating ham sandwiches, sitting around the space heater in the middle of the barn floor. We couldn't take a chance on showing a light, so we ate by the heater's glow, and by the narrow slants of moonlight that came in through the windows.

The wind sighed through the branches of the bare trees outside, and the slants of light moved slowly across the floor.

At eleven, Howie and Earl began to wrap yet another layer of electrician's tape around the chains of their fire-escape ladders—on top of the five layers they'd already put on—so that they wouldn't rattle against the Bible School fence. There was a game of hearts going, a very quiet one, the players holding their cards up to their noses and twisting around to get some light on them from the heater.

"What's that, an eight?" Dick muttered.

"Eight of diamonds," Dolores said.

"How can you tell?"

"Trust me."

"Howie, you going to be able to lift that thing with all that tape on it?"

"Going to be stiff as a board."

"Aw, pipe down over there."

"Don't know how we're going to be able to see it in the dark."

"Don't have to see it. Just climb it."

"Have faith, child," said Earl.

"And just be glad we got a moon."

"What's that one?"

"Six of clubs."

"Mmm. Thought you played that already."

At midnight, Ed sorted through his tools for perhaps the fiftieth time and carefully packed them into the fanny-pack he'd bought.

And at one o'clock we loaded all our gear into the back of Zeke's pickup truck, and filed onto the bus, and moved out.

CHAPTER 25

ROSIE LAY ON HER STOMACH ON THE SOFT couch, one eye open wide.

Before her, in the darkness, the TV set glowed like a little enchanted world, a wondrous, radiant, jewel-like landscape, Oz green, ruby red, sapphire blue.

She lay very still and watched it, her face bathed in reflected light. She was stunned, breathless. She lay so still, you might have thought she was dead—the glassy stare, the mouth frozen open as if about to cry out, the one arm flung above her head, the other dangling to the floor—but she wasn't. She was listening.

Because it was speaking to her. The most incredibly peaceful voice she had ever heard—speaking just to her, straight to her, especially to her.

It had been speaking to her for a long time now—almost forty-eight hours, in fact, ever since Wednesday, although she had long since lost track of time. Across the room, the panel in the door had slid open any number of times; breakfasts, lunches, dinners slid in to her and slid back out again, unnoticed, untouched, while Rosie lay on the couch and listened. She had forgotten all about food; the voice was so irresistible, she'd forgotten everything.

Everything—because it was doing much more than speaking to her. It enveloped her. Wrapped itself around her, mingled with the air. Barely a whisper; it was so soft, it hardly seemed like sound at all. It was more like a current, like a tide, flowing all around her in the darkness—pulling on her, welcoming her, drawing her to itself.

Changing her.

And the two burly men who had brought her here—how foolish of her to have been so terrified of them! This was wonderful. They had saved her life.

She felt as if an immense burden had been lifted from her. A yoke. A burden. As if her whole life up to this moment had been a dream, and a bad one, filled with images of herself always angry, always yelling and screaming about things. What things? What for? She could no longer remember; she was detached from it now, as if she were looking back at it through the wrong end of a telescope. It was as if she were rising slowly and gracefully up out of it, and all its grit and grime were falling away from her—left behind now, all the strife and argument, contention, doom and gloom—as if the voice were drawing her steadily upward, bearing her away.

She felt weightless. Emptied out. Floating. Flying. So weird . . . As though she were a whole new person; as though all her circuits had been blown and were being rewired from the ground up. Synapses, brain cells, chromosomes—her very DNA untwirling, twirling back together in a new configuration. Starting fresh; rewired delicately, patiently, with infinite and loving care.

She'd never been so fascinated in her whole life.

CHAPTER 26

T WAS A LITTLE OVER FIFTEEN MILES TO THE Bible School, all of it uphill. It took us an hour to cover it.

Pharaoh drove the bus. Beth went a little way in front in Zeke's pickup, with only her parking lights on; we could see the truck's taillights through the windshield, drifting right, then left, then right again as the road snaked its way up the valley.

I rode in tense silence, clenching my teeth, afraid to look out the windows as we teetered around the hairpin turns. There weren't any guard rails, just the road, cut into a narrow ledge on the sides of the mountains, with only a snowbank between us and the Abyss. It was a dizzy drop, down and down and down to the creek at the bottom.

From time to time there was a gnashing of gears as Pharaoh downshifted from third to second to first. From time to time there was a whispering as Hector and Dolores said a few Hail Marys. They had plenty of company among the Protestants.

I tried to empty my mind as much as I could; that's what they say you should do in Zen.

I couldn't empty it, though. It was full to overflowing.

Climb, twist, and climb again—until we came to a spot, just short of a blind curve, where a logging road branched off into the woods. The pickup's brake lights went on, and we halted.

A quarter of a mile to go. Pharaoh backed the bus in at the foot of the logging road until it was reasonably well hidden in the trees. Beth did likewise with the pickup; the rest of us got out and went on on foot.

They were going to give us thirty minutes.

We were up so high we could see all over. The moon was straight overhead now, and almost full; up there near it we could see the tips of the highest peaks, jagged, snowy, luminous. They looked like chunks of moon themselves, poking up against the black sky. The lower mountains in front of them were dark and forested—tremendous folds of earth all in a row, one after the other, all the way back down the valley.

Everything was still. Not a light showing anywhere; not a sound but the wind in the distance, and the crunch of our footsteps on the road.

We walked close together, elbows nearly touching—Ed on one side of me, Louise on the other, Gus and Joanie in front of us, and in front of them Muffy and Nathan and the rest, on up to Howie and Earl hulking along in the lead, wearing the ladders coiled over their shoulders like bandoliers—a motley little procession, all hatted and gloved and bundled up against the cold, carrying our axes and tools and rolls of wire and sacks of potatoes and screw-top bottles of motor oil. We looked like a lot of fugitives from a scavenger hunt.

Nobody talked. We had to be as quiet as possible, and anyway there was no need; we'd been over it and over it, and we all knew what we were supposed to do.

One foot in front of the other. Nothing left to do but to do it.

There was a moment, going around that curve, when the road ahead and the road behind were both out of sight, and for a moment it was possible to believe that none of this was happening. No past, no future, no Bible School; not even us; as if none of our species had ever been thought of. Only the mountains and sky, all crisp and sparkly as if they were brand new.

But a moment later we were around the curve; the mountain dropped away on our left like a curtain drawn aside, and the place came into view, right in front of us.

Prickles went down my back.

There was a space, about three hundred yards wide, between the mountain we'd just passed and the next one to the north; and in the space stood the long line of cedars by the roadside, the ones they'd trucked in and planted full-grown. Two rows of them. To hide the ten-foot chain-link fence with the barbed wire on top. And hide it they did; they hid everything beyond the fence as well, they were so tall.

Halfway along, there was a gap where the driveway went in through the chain-link gate, which was closed, locked, and wired for sound with the electric-eye alarm. We could see the guardhouse just inside; the light from its windows spilled out onto the snow.

We crept forward, hardly breathing. Howie and Earl slipped the ladders off their shoulders. Forty yards shy of the driveway they moved off the road, crossed the snowbank, and disappeared into the cedars.

The rest of us were right behind them.

The trees were set close together, with the fence running along between the outer and inner rows. There wasn't much room to maneuver in there, and no light at all. Howie, Earl, and Parker moved into position at the fence—though in the darkness they were only three bulky shapes—and boosted three smaller shapes—Wally, Gus, and Hector—up onto their shoulders. Gus took out a pair of wire cutters and clipped the top strand of barbed wire; Wally and Hector held the cut ends taut, so they wouldn't bang around, and wrapped them a turn or two around the slanting supports that held them up. Clip, hold, and wrap, and the second and third strands were done; then Gus took the ladders, hooked them over the top of the fence, one outside and one in, and gently let them down. The tape worked fine; they didn't make a sound.

And over we went, quietly dropping to the ground on the inside.

Peeping through the inner hedge, we looked out across a vast, moonlit, snowy lawn. It was Zeke's drawing come to life: a large rectangular enclosure, sloping up and away from us, with the cedars around the edge, all wedged in between the two mountains that loomed up steeply on either side. Away at the back were the three dormitories, all dark—everybody sleeping—with only night lights over their entrance doors. To the right was the parking lot. And next to it, in front of the dorms, the conversion building squatted broadside in the middle—a huge, ugly, squared-off block of concrete. There were some low shrubs scattered around it, presumably to soften its lines, but they didn't have much of an effect. It still looked pretty much like a mental hospital in Siberia. The windows on its upper floor glowed yellow; the ground floor had no windows at all.

The only other light came from the guardhouse, close to the hedge on our right. It had its back to us; its windows and door were on the far side, facing the driveway. We saw its silhouette against the lit-up snow—and also those of Ed and Joanie, sneaking around it on either side. Joanie stayed near the hedge; Ed went around to the left and stationed himself, in a crouch, within striking distance of the door.

Then Joanie bent down, made a snowball, and lobbed it at the electric eye on the front gate. It broke the beam, and from inside the guardhouse came a tiny "Bling!"

There was a pause; then the snow brightened as the guardhouse door opened and closed. Ed sprang, and we heard a faint "Mmf!"—and shortly Ed reappeared around the corner, dragging a dark form.

Silence. They waited a moment, and then Joanie lobbed another snowball; and at the same time Ed said, in a hoarse stage whisper, "Wow, look at this! It's a deer!"

That brought the other sentry out of the house, and Ed jumped him, too. There were sounds of a struggle, followed by a thud, whereupon Joanie turned and beckoned to us. She'd moved out into the light; we could see her grinning.

"Okay," Louise whispered, and the eighteen of us stepped out of our hiding place in the cedars. "Everybody ready?"

Hell, no.

"Then let's do it."

So we split into two groups and set off in opposite directions. Nathan and George and Ellen and I and Howie's gang went north with Louise; Muffy led the other nine south.

Our group's path took us past the guardhouse, where Ed was tying up the sentries; Joanie was already inside, starting to work on switches and control panels. Ed gave us a thumbs-up as we went by.

"Wait for the signal," Louise told him.

"Got it, babe."

We moved off into the darkness, single file, sticking close to the hedge where the snow was shallowest. It was a hundred and fifty yards to the front corner of the rectangle; we turned there and headed in along the northern edge.

Far away across the snow, we could just make out Muffy's group moving parallel with us on the south side. They were all but invisible against the cedars, which themselves were all but invisible against the black mountainside behind them; the only thing we could see clearly was Muffy's painter's pants, scissoring along in the moonlight. They stopped moving, and so did we, when we drew even with the concrete bulk of the conversion building.

Two-thirty. Right on time.

"Okay, Howie," Louise said; and he and Dub and Earl and Parker dashed off toward the dormitories, with their booby-trapping gear in hand.

The other five of us crept forward into the parking lot. Ellen and I opened our sacks of potatoes and we all fanned out, crouching among the cars and vans, and rammed a potato up the tailpipe of every one.

Meanwhile, Howie's gang had reached the lighted entryway of the farthest of the three dorms. Howie wired the door handles shut with a length of good strong steel wire, while Earl and Dub stretched a second length of wire, shin-high, across the doorstep. Parker opened up two quarts of motor oil and emptied them onto the concrete walkway.

That done, they picked up their gear and sprinted toward the middle dorm. One down, two to go; when they were finished, we would make our move. After that it was all going to go very fast; if it didn't, it wasn't going to go at all.

We crouched in the shadows at the edge of the parking lot, and watched, and waited. Dead ahead of us was the conversion building, across fifty yards of snow—blank and windowless on the end facing us; just the doorway in the center of it, with a single bulb overhead.

Across the way, Muffy's group was waiting, too, at the far end of the building. We could just see them around the corner—we could see Muffy's pants anyway—with the dark mountain as a backdrop. The mountain had a scar across its face. A logging road, probably—a bright thread of snow in the forest up there, picked out by the moon. I wondered if that was where Zeke had made his drawing from. Good view; he could have gone up there with a pair of binoculars and looked all he wanted.

We waited some more. We turned our collars up and pulled our hats down to our eyebrows. The wind wandered softly around the edges of things, ruffling the trees. It managed to make the silence louder. Nobody stirred; no lights went on; the whole place seemed as if it were wound up tight like a wind-up toy, ready to burst into frenetic motion.

Howie's gang finished the middle dormitory; now they hustled over to the last one, nearest us, and started to work. Only a few more seconds now. As they strung their wire and poured their oil, we heard the sound of engines in the distance, very faint, coming closer: Pharaoh and Beth were on their way in.

Out front, by the lights from the guardhouse, we could see Joanie swinging the front gate open for them to come through. Ed was inside, getting ready to cut off the phones.

Louise put her hand out and grabbed George's hand. Ellen grabbed on, and so did Nathan and I.

Every detail of it going to stick in your memory for a long

time, the sparkle of new snow, the look of the ribbing on a knitted cap, the mist of your breath. Your heart going like a jackhammer.

And then Howie's gang was done, and Howie straightened and lit his cigarette lighter and waved it back and forth.

Louise took out her lighter and answered Howie; across the way, Muffy lit hers.

"Now," Louise whispered.

And we all charged.

Up on the mountain where the logging road was, another light went on and off, and there was the *chunk* of a car door shutting. It was too far away for us to hear; the wind carried it off, along with the sound a few seconds later of more engines starting up. We'd have been able to see the pencils of light up there from their headlights, had we stayed where we were; there were so many of them, they lit up the whole road; but by then we were already across the snow and over the driveway, skidding to a halt outside the building's north door.

Very cautiously, I peeked through the small pane of glass set into the door. There was a foyer inside; a desk to the right; a sentry seated at the desk, nodding over a book in his lap. The foyer gave onto a corridor that ran the length of the building. It looked as if it belonged in an expensive medical clinic—cool white plaster walls, quiet carpeting, indirect lighting. There were doors all the way down it on both sides; each of them was marked with a number. All of them were closed.

And at the far end was another foyer, another sentry sleeping, and another exterior door, through whose window Muffy looked back at me.

I ducked back down and whispered all this to the others; then we braced ourselves, and Louise gripped the door handle, counted to three, and yanked it open.

George and Nathan went in fast. The sentry, jerking awake, looked up with a horrified expression; he was just reaching for the telephone beside him when Nathan slapped his arm away and George barreled into him and spun him out of his chair and into the wall; Nathan gave him a karate chop and he fell down.

At the far end of the corridor, Hector and Floyd were all over the other sentry, while Muffy and Gus and the others came boiling in past them, axes in hand, and headed for the first of the cell doors. They swung the axes; wood splintered; the doors came open.

And then all hell broke loose. Bells, my God, you never heard such bells. The whole building just exploded with noise—an incredible, vibrating, teeth-jarring din. We all jumped about three feet into the air, and when we came down we were yelling at the top of our lungs, and unable to hear either each other or ourselves, though you could have heard the bells from there to Albuquerque.

It was the boys on the night shift, upstairs in the monitoring room. They'd been having a quiet time of it; their electronic equipment was all humming and beeping smoothly in the background, and the banks of TV screens in front of them showed a pleasant lack of activity in the Management Units downstairs. Many of the subjects were sleeping; those who weren't were sitting quietly on their couches, rocking gently back and forth, or singing along with the program of devotional music, performed by the Gospel Crusade Choir, which was being shown them on their TV sets. No more temper tantrums down there, no more screaming or antisocial behavior; even the radicals were singing along. Remarkable progress; even better than their projections indicated.

Accordingly there was very little for the monitor-room boys to do that night. One of them had smuggled in a deck of cards, and they were whiling away the time playing Steal the Old Lady's Bundle, secure in the knowledge that the front gate was locked, the sentries were on duty, and the Lord's work was being done; so secure did they feel, in fact, that when they heard the first noises downstairs they didn't even look up from their cards, assuming that one of the sentries must have gotten up to stretch his legs. But then more noises came trickling up the stairwell, and they did look up; and one of them glanced at the TV monitors, where blazes of light had appeared on numbers one and two; the doors to those cells were open and there were people standing in the doorways. A lot of people.

In parkas and ski hats. With axes in their hands.

"Uh . . ." the boy said, pointing at the monitors.

The other two looked, and their eyes popped.

"Oh, my God!"

"Hit the alarm!"

"Call Miss Masters!"

"Which one is it?"

"There—no, there! The red one!"

The second boy flipped a switch and the bells went off, shrieking and thundering, while the third boy leapt to the phone and punched out Harriet's home number in Winnetka. Clapping his free hand over his free ear, he shouted into the phone, "Mayday, mayday! We're under attack! We—hello?"

"Quick! Where are the pistols?" the first boy shouted.

"What?"

"The phone went dead!"

"Where'd we put the—"

"*What?*"

Monitors three and four showed two more blazes of light. Then two more on five and six. The three boys scurried frantically around the room, looking for their tranquilizer pistols; at last they found them behind an oscilloscope, and, soundlessly shouting, they tore out of the room and down the stairs.

Downstairs it was a madhouse. The corridor was full of Soldiers by now; everybody was running at once, and yelling through the deafening racket of the alarm bells. Axes were swinging and more doors were breaking down—seven, eight, nine of them—and bearded, hollow-eyed men began to emerge, blinking, from the pitch-black cells. They were the preachers; they had to be, though they no longer bore any resemblance to the pictures of them we'd seen on TV; sunken-chested and weak and trembling, dressed in pale blue T-shirts and cotton pants, and barefooted, they looked as if they'd been shut away for the last ten years. They weren't glad to see us; far from it. They cowered in the doorways, bewildered and frightened, blinking at the light, cringing from the ear-splitting noise.

Muffy and Gus and Louise were screaming, inaudibly, into their ears. "Get out! Out!"

"What?"

"Hurry up!"

"Come on, man, you're free!" Producing nothing but further bewilderment. They had to grab the preachers and shove them roughly down the corridor; the rest of us quickly set up a bucket brigade and began to pass them from hand to hand, stumbling and protesting, out toward the north door.

"Move it! Get 'em out of here!"

Outside, the school bus and the pickup truck came tearing up the driveway, with Ed and Joanie running after them.

Ten doors were down; eleven; we were halfway down the corridor when the three boys in lab coats came charging out of the stairwell, waving their pistols and shooting wildly in every direction. The crowd in the hall swayed and surged. Hector took a flying leap and landed on one of the boys, and Floyd tripped another one, but not before Dolores faltered and went down, clutching her side. Dick gathered her up and handed her to me and I handed her on to Ellen, just as a dart whizzed past my ear; I turned around in time to see Muffy's elbow cracking into the third boy's jaw.

It had only taken a few seconds, but we needed every second we could get. The axes started swinging again, faster now. Another preacher blundered into my arms, pale and glassy-eyed. They were all going to need some serious counseling once we got them back to civilization. I swung the man around and passed him on, and I'd hardly turned around again before Gus threw me another one. The bells clanged and clattered as though the world were ending. Fourteen, fifteen doors came down; we were all working furiously, pushing and bumping and jostling against each other, desperately trying to get them out before the Harvest Workers in the dormitories, who couldn't possibly be sleeping any more, could get past the booby traps outside.

"Come on!" we all bellowed at each other.

And outside, in fact, they were getting past the booby traps already. Over at the dormitories—all of whose lights were blazing now—they had crowded into the entryways behind the wired-up doors; after a bit of dithering, they'd put their shoulders to the doors and heaved. The doors bulged outward once or twice and then popped open, and the Harvest Workers burst forth all at once, like corks out of bottles—and immediately fell over the trip-wires. That was the first of them. The ones behind them, unable to stop, jumped over them, and came down flat on their backs on the greased cement.

But there were plenty more right behind *them*, and they got through, though they had to trample on their fallen comrades in order to do so; and in no time at all they came raging across the snow, a great yelling mob of them, in their striped pajamas, their bathrobes flying, and brandishing trank pistols, broom handles, fire extinguishers, and whatever else they had happened to snatch up on their way out.

Howie and Dub and Earl and Parker planted their gigantic selves directly in the mob's path and stood there, eagerly, on the balls of their feet, watching them come.

Inside, all of us shrieked at each other to for God's sake hurry up. There were women coming out of the cells now—Zeke's people—and younger, more muscular men. But though their bodies looked fitter than the preachers', their minds were gone. They hadn't the slightest idea where they were or what was happening. And we didn't have time to tell them; all we could do was to yank them out as fast as we could, and keep on moving. Another swing of an axe, and Louise's face fell; her mouth said, "Zeke," and I caught a glimpse of a skinny blond man with a wispy beard, who looked scared to death. He ducked back into the safety of his cell and had to be bodily carried out by Nathan, who had started to cry.

Eighteen, nineteen, twenty; one after another we sent them careening down the hall; and then I was crying too, because there stood Rosie in the twenty-first cell with her hair all disheveled and a perfectly witless grin on her face. I'd known she was going to be there. I knew it, I knew it; and she stood there in the doorway a moment, weaving, until her eyes focused on a point somewhere above my right ear and she grinned some more.

"P.K.!" she said, in a peculiar, high-pitched voice. "Oh, this is terrific! I've got so much to tell you!"

"Oh, my God," I said.

Somebody gave her a shove; she stumbled against me for half a second, and latched onto my arm and leered at me. "Jesus loves you, d'you know that?" She waved a finger in my face. "He's got a plan for us! We've got to help Him!"

"Oh, my God!" I bawled, blindly swinging her around; and we did a little do-si-do, staggering around in circles, both of us yelling incoherently at each other—she happy as a lark, and I crying and gasping and damning it all to hell—until somebody yelled, "That's it!" and suddenly we were all moving, as the last of the doors went down.

"Beat it!"

"Everybody out!"

Rosie was six or eight feet in front of me now, being swept down the hall; I could see her bobbing along, still grinning, amid the crowd of rushing bodies.

"Mission!" she crowed. "America to Christ!" And then

she was sucked out through the exit door; and a moment later, so was I.

And even before I got through, I could see that there were entirely too many people out there.

Pharaoh had wrestled the school bus through the world's fastest seven-point turn in front of the building, flattening snowbanks and mowing down a good deal of shrubbery in the process, and had brought it to a halt with its nose pointing out toward the road. Ed and Joanie began throwing preachers aboard it like mad, while Ellen and Nadine and Sister Margaret and the rest of the bucket brigade fed them new ones as fast as they came out of the building.

Meanwhile, the Harvest Workers came stampeding in from the dormitories. Beth had pulled the pickup truck around the bus's tail end and parked it, crosswise, for a barricade; that left only a fifteen-foot gap, between there and the corner of the building, for Howie's gang to defend. And defend it they did. Howie stuck out a massive arm and clotheslined a number of them; Dub and Earl got busy butting and blocking everybody they could get at, while Parker began picking them up two at a time, one in each hand, and tossing them onto the heads of their comrades.

And for a while they held them at bay, the four of them, shoulder to shoulder like a human dam, with the screaming mob piling up behind them.

But you can only load people into a school bus just so fast. The doors are too narrow; you can only put them aboard one at a time. Even in the best of circumstances it takes a while, but when they're staggering around, stoned out of their minds on LSD, and blithering about Jesus, it takes a lot longer. Ed and Joanie did the best they could, but already things were getting out of control; the captives' legs were so rubbery they could hardly get them up the bus's steps; and behind them, while they struggled, the other captives kept wandering off, and falling down in the snow, and having to be rounded up and herded back into line.

Over in the gap, the Harvest Workers kept piling in. There were easily a hundred of them now, ten deep, throwing themselves in wave after wave against Howie's gang. Big as the four of them were, they couldn't hold them; by sheer weight and numbers the mob forced them back a step, a step, and another step, until at last they broke through and came pouring in around them in a torrent.

And that was what I saw as I came through the door. I was almost the last one out; the other Soldiers had plunged in already, and I stood there for a split second before I joined them, taking it all in—the moon, the stars, the mountains, the wide night sky, and under it a heaving roiling moiling thrashing sea of humanity, all screeching and hollering and beating each other to a pulp, with mops and brooms and table legs going up and down like pistons, and fire extinguishers squirting foam into the air.

I'd still been crying when I came out the door, but I stopped now, looking out at all these people who couldn't find anything better to do than to beat each other's brains out, and suddenly all the anger and rage and grief and sorrow in the world came boiling up in me all at once.

"All right, you motherfuckers!" I yelled at the top of my lungs, and threw myself into the middle of it.

It was a little like being in a heavy surf in the middle of a hurricane. I felt myself tumbling over and over, caught up in a tangle of whirling arms and legs, being tossed in all directions at once—meanwhile kicking and punching and tromping on insteps for all I was worth. Everything got all churned up together—bared teeth, whites of eyes, bloody noses; snarls, insults, howls of rage and pain.

Every so often I came up for air. Once, I caught a glimpse of Parker wading through the mob, still picking up people and throwing them right and left. Another time I saw Hector and Floyd, close together, making small abrupt movements that sent Harvest Workers flying. Louise was a few feet to my left; I saw her take somebody's fire extinguisher away from him and slug him with it, while Nathan finished him off with a wicked right cross.

A second later I got pounded by a few dozen elbows and knees; then somebody grabbed me by the collar and I got dragged under and spun around some more.

And all the time the bus was still there, its red lights blinking, its whole frame shuddering and rattling as Pharaoh gunned the engine. Captives peered down at us from its lighted windows; they looked mildly puzzled, as if they were wondering what all the fuss was about. Ed and Joanie were over at the doors, still madly stuffing them aboard; there was still a little bit of a clearing over there, and from what little I could see from where I was, they didn't have many left to go.

But the clearing was getting smaller and smaller. There were Harvest Workers all around the bus now, jammed up against its sheet-metal sides, roaring and wrangling right up under the windows. And for every one of them we knocked down, there were five or six to take his place; they kept coming and coming—far too many of them—circling in, closing us off.

We were starting to lose our footing, as the snow underfoot got trampled into packed slick ice. I started seeing tranquilizer guns everywhere; they were lousy shots, but it was fish in a barrel, and some of them began inevitably to hit their marks; and people were going down, one by one.

I saw George, with his hat knocked off and a nasty cut on his forehead, but still punching; and then he wasn't there any more.

I didn't see Muffy any more either.

Or Dub.

Or Howie.

Or Louise. One minute she was right there, and the next, she was gone.

I could see the guy who'd gotten her; he was taking aim at Parker next. I was almost close enough to reach him. He had a snub-nosed, rosy-cheeked, angelic face, a Boy Scout face, and as I floundered toward him I wondered how a face like that could get such a vicious expression on it. Who knows; I probably looked worse. I clutched at him, was yanked away, reached out again and got hold of his sleeve; I was trying to get his pistol away from him when somebody yelled, "Look out!" and another one came at me from behind. Floyd pulled him off me—I think it was Floyd—and sent him reeling; and then something clonked me on the back of the head and I saw stars.

I saw the moon, too, high overhead; then I stumbled into some shrubbery, and righted myself, and stood there a while, unsteadily, trying to catch my breath.

Everything was spinning. I felt as if half my bones were broken and the other half were bent. We were done for. We'd never get out. Everybody was still fighting—everybody who was still left—but the clearing was gone now. The Harvest Workers were swarming around the bus doors; they'd knocked Ed and Joanie down, and before Pharaoh could get the doors shut they were through them and hauling him out by his heels.

Ah, shit.

Ah, hell.

They'd be fighting now forever, world without end.

I wondered if they had enough cells to put all of us in, or whether they'd have to build an annex.

Right now, I felt so bad, it hardly seemed to matter. They'd have the whole planet before long; that ought to be enough room.

I raised my aching head and looked up at the moon again. Big and bright and swaying; I saw a pair of them. And another pair. And a . . . No, no, I thought, blinking my eyes until my vision cleared. Those weren't pairs of moons; they were lights.

They were headlights. Coming up the driveway, a thousand of them—headlights, and bullhorns, too, squawking like a flock of geese!

Where the hell could they have come from? By God, I

thought, they must have—up on the mountain—of course! While we were—! Just look at 'em—squad cars, paddy wagons, Colorado police jeeps with chains on their tires, and red lights flashing all over the place!

"By God!" I said, and sat down heavily in the snow.

"All right, boys, round 'em up. Move it."

It was Sergeant Fleischmann, stout and gray-haired and crabby, in a brown hunting coat and rumpled corduroy pants. He was standing by the lead squad car with his friend Connolly, barking orders at a flock of Colorado cops, sending them scurrying.

"You guys secure that building," he said. "Make sure everybody's out of it, and rope it off."

"Yessir."

"And get those goddamned bells turned off. Driving me nuts."

"Yessir."

The Harvest Workers stood and stared.

"Okay, Jenkins, you can read 'em their rights. Witherspoon, take some men and check out the rest of those buildings; if anybody's still in there, get 'em out here."

"Yessir," said Witherspoon.

"And make it nice and clean, huh? Going to lose my job for this as it is."

"Ah, g'wan, Bob, they'll probably give you a medal," said Connolly.

"Sure they will."

The cop called Jenkins picked up a bullhorn. "Okay, listen up, kids," he squawked, and proceeded to read us our rights.

While he was doing that, a boy in torn pajamas, with a plaster cast on his arm, came forward from the ranks of Harvest Workers and advanced on Fleischmann. "What are you—arresting *us*, too?" he demanded.

"Uh-huh," said Fleischmann.

"What for, man?"

Fleischmann rolled his eyes.

"You got a warrant?"

"Sonny, we're knee-deep in warrants, said Connolly, pulling a fat sheaf of papers from his coat pocket. "Whyn't you pick out one you like."

Fleischmann was looking past the boy and out over the crowd of us. "All right," he said, "which one of you clowns is Louise Macdonald?"

Louise was still lying in the snow, as were a lot of other people, but before anybody could point her out to him, there was a great commotion as a pack of cars and panel trucks came flying hell-for-leather up the driveway, skidded to a halt, and disgorged a mob of people clutching minicams, battery packs, microphones, and even pencils and note pads.

"And who the hell are *you*?" said Fleischmann.

"Mitchell. Denver *Post*."

"Channel Four."

"Eyewitness News Team."

"*Rocky Mountain News*."

Fleischmann gave Connolly a look. "What do they do?" he said. "Tap the phones?"

Connolly smiled innocently.

"Connolly! You son of a bitch!"

"Well, hell, I figured we'd want some witnesses. Just tryin' to cover my ass."

"Christ almighty." Fleischmann turned away. "Come on, boys, let's get 'em out of here. Put 'em on the bus if you can't fit 'em all in the wagons."

And so they herded us all together and moved us toward the vehicles for the long trip back to Denver, while the reporters yelled questions and got in the way and generally made nuisances of themselves.

"Give us a statement, huh, sarge?"

"Find any drugs yet?"

"Is that the preachers over there?"

"You one of the Soldiers of Elijah?"

"Hey, you," one of the cops was saying. "Pick those people up before they freeze. That's right. Go on. Yeah, you, too."

Nathan was bending over Louise. "Gimme a hand," he said, and the two of us picked her up and draped her over our shoulders as best we could and moved along with the crowd. One of Nathan's eyes was swollen shut and beginning to turn black and blue. His other eye was twinkling.

"Would you mind standing right over there?"

"Which one are you?"

"How do you feel about all this?"

The red lights from the police cars danced over everything. I smiled at the camera.

ABOUT THE AUTHOR

A former student of New York's Union Theological Seminary and prison chaplain, Katharine Stall now lives in Portland, Maine. She is currently working on her second novel.